BURN

BURN

MONICA HESSE

HOT
KEY
BOOKS

First published in Great Britain in 2014 by Hot Key Books
Northburgh House, 10 Northburgh Street, London EC1V 0AT

A CIP catalogue record for this book is available from the British Library.

ISBN: 978-1-4714-0059-9

1

This book is typeset in 10.5 Berling LT Std using Atomik ePublisher

Printed and bound by Clays Ltd, St Ives Plc

Hot Key Books supports the Forest Stewardship Council (FSC),
the leading international forest certification organisation, and is
committed to printing only on Greenpeace-approved FSC-certified paper.

www.hotkeybooks.com

Hot Key Books is part of the Bonnier Publishing Group
www.bonnierpublishing.com

For Rob

What was he trying to find?

He pulled out the desk drawer too roughly; it came out off its sliders, spilling pens and notepads all over the floor. An emptied box of thumbtacks scratched against his hands as he sifted through the pile.

It wasn't here.

Whatever it was, it wasn't here.

There was a beep. It was the security monitor, the one positioned on the wall, the one trained on the entrance outside. Figures appeared. They were coming, coming, they were too close. He couldn't stop looking. He had to find it. He had to—

Lona lurched against the mattress. It was that sensation of falling, like she had been levitating, and regaining consciousness sent her crashing back to the bed. That was one blessing of nightmares. They ended with whiplash, but at least they ended quickly. Her heart was racing and she couldn't stop it. Telling herself it had only been a dream – that it hadn't really happened to her – didn't help. It was the fact that it hadn't happened to her that made it so terrible.

Outside the sky was violet, an in-between time. Post-midnight, pre-dawn. Post-sleep, pre-awake.

Lona knew something about the subconscious, and the hazy way it could straddle reality and fantasy. In some of her dreams she was still Julian, still dreaming like she was on Path. Other times, she managed to wrestle her mind away from the Julian Path and have her own dreams. It had been confusing at first, for her dream life to be split between two people, but she'd trained herself. She now knew within seconds whether she was Lona or Julian in any sleep cycle.

But in this dream she wasn't Julian. And she wasn't herself.

She was someone else entirely.

Someone had stolen her dream. Someone had put her on a new Path.

1

"Are you going to make a wish, Lona?" Gamb poked her in the ribcage. "I've already made, like, forty-seven of them and it's not even my birthday."

The cake was shiny. The smooth buttercream reminded Lona of an ice-skating rink. It was almost too immaculate to eat, except that her stomach growled when she looked at it. It smelled like hot sugar and butter, and the vanilla extract that had been whipped into the frosting. She could almost taste it on her tongue, the sweet grainy sheen.

"Wait until it is your birthday, Gamb," Ilyf said. "The birthday fairy is going to be all, 'Oh, sorry, your wish allotment has been filled. You used them up six months ago when you stole someone else's.'"

Gamb was careless with his wishes. Lona didn't want to be. This was, after all, the only one she'd ever made. It was her first birthday. Her seventeenth year, but her first birthday. Pink and green streamers hung around the kitchen, and also an iridescent banner with "Happy Birthday" spelled out in bubbly gold and silver. It was the décor of a little kid's party, but she liked it. She liked the giant bouquet of sunflowers Ilyf had arranged on the table, and the paper cone hats Gamb ceremoniously put on everyone's heads, affixed with stretchy elastic.

Today she would turn seventeen, and she would get a new name. Lona Sixteen Always would become Lona Seventeen Always. If she wanted. Now that she wasn't on Path anymore, there was no reason to obey Path naming traditions – but there was no reason not to, either. It's not like she had any alternate options.

"She doesn't have to make any wishes if she doesn't want to." Under the table, Fenn's hand stroked the soft underside of her wrist. He leaned in closer and his breath tickled her ear. "Or you can make a million. Or a million and one." His fingers traveled higher, skimming over the crease of her elbow. It was a gesture of comfort, a remnant from the way Pathers used to be stroked by Coping Technicians, but it still felt sharp and shivery on her skin.

Fenn reached into his pocket and produced a lighter for the candles – eighteen in total: seventeen for every year of her life, and a symbolic one to grow on. Gamb turned off the light so that the room flickered, and Lona's face felt warm from the heat. As many wishes as she wanted. Gamb sighed at her indecision. "Give her some *time*," Ilyf ordered him.

"I don't need anything," she protested.

"You suck at birthdays," Gamb said. "You're not supposed to wish for something you need. It's supposed to be about something you *want*."

"Before they melt," Ilyf encouraged. A spot of pink wax had already dribbled onto the frosting. "It's just a birthday tradition. It doesn't have to be a big deal."

A birthday tradition. Lona closed her eyes. She should make a wish, for the full, traditional birthday experience. But her deepest wishes had already come true. She was alive. Fenn was alive. Fenn was here, at this moment, his hand still skimming her arm. She and Fenn and Gamb and Ilyf were the first living graduates of the Julian Path. They were so much luckier than they could have been. What more was there to wish for?

I wish I could know my real name.

The thought appeared in her mind unbidden, an unexpected guest at the door. That's what she wished for. Her name. Not Lona, which was the arbitrary conglomeration of letters assigned by the Julian Path when she was an infant. But her real name. The one her mother intended for her in the hours before she relinquished custody of her newborn daughter to a government program. The one that signified someone had cared about her. That name.

Lona watched as one of the candles listed slowly to the right, a snow bank of white frosting piling up against its side.

I wish I could know my real mother, too.

There. That's the wish she wanted more than anything. The wish that was too extravagant to say out loud. It could only be conceived of in secret, on birthdays.

Before she could take it back, she drew in a breath and blew. Seventeen candles went out, leaving puffs of smoke and the smell of wax and sulfur. The eighteenth flickered, but eventually it died too and the kitchen was bathed in gray.

Gamb immediately smeared a glob of frosting on Lona's face. She licked it off the side of her mouth, feeling the sugar particles roll around on her tongue.

11

"We forgot to sing Happy Birthday!" Ilyf cried. "We were supposed to do it with the candles." They were all still amateurs at the patterns of birthday parties. They'd only had three to practice on – Fenn's, Gamb's and Ilyf's when they'd all turned nineteen the previous year.

"I don't think there's an official rulebook, Ilyf," Gamb said. "I think Lona still gets to turn seventeen whether we sing the song or not."

"But we have to," Ilyf insisted. "Tradition."

They started in three different keys – Ilyf, determined and slightly flat; Gamb in a ridiculous falsetto; Fenn, softly and just to Lona. She clapped when they were done, and Ilyf sliced around the candles to give Lona the biggest piece, with the sugar rose.

"Are you going to tell us what you wished for?" Gamb asked, but he lost focus before Lona could think of a pretend wish she could use instead of her vulnerable real one. "Hey – listen. When I do this, I can play a song." He took his paper hat off and strummed the elastic, stretching it to longer and shorter lengths. "*Oh my darling, oh my darling, oh my darling Clement*— ow." He sucked at the finger he'd snapped.

Ilyf rolled her eyes. "The package did say 'not suitable for children under four'."

"The package wasn't considering the musical possibilities of these hats."

"Anyway. All the candles went out on the cake, Gamb. So Lona doesn't have to tell us her wish. We'll see it when it comes true."

"The important ones already have," Lona insisted.

"Please don't tell me you wasted a wish on, like, world peace or ending poverty," Gamb said.

"I wished that I could play a musical instrument."

"You – wait, what?"

"The elastic chin strap, Gamb. I wished I could play the elastic chin strap."

She darted her hand out before he could back away, and—

"*Ow!*" He rubbed his face where she'd snapped at it. "Let the party record show, the birthday girl is going to be punished, as soon as it's not her birthday."

2

She wrapped her arms around her knees, watching her breath come out in white clouds and disappear. December 15, but no first snowfall yet. The forecaster said maybe next week.

"There you are." The screen door squeaked behind Fenn as he stepped out onto the porch.

"Just watching for snow."

"Do you want a blanket? I can go get one."

"No. I like feeling how cold it can get." When Fenn and Lona had been in the Julian Path, their sensory perceptions had been dulled. For their own comfort, things were cold, but never freezing. Off Path, Lona liked feeling the thousand tiny pinpricks of a windy night, the way the frigid air found the gaps in her clothing and gave her goosebumps.

Fenn sat beside her on the porch swing. His skin was still inside-warm against her shoulder, and his eyes were still summer-green against the bleak winter landscape. Today his shirt was flannel and brown, the color of the wet earth and a few shades lighter than his hair.

He used the heel of his foot to rock the swing back and forth, and she leaned into his body. "What does this cold taste like?" he asked.

She smiled and breathed in. "*This* cold? Peppermint. Or wintergreen, maybe. Something spicy. What do you think?"

She felt his ribs expand as he inhaled. "Cloves? If it were snowing, I'd definitely say peppermint. But the brown – the fact that everything is muddy and damp and thick – it makes me think of the cloves in the ham Julian's grandma used to make. How if you put them in your mouth, they tasted spicy and hot and cold at the same time."

"You win." She loved that about him, the attention to detail he gave things like sights and sounds. The night was exactly clove-flavored. "What musical instrument does it sound like?"

"Not a flute." He cocked his head away from hers to listen, exposing his neck. "Maybe a clarinet? Or maybe—" She tilted up and brushed her lips against his bare skin, watching it ripple with goosebumps. He groaned. "No fair. Now I can't hear anything but my heart pounding."

"Are you saying the night sounds like drums?"

He laughed, then reached into the zippered pouch on his shirt, producing a small package and two slender envelopes. "I didn't know if you'd want to open these in front of everyone."

"More birthday?"

"The first card is from Talia."

"I'll see her in a couple days for Tuesday dinner."

"She wanted you to have something to open on your actual birthday."

She slid her thumb under the envelope flap, pulling out a blue card from the Monitor who'd helped Lona and Fenn shut down the Julian Path six months ago. And who, though it still

15

seemed strange, was technically Lona's legal guardian. "Gabriel signed his own name." Lona showed Fenn the card with Talia's block print and the shaky scrawl of a four-and-a-half year old, belonging to Talia's other ward. "I think, at least. I think that's supposed to be a 'G'."

She guessed who the second card was from even before opening it. The cover said "Happy Birthday" and nothing more, and the inside was blank except for a "J". Julian. This card was the first time she'd heard from him in months. The postmark was foreign, though, which meant he'd remembered her birthday in advance, in time for the card to cross an ocean. That was something. Even if he never called.

"Who's this from?" She picked up the final package. It was small and square but heavy for its size, wrapped in green tissue paper that whispered against her fingers.

"Me."

"The party was supposed to be my present!"

"This is your *other* present." She tore off the wrapping. Inside was a book, plain and brown, no title on the cover or the spine. "Open it."

The first page was creamy and textured. "For all of your birthdays," Fenn had written in careful cursive. There was no text on the next page. Just two pictures of infants, each propped up against a beige background – one bald and wailing, the other dark-haired and solemn. As Lona turned the pages, the infant in one set of pictures grew a pointy nose, sandy hair, grey eyes. The other grew curly hair, and his nebulously colored eyes became a bottle-glass green. By the fourth page, he was as she remembered him the first day they met, standing by a calisthenics machine.

"Fenn – it's us. It's all pictures of us. How did you—"

"Do you like it?"

She turned another page, sixteen in total. Mirrors hadn't been illegal in the Julian Path, but they hadn't been prevalent, either. There was no point in providing anything that would have encouraged individuality – not when the goal of the Julian Path was to teach them all to be like Julian. Lona had never seen these before.

"I had Talia dig them out of our files before they shut down the system," Fenn explained. "Our yearly progress photos – the ones they took for records." He looked worried suddenly. "I hope you like it. Ilyf said I was supposed to get you jewelry for your birthday."

"Fenn, I love it." Jewelry. As if there was a bracelet that could be half as beautiful as this album. "I wouldn't have thought to ask for it, but it's exactly what I needed."

"It is?"

"You have no idea."

Only Fenn would think to give her something so grounding, so affirming of her own past. Because he had shared her Path. He was her first and only friend there.

"Can I—" He still did that sometimes, asked permission before he kissed her. It was a residual habit, a leftover taboo from when they lived in Path and excessive touching was frowned upon. This time, he didn't complete the sentence before his mouth found hers and she inhaled the earthy scent of his skin. She didn't know whether Fenn actually smelled like grass or whether she just associated it with him because he taught her to appreciate the scent. Either way, when he was close she smelled prairies and meadows, and the dry rustle of wheat or corn. His lips were soft; his fingers wound through her hair and tightened when she leaned in closer to him.

"Thank you," he breathed, when their lips parted. He still did that sometimes, too. He was grateful for the simplest experiences, in ways one could only be if one knew what it was like to live without them.

"Are you going to bed soon?" he asked.

She nodded. They had their own rooms, but sometimes when Lona had a bad dream, Fenn would slip in and crouch low beside her bed. She would wake to his hand stroking the small of her back, or his voice whispering in her ear. She did the same for him. Nightmares were a symptom of withdrawal from the Path, but they nursed each other through the worst of them. She had gone from fearing physical touch to feeling as though her life depended on it.

Her nightmares were mostly gone. There was only one recurring bad dream left, and it was always the same: she was kneeling on the floor in a sterile white room, hunching over the lifeless body of a beautiful girl as blood seeped onto Lona's pants, spreading until her clothes were soaked. Genevieve, the girl who loved Fenn and who ultimately died proving it. That dream replayed in her sleep almost as it had happened in real life, except that in real life Lona couldn't will herself to wake up. It was sad and strange to live in Genevieve's house, left to them after her death, but Lona didn't want to move. Grief, like cold, could be a reminder of being alive.

"Have you had the dream lately?" Fenn could read her

quietness sometimes, know what thoughts sent her into herself. He knew how Genevieve's death haunted Lona's sleep.

"Not for almost a week."

Now is when she should tell him about the other dream, the one that woke her last night in the dim, quiet hours of her seventeenth birthday. She could still feel the thumbtack scratches on her hands, still remember the clinical beep made by the sound of the security system. She could still feel the man's panic as he searched through the ravaged office.

What was he trying to find and why was it so important he found it before they did?

She should tell Fenn about that, but she couldn't. She didn't want to mar such a beautiful day, and she didn't want to remember the dream. She just wanted it to go away.

"Are you sure?" Fenn asked.

"I'm sure," she said, technically answering his question honestly. "I haven't had the dream about Genevieve."

That night, in her bed, she dreamed of cake. She dreamed of doughy sweetness, shortening and sugar, and running her tongue over her lips, tasting happiness.

3

"Slide it through the metal detector."

Lona looked down at the plastic-wrapped paper plate in her hands. "It's just cake."

"Slide the cake through the metal detector."

She sighed, but set the plate on the conveyer belt next to her shoulder bag. The regular security guard wouldn't have made her do this. Veronica knew her – she would have gazed up just long enough from her knitting project to smile and wave Lona through.

When this new guy handed back her plate, the frosting had a thumb print in the middle, the clingy plastic wrap dipped down into the hole like a moon crater. "We just have to check," he said defensively. "People could hide keys or knives in there."

She made her way back to the residential wing. It was craft hour; some patients were painting watercolors in the common area. Mrs. O'Hare's Monet was beautiful. She was a retired art teacher. It must be sad for her husband, who Lona saw visiting sometimes. Mrs. O'Hare remembered everything about how to hold a paintbrush, but had no idea who he was.

Before Lona could open the door to the intensive care wing,

it flew open and a bosom-heavy nurse smashed into her, trilling a theatrical scream.

"Christ, Lona." Rowena was her favorite nurse on the ward. A retired opera singer who still behaved like she was on stage. "Oooh, what's that? Someone having a birthday?"

"I did," she admitted. "Yesterday."

"Happy Birthday! Party?"

"A little one."

"Am I going to be disappointed when I ask if that cake is for me?"

"I'm sorry. I should have brought more." She'd planned to. But when she got up this morning Gamb was eating it with a fork, digging out the frosting flowers without even having the decency to look guilty. Lona salvaged the only intact piece she could.

"Oh, my butt doesn't need it anyway." Rowena absentmindedly ran a hand over the thick padding of her hips. "He'll be excited to have the cake. And the company. Nobody else ever comes to visit him." She checked her watch. "You all should stop by the common room later. After crafts we're showing a movie."

Lona nodded, but she doubted she would come to the common room. The idea of lingering nauseated her. She made these visits in secret. Fenn wouldn't understand why she came here; she could barely understand. She hated herself every time she walked through the door.

His hair had gone white, the fast-forward aging that happens sometimes with trauma victims. Not salt and pepper but salt and nutmeg, with flecks of his original warm brown. Today he wore a fleece tracksuit that zipped up the front – he was allowed to have zippers but not buttons, which could be removed and swallowed – and a pair of white Velcro shoes on his feet. He was not allowed to have lace-up shoes.

"Hi, Warren."

He looked up from the picture book on his lap. She knew the title without having to see the front; it was a favorite. *Dilbert Ducky's Big Adventure*. Sometimes he pressed the book into Lona's hands, asking her to read it to him, but not today. Today his eyes lit up when he saw the cake in Lona's hands.

"Cookie!"

"Close. It's cake. It's birthday cake, Warren. Yesterday was my birthday." She crumpled the plastic wrap into a waste can and searched for a plastic spoon in the drawer where he sometimes collected them. He wasn't allowed forks. "Do you want to feed yourself?"

He opened his mouth like a baby bird. She spooned a small bite in, using the hard edge of the utensil to scrape a smear from the corner of his lip.

Why was she here?

Six months ago, she couldn't have imagined this. Six months ago, Warren was just the Architect, the man who designed the Julian Path as a monument to his dead son. He was also Genevieve's father. The Architect responded to the trauma of her death by erasing all of his memories with an electrical remmersing prod.

The first time Lona visited him, she wanted to see him miserable. She wanted to hate him. But then Rowena led her to his room, rapping brusquely on the door and shoving Lona inside. He was still in his crank-up bed then – he hadn't yet learned how to walk – stroking a plush pony.

"You have a visitor, Warren," Rowena had said, pushing Lona down into one of the chairs next to the bed. "First one. I'll stop back in twenty minutes to see how you're doing."

The Architect looked at her and his blue eyes were wide and benign. "Hi-hi!" he said. "Hi!"

She wanted to hate him. But when she opened her mouth, what came out was, "Hi, Warren. My name is Lona. It's nice to meet you."

"Story?" he asked hopefully when the cake was gone.

"There's a movie outside. I think it's *Bambi*. Do you want to watch it? The beginning is scary but you'd like when the baby deer and the skunk become friends."

He shrunk back against the armchair. "No. No out. Story."

"Fine. A story. Not Dilbert, though. I can't read that again."

He held out the duck story hopefully.

"No, *not* Dilbert. Something else." She picked through the selection on the shelf. "How about this one?" She pulled out an unfamiliar hardback that had a pig and a porcupine on the cover. One of the nurses must have brought it from the library. She settled on the arm of Warren's chair, making sure to hold the book so he could see the illustrations.

"*One day, Oink decided to conduct a science experiment,*" she began. "*He asked his friend Spike to help set up his laboratory.*"

"Nehhh," he interrupted. "Nehhh!"

"Right, Warren. It's an exciting story."

"Nehhh!"

She'd thought, once, that the exclamation was his daughter's name – that he was trying to say "Neve", the nickname Genevieve preferred. Doctors told her this wasn't possible – his brain scans on memory tests were flat. He didn't remember Neve. "Nehhh" was just an exclamation.

The book was funny, a *Sorcerer's Apprentice*-like tale that involved Oink and Spike surfing waves of expanding soap bubbles as they tried to stop their Magical Multiplying Solution. When Lona reached the end, she turned back to the beginning, without prompt, to read it again. Warren always liked to hear stories twice in a row, sometimes three or four times. When she finished the second time, she made a big show of closing the cover and putting it back on the shelf so he would know he wasn't going to get a third reading.

"Okay, Warren. It's time for me to go now."

He shook his head furiously and squirmed; he'd tucked something behind his back. She looked down to the floor. Her bag was missing. "Warren. We've been over this before. I'm still going to leave, even if you hide my things. It just makes me waste time looking for them, which makes me late, which makes me not want to come back." Warren tucked his head in shame, slowly pulling the bag from behind him.

"Thank you. I'll come back soon. Maybe next week."

"Soon."

"Soon."

He didn't have any concept of time. Lona could leave to get a soda from the vending machine down the hall, and when she returned he was just as happy to see her as if she'd been away for months. He didn't have any concept of anything. Warren had gotten what he always wanted for the children of the Julian Path. A clean slate.

Clean slate didn't mean purified slate, though. His had been wiped down, but it was impossible to remove the grime that had already burrowed below the surface. He was still responsible for his daughter's death. He just didn't have to spend every day remembering it.

Rowena appeared at the door, now wearing a pipe-cleaner necklace that someone must have made her in crafts. "We're doing root beer floats with the movie," she cajoled. "Are you sure you don't want to join us?"

Lona slung her bag over her shoulder. "Thanks, but I have stuff to do."

"Stay!" Warren pleaded. He'd grabbed the edge of her coat; his fingers were stubby and sticky and brown with cake, and looking at them suddenly filled her with revulsion.

Why did she keep coming here? It made her uneasy that she couldn't articulate it. She didn't enjoy spending afternoons with a 170-lb toddler, reading the same books over and again. The visits didn't feel like virtuous acts; they were filled with irritation, not compassion. But she was still choosing them, again and again, even though Warren didn't deserve them. Even though it meant lying to Fenn. Even though it would devastate him to find out.

"Lona?" From the tone of Rowena's voice, she could tell it wasn't the first time the nurse had called her name. "I asked if you wanted a root beer float for the road."

Lona shook her head and moved toward the door.

"Bring a friend next time," Rowena suggested cheerfully. "It would be nice to see more young people here."

"I don't have any friends who know I come here."

"Tell them you can get community service credits for volunteering," Rowena offered. "We've partnered with schools before."

"No," Lona said, because she'd phrased it wrong. What she should have said was, *If my friends knew I came here, they would no longer be my friends.*

4

A car was in the driveway at home, a blue station wagon Lona didn't recognize. She hung her coat by the front door and sniffed the sleeve of her sweater. The hospital had its own odor, like lemons and stale bread. She wanted it off her.

"Hey, are you back?" Fenn called from somewhere in the house, but she couldn't answer him smelling like hospital. It felt like reveling in her dishonesty. She ducked into the hallway bathroom, stripping off her sweater down to the short sleeves she'd worn underneath, scrubbing her face and arms until they were red.

In the kitchen, Fenn poured coffee for a small, wiry woman with a long ponytail.

"Talia!"

It was funny – Lona used to think the ex-Monitor had a hard face, one that reminded her of a weather-worried stone. Six months later, the fine lines around her mouth looked like laugh lines, not frown. The clothing helped. As a Monitor for the Julian Path, Talia had worn regulation black; today she was dressed in a green pullover and jeans.

"Where did you end up?" Fenn eyed her, briefly, before

pouring her a cup of coffee. "I thought you'd be back an hour ago."

"You probably just missed us." Talia slid the sugar to Lona. "Gabe and I were out doing errands all afternoon, but we were in the neighborhood so we decided to stop by and show you guys the new car."

Just missed them? Oh. Right. Her stomach fluttered as her memory returned. That was the fake destination Lona had given Fenn: going to drop some papers off at Talia's.

"I should have called first," she stammered. "When you weren't home I went to the mall instead. Just wandered around, didn't buy anything." She thought she saw Talia look at her, out of the corner of her eye, but tried to ignore it. "Are we doing Tuesday dinner a day early?"

Finally, Talia stopped looking at her and turned to Fenn. "If the chef says we're invited. We might as well; we're already here."

"It's just spaghetti. I'll add more noodles."

The back door banged open and a small boy flew inside, a mess of knees and elbows. Behind him, Gamb's arms extended like talons, swiping at the air. "RAAAWWR," he snarled. "I am a Ty-Gamb-isaurus Rex. I am going to EAT YOU FOR DINNER."

"Gabriel, tone it down in the house," Talia called as he rounded a sharp corner, but she was smiling. Talia had been terrified of taking full custody of Gabriel; she'd never been approved for parenthood. She insisted she was better equipped to deal with machines, not people. It made Lona happy she'd been wrong.

"How is he doing?" Fenn asked.

28

"He's a weird little dude. Really precise, I guess the best word would be? Like this afternoon I said, 'Okay, go get in the new car,' and he said, 'It's a *station wagon*.'"

"Do you ever think he remembers anything?" Fenn had lowered his voice to almost a whisper. "From before Path?"

Before Gabriel was admitted to the Julian Path, his mother tried to drown him in the bathtub. Erasing his memory prepared him to accept his new life as Julian – his Path name had been Djna, signifying he'd been born April 10, and Sector 14 like Lona.

"I don't know. Sometimes I think he does. I'll be reading him a new book and it will seem like he recognizes the plot already. Things like that. The therapist says I'm just imagining things. And why would I want him to recover his previous memories, anyway, when his childhood before was so shitty? Besides, it's possible he's just really freaking smart, and he knows that all kids' books are eventually going to end with the bunny deciding to come home.

"How's *your* school going?" Talia continued, turning her attention back to Lona. Her tone was casual; Lona hoped that meant she believed her story about going to the mall. "If we're doing Tuesday dinner now, we might as well get the official stuff out of the way. You're not behind on any assignments, are you? And you've scheduled your college entrance exams?"

Part of the court arrangement that allowed Lona to live in the farmhouse instead of with Talia required that she finish the rest of high school through self-paced home study, keeping a certain grade point average and maintaining weekly check-ins. Talia was caring, but efficient. She didn't try to parent, and Lona liked that about her – that she hadn't forced some unnatural intimacy.

"School's fine. Boring. The proficiency tests for eleventh grade are easier than what Julian was doing in ninth."

"If Lona proficiencies out early, we can start college together in the fall," Fenn explained. "We actually have a campus tour and interview scheduled for tomorrow, with the dean who contacted you a couple months ago."

"That's great." Talia looked pleased. "I was hoping you'd get in touch with him. High school's a nightmare however you spend it. Better to get it out of the way early."

Fenn opened the lid of a pot sitting on the stove and Lona smelled fresh tomatoes. He'd become the best cook in the house. He had the most time: Lona still had classes, and Ilyf had recently been recruited to work for a computer security company, something complicated with weird hours, and Gamb couldn't be trusted to microwave a potato without a kitchen disaster.

He dipped in a spoon and frowned. "I think this needs more basil. I'll go grab some from the greenhouse."

"Lona and I can do it." Talia was already scooting back her chair and looking meaningfully at Lona. "I should earn my supper."

There hadn't been a working greenhouse when the house belonged to Genevieve's family. Just a glass building down a path from the main house, unkempt, littered with leaves and mouse carcasses. Fenn cultivated it, making neat rows of cucumbers, tomatoes and asparagus, each labeled with seed packets on raised wooden beds. It was warm in here even when it was cold outside, the sun getting trapped by the glass, holding in moisture.

"Are you sure everything's okay?" Talia pushed aside the tomato vines to try to reach a particularly red fruit in the middle.

"Why wouldn't it be?" She froze, worrying that Talia could smell the hospital on her.

"Gabriel and I weren't running errands for very long before we came over," Talia said. Her voice was even. Not an accusation, but an invitation to Lona to explain more. "We only went to the bank."

"Then I guess I must have really just missed you. Bad timing."

Talia nodded, slowly. "Lona. If anything is bothering you, that's what my job is. In case there's something you didn't want to mention in front of everyone else."

She felt a sudden, desperate urge to mention where she'd been that day. She wanted to tell someone how she visited Warren and fed him cake, and she wanted someone to stroke her arm and tell her it was okay. Or to shake her and ask her what she was doing and tell her to stop. Or at least to help her understand why.

If she could tell Talia about Warren, then maybe she could tell her other things, like about the dream from two nights ago. She could explain how scared and out of control that dream had made her feel. *She could still feel the thumbtacks scratching on her skin.*

"What is it, Lona?" Talia asked.

"It's—"

"Yes?"

Lona swallowed down the urge to say more. That should be her penalty, for doing something she knew would hurt everyone else. Her penalty was silence.

There was one thing she *could* mention today, though she was shy about asking. Speaking out loud meant vocalizing beyond birthday candles that what she wanted was important.

"There *is* something I was hoping you could help me with. As my guardian."

"That's what I'm there for. To guard you."

She stalled by plucking a few basil leaves off a plant, tucking them into her hand and feeling the coolness against her skin. "I know my Path admission records didn't have any information on my parents. But I wondered if there could be more that wasn't included with those records."

"Lona, we went over this six months ago when you first brought this up. I found you myself, outside the Center, in the middle of the night. If anyone would know any more about your admission, it would be me."

"I know. But maybe not admission records. Maybe hospital forms? Maybe they did genetic testing, or they have samples of my DNA or something."

"Even if they did, it wouldn't matter unless there was someone to match the DNA with. You'd already have to have a parental candidate in mind."

"I know. I just thought. I don't have access to any of my own records until I'm eighteen. I looked it up. But I thought that as an employee – and as my guardian—"

"Lona, in nineteen years working in Path I don't think anyone was ever left with as little information as you came with. Most people at least left a note pinned to their kids' blankets."

She wasn't trying to be cruel. Talia spoke bluntly whether

it was harmful or not. Her career had, after all, been spent around machines. The underlying message wasn't comforting, though: *Nobody has ever abandoned a child as thoroughly as your parents abandoned you.*

"But you could try."

"I'll try. If you're sure you want me to."

"Why wouldn't I want you to?"

"Because you might not like what you found out. If you could find out, but what you found was a background like Harm's, which would be better – to know that or know nothing?"

Harm. Lona shuddered at the name. Harm the beautiful, Harm the ex-Pather, Harm the sociopath, who had lived with Julian along with seven other Strays. In the last memory she had of him, he was launching himself at the officers who were trying to remmerse her, ripping at skin with his teeth and nails. Lona remembered his file. He was abandoned when he was a few weeks old by a mother who already thought he was evil.

"I think I'd rather know."

Talia nodded. "Okay," she said. Then she pointed toward the house. In the kitchen, Fenn's head was bent over some culinary task. All Lona could see was the top of his curls, but those curls made her smile. He looked up, as if he'd felt her eyes on him, and waved with a slotted pasta scoop in his hand. "I'm just saying that you've had two families in your life. One didn't want you," Talia said. "And one of them obviously does. And I know which one I'd pick."

5

"I don't understand. You're saying that you need Lona Sixteen Always to help you achieve the goals they set for you."

"Seventeen. She just turned seventeen, Anders. But yes. I'm saying that."

"But you're also saying you don't want me to bring her to you. I could. They put me here to help you."

"They put you here to watch me. They never wanted to help me, or anyone else from—"

"They put me here to ascertain you're doing what's expected. Sir."

"Haven't I always done what's expected of me?"

"I'm just saying I could get her for you. Last time a group of kids got her from a government facility. This time we're the government and she's staying with a bunch of kids."

"It's more effective to wait until she comes to me. If you go get her, I'll have to put her to a bunch of tests you haven't even finished developing, to make sure she has what we need."

"You make it sound worse than it is."

"I think I'm the better judge of how bad the tests are."

"So you'll wait for her?"

"If she comes here, we won't need those tests. The proof that she has what we're looking for will be in the fact that she found us at all."

"Speaking of that. How is the prisoner?"

6

The desk drawer made a startled grunt when it pulled off its sliders, the sound of an old man being woken from a nap. The tacks were on the floor. His plastic name badge banged against his knee. It hung from his neck on a strand of metal balls, like a soldier's dog tags, like the worry beads carried by old women on the bus. He pushed it aside.

The voices were getting closer. The footsteps, too. Where would they have hidden it? Once they'd taken it from him – stolen it, no matter what they said – where would they hide it so he couldn't get it back?

He should hide. Under the desk. Between the filing cabinet and the potted plant. This was absurd. He wasn't a child playing hide and seek, and they weren't children, counting to thirty and chasing him to home base.

They were coming. They were coming. There was nowhere to hide.

"Lona." The hand on her shoulder wouldn't stop jostling her. "Lona, wake up."

She gasped for air, clawing blindly in front of her until her hand closed on fabric. Her heart thudded against her ribcage; she felt a scream fighting to come out of her throat.

"It's nice to see you, too," Fenn said. She looked at where she'd grabbed his shirt – at the buttons by his chest, as if her intention had been to kiss him, not to strangle him.

"Good morning," she said shakily, trying to laugh at herself, or at least make him think she was. She unclenched her fist, laying her palm flat against his chest, feeling the steadiness of his heartbeat and trying to slow hers to match.

It wouldn't slow. Why had she had that dream again? The dream that didn't belong to her, like she'd accidentally taken someone else's shopping cart. And this time it had gone further. This time the door had opened. This time she was seconds away from learning who was coming inside. *Big belly. Chapped hands. Short hair that brushed against his collar as he sorted through the drawer. Who was he?*

"It's almost afternoon, actually," Fenn apologized. "That's why I had to wake you. We'll be there soon. I was shaking you for almost a minute. Exhausted?"

Ex-hau-sted. She heard the words as a rhythm, and it took her a moment to realize why. The train. They were on a train; his voice matched the rattle of the cars going over the track. They were visiting a college. She wasn't searching through a messy desk; she was on a train, visiting a college. "I guess so," she said. "I must just be really tired. How soon will we be there?"

"Ten minutes. The stop after this one."

Ten minutes. She couldn't help but feel annoyed. If Fenn had let her sleep for two more minutes, she could have figured out who was coming to get the man, and why, and what he

37

was trying to find. She felt sure this dream had a definitive end, one she just couldn't get to.

"Do you have your transcripts?" he asked.

She groped for the vinyl bag beneath her seat. The hard plastic folder was in the outside pocket. She'd known it would be there – checking was unnecessary. But it was reassuring to have something tangible to moor her, even if the tangible thing was just a sheath of her grades.

"Next stop, Thirtieth Street Station," the conductor's voice blared over the tinny speakers. "Thirtieth Street Station, next stop."

"Hey." Fenn took his hand in hers, drawing circles in her palm with his thumb. "Hey. Are you nervous? It's just an informal interview. We don't have to go to this school. We don't even have to go on this tour if you don't want to. We can just go home."

She was being ridiculous. About all of it – wanting to get off the train, and about her dream. *Dream*, she repeated to herself. That's all it was. A dream. Not a message. Not a program. Not a Path. It was just her own mind, trying to make sense of everything that had happened to her in the past six months.

"I'm just jumpy," she assured him. "I want to be here. Of course I want to be here."

It was a beautiful campus. Lona could tell, even in the brown cold of December. It had archways made of stone, classrooms with old wood floors and unworking fireplaces. The tour guide, Jessa, told them the architectural style was called "American Gothic", modeled after the oldest universities in Britain. The buildings surrounded a green, which, Jessa giggled, might be dead and brown now, but really was green in the spring, with grass that students spread blankets on. Today was the last day of finals, and most of the campus had already emptied out.

Fenn squeezed her wrist. She could see him imagining them there, sprawled on the grass with a Frisbee and their textbooks and a bag of potato chips.

"What should we see next?" Jessa asked. She was from a town called Jessup. That's how she introduced herself. Jessa from Jessup, Maryland. She wore a puffy coat with the crest of the university on it, and a black outline of the dead president it was named after. Her cheeks were round and pinchable; Lona bet you could look at pictures of Jessa as a baby and know exactly what she looked like now. She liked to smile a lot. Especially at Fenn, Lona noticed – she smiled and looked for excuses to grab him by the sleeve as she pointed out campus landmarks. She didn't notice the barely perceptible way he recoiled – Pathers generally didn't like to be touched.

"Let's see." Jessa counted off the tour stops on her fingers. "We saw a dorm. We saw the green. We saw the student union, and the duck pond with the running trail. We saw a lecture hall. We saw the humanities library – did you want to see the science library? It's in a different architectural style – really modern. Some people like it better."

"I'm concerned about safety," one of the mothers asked. "You said the libraries are open until midnight, but I don't want my daughter walking through an empty campus that late at night."

"*Mom*," the daughter protested out of the side of her mouth. They looked alike. Both had the same thin noses, pale hair, long torsos, running shoes.

"What? I'm your *mother*. It's my job."

"No, no, it's a great question," Jessa said. "Campus is very safe. But if you're ever nervous about walking somewhere alone, that's why we have these yellow emergency call boxes all over the green. Pressing the red button immediately sends a public safety officer to your location. Or, if you call ahead, one of them will come and escort you back to your dorm."

The mother opened her notebook to make a satisfied check mark next to one of the questions on her list. This was her fourth on the tour. Check, check, check, check.

What would it be like to go through this tour with a parent? She and Fenn were the only ones without them in the group. She wouldn't know what to do with that level of protectiveness. It would drive her crazy. But at the same time, she wondered what it would feel like to have the genetic closeness. To not only know where you'd come from, but to see it every day.

"What are you two interested in?" Jessa asked, turning to Lona and Fenn.

They'd been mostly silent, hanging back while the other prospective students asked about "social life" and "dorm curfews" – coded language that made it clear they were really just asking about parties. Lona hadn't had a curfew for six months. "I could show you the athletic center," she continued. "Did either of you play any sports in high school?"

Lona hesitated; so did Fenn. This was the type of question she never knew how to answer. Julian had swum in high school, but was that really what Jessa was asking? She decided on "Not really" at the same time Fenn said, "We swam."

"Me too." Jessa clapped her hands. "And you're from

40

Maryland, too, right? What high school? I wonder if we swam each other."

Another question that should have been easy, but wasn't. Lona and Fenn's bodies had grown up in Maryland. Their brains went to school in Illinois, where Julian lived with his family.

For a few months after Path shut down, when everything was messy and there was no protocol, Lona had been sent to a therapist for coping skills on assimilating to the outside world. "Just tell them it's complicated," the therapist advised. "You're not under any obligation to share your whole life story with anyone. Tell them it's complicated, smile and move on."

"It's complicated," she tried now, and Jessa looked confused.

"We both grew up in several different places," Fenn filled in.

"Are you military brats or missionary kids, or. . .?" The question mark dangled as she waited for Lona to fill in the blanks. "Child actors?" she laughed. "Witness protection program?"

Lona should have lied and agreed to the military option. Now her silence was getting obvious – she could see Jessa getting embarrassed.

"You know what?" Jessa fumbled in her bag for her phone, checking the time. "Lona has her interview in fifteen minutes. Why don't we just go to the dining hall, and we'll all grab some hot chocolate and chat until then? That's what everyone's interested in anyway – how the food is. Ours is pretty good. There's always a kosher option, and the east dining hall has vegan—"

As Jessa rattled off more statistics about the dining hall, Fenn grabbed Lona's hand. "What does this campus taste like?"

"Besides kosher vegan hot chocolate?"

41

"I was thinking apples. Green ones, almost too tart." His nose was red in the cold. This – this college, this green, these American Gothic buildings – they all represented a fresh start to Fenn. Clean blackboards, clean slates, new apples. She loved the way he saw the future stretching out in front of them in wide expanses.

"If this campus were a fabric, what would it feel like?" she asked.

"The inside of a sweatshirt," he said. "Before you've washed it, when it's still really soft."

"I'd like to see another dorm first." The mom in the running shoes was asking another question. "The one we saw was all boys – can't you show us a girls' dorm?"

"No problem," Jessa said. "I'll take you to my room; it's on the way to the dining hall. Just ignore my roommate's messy desk. She's a total slob."

Lona's skin went colder than the weather should have allowed. *Messy desks. Thumbtacks. Footsteps. Coming.*

A dream, she told herself. *Just a dream.*

7

"If you just want to come with me." The assistant appeared in front of the couch where Lona sat. "The dean will be back any minute."

She followed the boy past the front desk, through a maze of corridors, and to a door at the end of an alcove. "Do you want anything?" the boy asked. "Some water?" He'd introduced himself but Lona had already forgotten his name. Something with a P. Lona did want a drink, but the water cooler was all the way back by the reception desk. She wished he'd asked sooner; now she'd feel rude making him retrace his steps to the front of the building.

"I'm fine."

"Cool," the boy said. "You can just wait in his office, then. And don't worry. He's not as weird as some people say he is."

He winked and Lona nodded like she got the joke. Did people say the dean was weird? She didn't know anything about the man who was going to conduct her admissions interview. Talia said he'd been made aware of her and Fenn's unique circumstances, and that he didn't mind them. That was all she knew.

It seemed warmer in the dean's office than in the reception area. She wondered if it was possible that books gave off heat. The office was stacked with them – dense textbooks, chunky readers, slim philosophical treatises, dog-eared paperbacks with cracked spines. On the shelves, but also on the floor and on the windowsill.

Lona shrugged off her coat and moved to sit on the only visitor's chair, but it, too, was covered in books. One, sticking out from the middle of the pile, had a bright blue cover of a little bird perched on the head of an exasperated dog. A children's book. She started to slide it out, wondering if it was something she'd read to Warren.

"That's one of the greatest sociological explorations of our time," a voice said. Lona dropped the book. It splayed open on the floor, one of its pages sticking out like a broken limb.

"I'm so sorry." She knelt quickly to pick it up.

"Don't worry. It's my great-grandson's. He's as likely to eat it as read it at this point in his life; I don't think he'll mind a couple scars."

The man who had entered the room had dark skin and white hair, shaved close to his head. Thick glasses draped from a chain around his neck. He was slightly built – she could see the way his layers of sweaters and tweed hung on his frame.

"Dean Greene." She extended her hand in the greeting she and Fenn had practiced. "I'm Lona. Your one o'clock admissions interview."

Dr. Greene waved his hand, unconcerned with her formalities. He navigated the path to his desk, easing himself into his chair, gesturing to Lona to remove the books and sit. "I haven't been a dean since I retired ten years ago. Just call me Quincy. Or 'professor', if a first-name basis makes you uncomfortable."

"You're . . . retired now?" At least she could tell Fenn not to stress about the interview. Their applications couldn't be taken seriously if the admissions interview was conducted by someone who didn't even work at the university.

"I wasn't joking when I said that book was an interesting sociological study. Have you read it?" She looked down at the book still in her hand and scanned the cover. *Are You My Mother?* it said. The title was familiar, but Lona couldn't remember the plot.

"It's about a baby bird – a generic kind of bird, although it looks somewhat like a duck – who hatches when his mother is away from the nest," Quincy continued. "So he sets out to find her, and of everything he encounters – a cat, a cow, a boat, a plane – he asks the same thing."

"Are you my mother?" Lona guessed.

"Self-explanatory, yes. It's for three year olds. You can probably surmise what happens."

"He eventually finds his mother and they're happy." A plot Gabriel would have been able to predict.

"Exactly so." Dr. Greene pounded the desk with his fist. She could see how he would have been a likable professor. Animated, encouraging, irascible. "On its surface, it's a quest about a bird looking for his mother. A tried and true, potentially overused, trope of storytelling. But if you think about it a little more closely, other strains of inquiry emerge. Why *can't* the cat be the bird's mother? What defines the intrinsic birdness of a bird? What message are we sending, saying birds can only be happy with other birds – rather than exploring what might happen if birds were taught other things? Maybe they would become more interesting birds."

"Maybe the cats would eat them," Lona said.

Dr. Greene chuckled. "If you're saying I'm being foolish, you're right. As a professor, my field of study focused on issues of nature and nurture, and how both come into play in questions of happiness. How much memory – even the memories we don't remember – can shape who we are. Forgive me, though. Professors – the old, saggy ones like me, at least – tend to see their work in everything they look at. Including children's books."

Dr. Greene might have been rambling, but the ramblings were the themes of Lona's own life. Should she look for her mother (that tried and true, potentially overused trope)? Should she let herself be distracted by a dream that felt like a memory? Even if the memory wasn't hers?

She realized the room had gone silent as she mulled these questions. "I'm sorry. I got lost thinking about what you'd said."

"A student stunned speechless by my brilliance!" he exclaimed. "Maybe we ought to admit you right now."

Yes. The interview. That's what she was here for. Not to debate the sociological implications of a children's book. "You said you retired?" she asked. "Do you still do work for the admissions office?"

"Oh, I come in from time to time when a project particularly interests me," Dr. Greene said. "I requested this interview. Actually, if you want to be precise about it – and we might as well, mightn't we? – I requested your application."

46

"Mine?" she blurted out. "Why?"

Dr. Greene leaned back in his chair and raised his eyes toward the ceiling. "'I own that I have been sly, thievish, mean, a prevaricator, greedy, derelict. And I own that I remain so yet'."

It sounded like a quote from something, but Lona knew she hadn't read whatever it was. Dr. Greene smiled. "It's from Walt Whitman. A poem about atonement. Not one of his better-known works, but if you're ever asked to memorize something, this one is only seven lines long."

"It's—" Was this part of the interview? Was he quoting poetry to see if she could analyze it? "It's funny. You expect him to say he'll never sin again, but instead he says he's still sinning."

"He still is sinning. But he's acknowledging it this time, which – at least he believes – makes it less evil." Dr. Greene paused. "Lona, I requested your application to atone for my sins." He leaned in. "I was on the committee that reviewed the Julian Path. I helped choose Julian."

Lona froze. She had been told that her interviewer would be made aware of her special circumstances. She hadn't realized quite how aware he would be.

"I was young then," he continued. His eyes were serious. "I thought I was old, but you always think you're old at the time and then look back and realize you were young. I registered my complaints, but they were more like grumbles. I could have done more."

She felt a surge of anger, the way she always did when something reminded her of the Julian Path. Here was a man who had helped to decide her fate, getting to decide her fate yet again with this interview.

47

"I wasn't going to tell you. But when you came in and I saw you – forgive me, for this in itself is selfish – I thought you deserved to have all of the information." Dr. Greene was silent then, waiting to see how she handled the news. Lona was sure if she stood and walked out now, he wouldn't try to stop her.

"This is your atonement? Giving me a chance to interview for a spot at your college?"

"The slot is already yours if you want it," he said. "Or slots, rather. Obviously, I've reserved one for Fenn Beginning as well."

"Don't we need to complete the interview?"

He raised his eyebrows. "Do we? I already know that you attended – virtually, at least – an excellent school with a strenuous curriculum. And I can't say that you lack an interesting personal history. I think I know all I need to know. Unless, of course, you have some questions for me."

Did she? Fenn had bought a book about preparing for college interviews. She was supposed to ask about classroom sizes and student–professor ratios. That seemed inconsequential now.

"Did you ever come to a decision?" she asked. "About how even the memories we don't remember can shape who we are?"

He brightened at the question – obviously not one he'd expected. "Not officially," he said.

"Not officially?"

"My disciplines were sociology and anthropology," he said. "We conduct studies. We're not philosophers – we can't just make something up and call it a finding. And I never could figure out how to conclusively learn whether the things that we don't even remember impact who we are. Because – problematically – we don't remember them." He shrugged ruefully at the paradox.

"Unofficially, though, you have thoughts."

He tapped his nose. "You're very perceptive. Unofficially, I think that the things we don't remember are the things that most define us. Because they are the things we'll go looking for – the holes we don't know exist but are always trying to fill." Dr. Greene produced a soft cloth from his desk, using it to clean his glasses. "Are you asking for yourself? Or someone else?"

She didn't know. She didn't know if she was talking about her, or Warren, or Gabriel, or anyone else. The dream she'd had had been so lifelike. *It's just a dream*, she kept telling herself. But it felt so much like a memory. "I'm asking – I think I'm just asking because I'm curious."

"Curiosity is a wonderful trait."

"I'm not sure." She thought back to Talia's question the other night. "If you could be curious or you could be happy, wouldn't you rather just be happy?"

"You say it like they're mutually exclusive. Some people are only happy if they're searching." He tilted his head. "You like big questions, don't you?"

"Do you know anything about dreams?" she pressed on.

Dr. Greene laughed, and, without answering her question, stood from his chair. She sensed the conversation was over, so she picked up the binder of transcripts that had gone unmentioned during the whole interview.

"My dear." Dr. Greene opened the door, patting her gently on the sleeve. "If we're not philosophers, we're certainly not Freudians."

8

She'd almost circled the duck pond near the admissions office twice waiting for Fenn, having left him a message to meet her there after his interview.

The air was cold and she found herself jogging to stay warm, trying to keep pace with a bunch of girls in earmuffs and nylon jackets who looked like they might be part of the track team. As she rounded the curve near the science library, her phone buzzed in her pocket. Talia. She slowed to a walk, resisting the urge to sit, which would only make her cramp up.

"Hi, Talia. I survived. Fenn's in there right now."

"The interview? It doesn't sound like you survived. It sounds like you're being tortured."

She forced herself to take two deep breaths. "I went for a run around this pond. Just self-imposed torture."

Lona talked about Dr. Greene first – how he'd been odd and silly but fascinating – and Talia swore she hadn't known anything about his connection with the Julian Path. Then she moved on to the campus, to the worried mom and all of her safety questions, and Talia laughed.

"Do you think you want to go there? Do you think you'd

be happy there?"

It was another version of what she'd thought about in Dr. Greene's office. What would make her happy? "I think so," she hedged. "If I'm going to go to college, I think I'd be happy at this one. I want to see what Fenn thinks. He should be getting out of his interview soon."

"Lona, wait." There was something new in Talia's voice – a misgiving, a trepidation. "I didn't call you about the interview. I'm glad to hear about it, but I called about something else."

"What?"

"You asked me to see if I could find any records. About your mother. And I said I'd try, but that there might not be—"

"What did you find, Talia?" She lurched to a stop. This was happening so much faster than she'd thought it would; it had only been a day since she'd asked. "Were there records?"

Talia hesitated. "No. But—" But? *But?* The wind was searing through Lona's coat yet it wasn't the cold that made her teeth chatter. "I found a video."

She slowly sunk to her knees, into the soft, woody pine needles covering the trail. "Of my mother?"

"I haven't seen it yet. It's being messengered to my house right now."

"Right now?"

"Lona. There's a good chance there's nothing useful on it." Talia was speaking slowly, like she spoke to Gabriel, or like Lona spoke to Warren when she wanted to make sure he understood that she wasn't going to read a story another time.

"But it's of my mother?"

"It's of the Path building, the night you were born. The

security footage. I'm shocked they still have it, honestly, except video files take up so little space, I guess there was no need to throw them away."

A herd of footsteps sounded from behind. Lona was vaguely aware of bodies pressing around her. The track team, a dozen girls in matching colors. One of them turned to give Lona an irritated look. She was still sitting on the ground, blocking the entire path.

"It's probably nothing," Talia said again. "It's old, and probably too dark to see much. Lona?"

"Yes?"

"Tell me you understand."

Probably nothing still meant possibly something.

"Lona, tell me you understand."

It was more than she'd had five minutes ago.

9

Lona leaned her forehead against the cool of the glass, watching the trees outside speed into a blur of green. She'd barely made the train, sprinting onto the last car just before it pulled out of the campus's station.

"Your card didn't go through. Miss?"

She looked up. A man with a mustache and a blue uniform was standing in the aisle. "When you went through the turnstile," he explained. "You went too fast – the machine couldn't deduct payment from your card."

"Oh. I'm sorry." She dug her train pass out of her pocket and handed it to the conductor, who swiped it with his mobile reader.

"You should never run to catch a moving train," he reprimanded her. "Take my mother's advice – if she ever saw someone do that, she'd say, 'Well, he must be late for his accident.'"

"Are we almost to the Forest Glen stop?"

He shook his head in irritation. "Half an hour. Be more careful."

She watched him stride into the next car, and the realization of what she'd done began to sink in. Talia had told her not to come, but she'd insisted on it anyway, leaving the pond and running straight to the train. And Fenn – she cringed with guilt when she thought of Fenn. He was probably standing at the duck pond entrance, alone, waiting to hear about her interview. She'd left without even telling him – how could she have done that?

She pulled out her phone to remedy at least that small thing. *Something came up with Talia*, she typed, feeling like the apology deserved full sentences. *I caught an earlier train. I'm sorry.*

How many truths was she omitting now? That she'd started looking for her mother again? That she went to visit Warren when she said she was running errands for school? That she was having bad dreams, of a man she'd never met? Fenn would never lie to her this way. She thought of him again, waiting for her under the pine trees, holding his binder full of transcripts. *I'm sorry*, she typed again.

"I told you not to come," Talia said when she opened the door. Lona was worried she was annoyed, but after a second she sighed and beckoned Lona into the living room, where Gabriel was playing with blocks on the floor.

"Lona!" He pointed proudly to the tower in front of him. "I made a castle!"

"Hi, Gabriel," she said mechanically. She was too jittery to summon the right excitement.

"Help me?"

"Hey, dude." Talia crouched to his level. "Let's relocate this building project upstairs, okay? Lona can't play right now."

Lona knew she should offer to help move the toys, but all she could do was stare at the television mounted on a stand across from the couch. Next to it was an antiquated machine, the type Lona hadn't seen since Julian was little. Talia must have requested it in order to play the footage. Inside the machine would be a disc. On the disc would be her mother.

"It's all set up?"

Halfway up the stairs, Talia stopped. "I'll be down in just a minute, after I get him situated. If you want to wait—"

"I just press play, right?"

"Are you sure you want to watch it alone? I can come back and—" Her face wrinkled in concern, but she cut herself off when she saw Lona's expression. Lona was sure. All of this felt too uncertain and too raw. The footage might make her cry and she didn't want to do that with company.

She waited until the door of Gabriel's bedroom closed above her and leaned in close to the television, until she could almost feel the heat coming off it. Her finger hovered over the play button, quivering. *This was your wish*, she reminded herself. *This is why you blew out the candles.*

There was static on the screen. And then there was blackness. As her eyes adjusted, she could make out more than blackness – the outline of a brick building, ghostly in streetlights. This was the building she'd grown up in, as it looked on the night of her birth. She'd grown up watching someone else's life on a screen. Now she was watching her own.

In front of the entrance, a car pulled up, the passenger's side facing the camera. It was a light-colored sedan, gray or beige. There was no audio to accompany the footage, so the car drove into the frame silently and pulled to a stop.

Her fingers hurt. She looked down and she was clutching the sides of the coffee table so forcefully her fingernails were bending.

She waited for someone to get out of the car. Would it just be her mother? Or had someone come along to help? Would her mother look sad? Would she stop to give her a last kiss?

The car pulled away. *No*, Lona thought. It couldn't pull away. She hadn't seen anything. The person inside hadn't done anything. *She hadn't even glimpsed her mother's face*.

But the driver *had* done something. Because the car was gone, and in its place, directly in front of the Path center, a tiny bassinet sat in the doorway. Herself. Lona, asleep and impossibly small, barely a smudge on the grainy screen. If she squinted her eyes, she thought she could see the baby on the screen raise a tiny fist in a wail.

She rewound the video and watched it again for clues. And then again, and again. But she could never see the driver open the door, or remove the bassinet. She could never see anyone ring the buzzer that must have been next to the door. She couldn't even see the license plate.

Talia had been right. This was a dead end.

"My hair was amazing, right?" Lona hadn't heard Talia come back down the stairs, and she jumped at the sound of her voice.

"Your hair?"

"You didn't wait for me to come on the screen with my hideous bangs?" Talia joked. "Nobody ever told me your hair wasn't supposed to grow horizontally." Her voice grew quieter as she placed a careful hand on Lona's shoulder. "You weren't

56

outside alone for very long. I promise, Lona. Whoever left you rang the buzzer – I hoped you'd keep watching because I came down and got you less than two minutes after they drove away."

"You already watched it. You watched it without me."

Talia shrugged in apology. "I know I shouldn't have. I just – if something bad had happened on that screen, I didn't want you to be the first one to see it." Lona softened at the concern in Talia's voice. "I'm really sorry, Lona. I'm sorry there wasn't anything useful."

"You tried. And you warned me. You said there probably wouldn't be anything." But she felt deflated. And annoyed. Not at the Talia now, who had watched the video after all, but at the one seventeen years ago, who came downstairs two minutes after the car that left baby Lona had driven away. Why couldn't that Talia have come down earlier? Why couldn't that Talia have seen something?

"Can I make you something?" Talia offered. "Hot chocolate or coffee? With animal crackers? Watch, as I try to solve the world's problems with snacks."

Lona shrugged loose of Talia's hand. "Thanks. But I should go now, anyway. To get back to the train station before it's too dark."

"Are you sure? How about I drive you home? We can stop for dinner on the way."

"No, you'd have to pack up all of Gabriel's stuff," she began, and when she saw Talia opening her mouth to protest, she hurried through. "And I kind of think I want to be alone. If that's okay."

Talia nodded, but looked unconvinced. "Call me if you change your mind. I'll pick you up at any stop."

Lona knew she wouldn't, though. She was feeling weary, saddened by the loss of something she'd let herself want even more than she realized.

She walked the fifteen minutes back to the train station on autopilot, and sank into an empty seat next to a commuting business man.

The whir of the train made her eyelids grow weighty. The colors outside the train window blurred together until finally she gave into the heaviness and fell.

There was nowhere to hide. There was no time to hide, either. It was too late. He wasn't going to find it before they got here. He had failed.

The door began to open. He stood up, leaving the contents of the drawer spilled on the floor. There was no sense in trying to put it away. No sense in greeting your enemy with your knees on the floor. No sense in letting your enemy know they are your enemy.

The man who walked inside jumped backwards after he opened the door. He said, "Oh!" like he'd walked in on his own surprise party. Like this was a pleasant reunion for all of them. "I was just looking for you," the man said.

"Hi, Warren. You found me."

10

"The prisoner still isn't responding. Sir."

"Give it time, Anders. Anders. You don't like when I call you by your first name, do you? You want me to call you *Doctor.*"

"No. Sir."

"It bothers you that you have initials after your name, and I am the one they put in charge."

"It bothers me that the project has been stalled for weeks and you're still not achieving any retainment. The advancements are useless if the subjects aren't retaining anything."

"I already told you that I didn't want to force it. I want Lona to come to me. I was put in charge of this project, because I have special knowledge of how to achieve these goals."

"The decision to bring you in was a highly unorthodox one, and it's one that's reversible. If they don't feel that your methods are working, there are other methods to be tried. All of those alternate methods will involve you going back to the place you were rescued from. How would you feel about that? Sir."

"I thought you knew. I was recruited because I don't feel."

11

Lona locked herself in the bathroom at home, curling into the small space between the sink and the bathtub, trying to surround herself with concrete, literal things. Things she could touch. Things that made sense. The dream had been scary when she didn't know anyone in it. Now that she knew Warren was in it, it was terrifying. She couldn't ignore it anymore. Something was very wrong. She didn't understand it. But something was very, very wrong.

"Lona?" Fenn knocked on the door. "You're back?"

She scrambled up to the sink, scraping a wash cloth over her cheeks and checking to make sure her eyes weren't too bloodshot before pulling the door open.

"I'm back. I'm fine." She heard how curt she sounded. She knew she should be apologizing. But it was hard to get out even short sentences after everything that had happened in the past three hours.

She squeezed past him into the hall. Fenn stepped back, but it seemed like it was at the harshness of her words, more than to let her pass. "You left me," he said. "You left me in the middle of campus with no warning."

"I know."

"You *know?*"

She pushed past him. Everything seemed pixelated. Everything seemed fuzzier than the sharp lines and pure colors of her dream. She needed to stay in reality. She needed to keep touching real things. She went to the kitchen, pouring a glass of water, making herself concentrate on the feeling of the liquid as it slid down her throat and all the way into her intestines. "You *know*." He pressed. "That's your excuse? Where *were* you?"

"I told you. I left you a message." *Breathe. Feel the water on the back of your tongue.* "I was going to Talia's."

"Is Talia okay? Are *you* okay?"

"Talia's fine," she managed.

"Then what happened?" She stalled, setting the glass on the countertop and watching the circle of water pool around the bottom. Wasn't that the essential question? *What was happening to her?* "Lona?" he asked again. "What's going on?"

It should be so easy to tell him. But none of this seemed easy. "*Lona?*"

"I don't want to talk about it."

"You don't—"

"*Stop it.* Stop asking me." She watched the words fly out her mouth and couldn't take them back. "I'm sorry that I left you, I'm sorry you were waiting for me, I'm sorry I don't want to talk about it, but I don't. I don't want to talk about any of it!"

"Then what do you want to do?" he asked.

"I want you to leave me alone!"

Fenn hadn't said or done anything wrong. She knew that. It was the questions she didn't know how to answer, and the panic that thinking about them prompted. Fenn's face – she could barely stand to look at the hurt and confusion in it, especially knowing that she'd caused it.

Back when Lona first left the Path, they'd had a few arguments. Times when she wondered whether the boy she'd grown up with had completely disappeared. They hadn't in a while, though. Not since the Path was shut down. Not since they were supposed to be normal. They had left the Julian Path and they had been cured, or if not cured, then better. This was their first real fight, she realized.

"Fenn, I didn't mean—" she started, but he waved at her not to bother.

"You don't need to," he said stiffly. "You don't have to explain where you were. I don't have to know everything about you."

"Wait, that's not what I meant," she said. She wanted him to know everything about her. That's how it had always been. She just didn't know how to fix this.

"It's fine, Lona. It's fine." He turned and disappeared; a few minutes later she heard the sound of his door closing.

The water had helped. She could feel steadiness returning to her stomach. She could feel herself becoming herself again. Or becoming whatever terrible person she was turning into.

12

"Warren, look! Lona's back again today. A visitor twice in one week!"

He looked up from the area rug in the middle of his room, the toes of his stockinged feet curling into the carpet.

"Shoes off." He pointed to where his Velcro sneakers sat by the side of the rug.

"Maybe you can show Lona what you mean." Rowena nodded encouragingly, before muttering an explanation to Lona. "He learned last night, all on his own. It's all he's been doing all morning long. Shoes on. Shoes off."

"Is that impressive?"

"Don't know. We've never had a case like this. But it's not like he's brain damaged. He's just an infant. There's no reason he shouldn't be able to learn things over again."

"Like, about his previous life?" Lona picked a loose thread from the headrest of the armchair, twisting it between her fingers. "Learn stuff like that?"

"I said things, not memories." Rowena spotted a few dirty dishes on Warren's kitchenette, efficiently sweeping them up on her way out the door. "Those old memories are gone for good."

Rowena left and Lona didn't know where to begin. She hadn't talked to Fenn since their fight last night. He'd gone to bed without saying good night for the first time she could remember. She'd thought about knocking, but what would she say? And now she felt unfinished, like something was missing, like her house key or her wallet, but what was missing was the sense of peace she usually got from thinking about Fenn.

Now she was cracking up and the only person who might be able to explain what was happening was the man in front of her. And right now all he wanted to do was take off his shoes.

Lona kneeled on the carpet next to him. It smelled antiseptic and musty. "Warren?"

"Shoes off." He pointed at her feet. "You shoes."

"Warren, I need to talk with you about something."

"You shoes."

She was wearing lace-up boots, good for cold weather, bad for this children's game. She unknotted the bows and yanked the boots off, lining them up next to Warren's sneakers. "Okay. My shoes are off. Just like yours. We both took our shoes off."

"Now on." He picked up his right tennis shoe and crammed his toes into it, using his index finger as a shoehorn against his heel.

"Warren, I had a dream that you were in yesterday. Do you know what a dream is? Warren?"

His tongue protruded from his mouth as he triumphantly shoved his foot in the rest of the way and sealed the two Velcro straps down on his foot, neatly parallel, like the "equals" sign in a math equation.

"In the dream, you were coming to find me. Except I wasn't

me. You were coming to find someone else." *How would that explanation make sense to him? It barely made sense to her.*

"Story?" Momentarily bored with the shoe game, Warren trundled to the shelf. He picked up a book Lona hated. It was about a marching band, and on every page, squishy rubber buttons that looked like clown noses simulated the noises of the instruments. It was loud and irritating, becoming completely insufferable after more than one reading. A few visits ago, she'd tried to stuff it behind other books on the shelf. He must have found it.

"Let's not do that story now. Let's—"

He shook the book open to a random page, blasting a screeching saxophone with the palm of his hand. With his other hand, he palmed through to a different page, beating down on the tuba button.

"Warren, please, I need to talk—"

Now he was pulsing both buttons at once. Her head throbbed from the noise. He raised his hand above his head and slammed it down onto the red-orange clown nose. The tuba emitted a wet, noisy wheeze. He'd crippled the soundbox.

"Warren!"

Before she could stop herself, she violently wrenched the book out of his hands and flung it across the room. "Stop it, Warren. This is *important*. I need to *talk* to you."

His mouth gaped open in a silent grimace, tears squeezed out of the corners of his eyes. She'd made him cry.

"Warren, I didn't mean—" She reached toward him but he fearfully burrowed further in the corner.

Lona tried to calm herself. The Architect had been in her

dream. This man was not him. She needed to keep reminding herself of that. This man wore his skin and shuffled around in his body, but it wasn't him. The man from Lona's dream didn't exist anymore.

Lona sunk to the carpet, folding her legs in, making herself small and unassuming. "I wish," she said softly, "that I had some shoes with Velcro on them."

Warren peeked out from around the corner. Lona ignored him, focusing on the rug in front of her. "I wish I did, because I know how to do a special trick, but it won't work on my shoes, because my shoes have boring laces."

Warren crawled out from his chair and extended his legs toward Lona, the pant legs of his lilac sweat suit riding up his calf.

"See, your straps are in lines." She gently reached to his feet. "But you can also do them *this* way." She peeled back the Velcro and switched the straps so that they crossed each other, forming a multiplication sign instead of an equals. "X marks the spot."

Warren bobbed his head up and down, insisting that she do the other one before practicing on himself. Lona leaned her head against the wall and glanced at the alarm clock on Warren's bedside table. Almost five. She still needed to stop by the electronics store for a new calculator. Hers had recently shorted out in the middle of practice text. Last week she'd also promised to buy some new earphones for Fenn. *Fenn.*

"Story?" Warren looked up hopefully from his shoes, which he'd managed to Velcro together.

"Okay." She sighed. "A short one. The one from the other

66

day? The pig and the porcupine and the science experiment?"

She found it by the chair where they'd left it and opened it to the first page. Oink sat in his lab, daydreaming about the experiments he was going to conduct. His elbows rested on his messy desk as thought bubbles floated from his head.

"Here's his lab." Lona held up the book so he could see the pictures. "See how messy it is?"

"Nehhh! Nehhh!"

Warren reached out and stroked his fingers down the page. He did that with books, treating them as tactile objects. Most of his had fingerprints streaking down the illustrations. This one he seemed particularly interested in, jabbing at the scientific clutter of Oink's office.

"Nehhh!"

Lona froze. The office was familiar because it reminded her of her dream. Her dream had been in a lab. It wasn't like the labs from Julian's high school science classes – it didn't have test tubes or Bunsen burners. It had electrical equipment, and reams of paper pouring out of a machine with a needle that looked like it was designed to measure earthquakes or lies.

She mechanically turned the page. The next illustration showed Spike the porcupine at home making a sandwich. Warren shook his head, trying to flip back to the previous page.

"Nehhh!"

Warren didn't have the typical linguistic problems of a developing toddler. He didn't say "pesketti" instead of "spaghetti", or "lello" instead of "yellow." Lona had only ever heard him make one repeated error. Sometimes, when he said a word that ended in "D", he would cut off the end sound, just the last consonant. "Bed" became "Beh". "Good" became "Gooh".

When Warren said "Nehhh," that's not what he was saying at all.

He scrambled on the floor, through the mess of the spilled drawer. His ID badge swung from his neck, the plastic photo clunking against his fat stomach. They were coming. The photo showed the top of straight strawberry blond hair. The last name started with a C, or an O, maybe. It was obscured by the fabric of his pants.

The first name was Ned.

He knew. That bastard. Somewhere in the deep corners of the Architect's broken brain, he knew exactly what Lona was dreaming about.

13

Fenn was in bed when she got home, his body curled like a C facing the wall. Lona stood over him for a few seconds, debating. Technically they were still fighting. But after what she'd just been through with Warren, she needed to feel comforted. She tossed her coat and the crumpled plastic bag containing her new calculator onto the floor and slid in behind him.

He stiffened when her hands touched his back – so he wasn't sleeping – but he didn't pull away. After a few moments she nestled between his shoulder blades and felt the expansion and contraction of his ribcage and how it mirrored her own. Their breathing always matched, like two instruments playing the same piece of music. In the Julian Path, the pods they lived in sounded like breathing. They made a whooshing sound, an electronic hum disguised as an inhale and exhale, the sound of two hundred Pathers living the same life at different times.

"Hi," she said quietly.

"Hi." He didn't ask where she'd been all day.

"How are you?"

"Fine."

"Fenn. Yesterday—" She could see the dark shadow of his

head nodding back and forth, telling her that she didn't have to continue, but she pressed on. "Yesterday I was at Talia's because I asked her to find my mother. She thought she had, but she hadn't."

Fenn immediately flipped over; she could see his eyes glinting in the dark. "Lona, I didn't know you were still looking for her. Why didn't you tell me?"

She shrugged, even though she knew he couldn't see. "I was embarrassed."

"About what?"

"I don't know."

"You're allowed to want things, Lona."

"I guess – I just didn't want you all to think you weren't enough."

He was stroking her hair now, and she closed her eyes, feeling their argument yesterday begin to melt away. "Is that where you were today again?" he asked. "Something with your mother? Is that where you've been all of the times that you've disappeared?"

Her eyes flew open. "All of the times?" She hadn't realized how many of her absences he'd noticed. She thought she'd been hiding it so well.

"When you disappear and don't tell any of us where you go. It seemed like something has been preoccupying you. And I'd been worrying – does it have to do with me?"

Tell him, she instructed herself. *Tell him about Warren, now, in the dark when he can't see your face and you're already sharing secrets. Just say it and lift the heavy weight from your chest.* But she still couldn't. The Julian Path had almost killed Fenn. She didn't know what hearing about this would do to him. The act of not telling him was selfless, she tried to convince herself. Her silence had nothing to do with just wanting to make things better between them.

"Yes. That's where I've been."

But as soon as the lie slipped out, she was flooded with guilt. "Fenn, there's something else. I've been—" She stopped and swallowed, trying to collect her thoughts. "I've been having strange dreams."

Fenn's hand on her hair trembled. "Why didn't you tell me?" he demanded. "We tell each other about those."

He thought she meant her usual bad dreams. He thought she meant Genevieve on the tile floor. "I had that dream last night, too," he said. Lona was surprised. Fenn hadn't even been there when Genevieve died. Apparently the experience was bad enough that Fenn absorbed it into his own subconscious.

"Then you broke your own rule," she said. "You can't be upset that I didn't tell you about my dream when you didn't tell me about yours."

In the darkness, Lona could see the shadows change across Fenn's face. A wave of nausea, maybe, or disgust. "We tell each other about the *bad* dreams. I didn't tell you about that one because in my world, that passes for a good one."

"Fenn." She stiffened. She knew that he was relieved when the Architect had remmersed himself, and she knew that he'd been angry with Genevieve before she died. Still, she couldn't imagine why Fenn would now say something so horrible.

"The bad ones are where it's you who was shot instead." His voice broke. "I hate myself, because I wake up from dreaming

71

about Genevieve dying and my first sickening emotion is to be grateful that it wasn't you." He touched her face, softly with the back of his hand, running his knuckles from her ear down her cheekbone and over her chin. "Lona. Even dreaming that you die kills parts of me. Every time."

"But I didn't die." She cupped her hand over his. "I'm here in this bed with you."

"Do you think we really get to be that lucky? Sometimes I can't believe it – that we got to come out of that program and I get to have you and we get to move on with our lives. I keep waiting for the other toll, the other tax for being so lucky. I keep waiting for someone to tell me that I don't get to have you after all."

He brought his mouth to hers, parting her lips with his tongue, tasting her while his fingers wound through her hair. She started to speak, to offer some kind of reassurance that everything would be okay, but his mouth pressed down harder, relentless. Through their swollen lips, she could feel his teeth mash against hers, hungrily. That's what this kiss felt like. Hungry. Feral. Desperate. He had kissed her a hundred times before but not like this. Fenn was usually gentle and careful, letting her take the lead. This time, when he finally moved his mouth from hers, it was only to kiss her throat, just below her earlobe, his tongue exploring the hollow underneath her jaw. By then she'd forgotten what she was going to say. Her breath came out in jagged gasps and so did his.

He moved his hand from her hair, resting his forearm next to her face and transferring his weight onto her. She could feel the warmth of his skin through his T-shirt, and below that, the pounding of his heart. His other hand ran the length of her body, from her neck down to her waist and thigh. He always treated her as something precious, but usually it was like a glass figurine, a paper snowflake, something that would break or tear if it fell to the ground. Tonight he acted as though she was something precious like water. Food. Something he could not live without.

In the early days after Path, kissing Fenn had reminded her that she was alive. Not just tied to him, but tied to the earth – a real physical being with her own desires and agency, not just a mind living in a pod. Now it reminded her of that again. Of how lucky she was to be here. Of things that were worth holding on to and things that were worth searching for.

"Fenn," she said, breaking her mouth away from his. "I can tell you more about – about where I was today."

"Do you still want to be with me?"

"Yes."

"Only me?"

"Of course."

"Then it's not important."

But it was.

14

It was almost two in the morning. Fenn's eyes were closed; he'd fallen asleep as soon as she'd told him everything was all right. His arm was draped around her waist and the corner of his mouth was twitching in what looked like a happy dream. She envied him. Her mind was moving too fast for sleep.

One time for Julian's birthday, he and his best friend Nick had gone to a visiting carnival. He was turning ten, she thought, or eleven. They went on two rides and then Nick got sick to his stomach, so they spent the rest of the day playing games. Nick liked Whack-a-Mole, where the goal was to use a mallet to smash down a plastic mole that kept coming out of different holes. That's what she felt like now. Every time she managed to make progress on one thing in her life, another popped up, unexpected, never what or where she thought it would be. She had made things better with Fenn, but only because she had lied. She hadn't found her mother in a security video, but she might have found the subject of her dreams in an old man's scrambled brains.

Lona shivered. It had been a long time since she'd used a memory of Julian's as a reference point for her own life. It was so comforting, to sink back into the time when she had been a passive participant in her own life rather than an active one. She tried not to let herself now, though. She wanted her own memories, her own identity.

She wanted to feel like she was taking control of her own destiny. And her destiny was there, right in front of her. Or destinies, rather. Three distinct paths and she needed to choose one.

She could go to school with Fenn. They could study at the café with the bad open mike guitar players, and they could go to end-of-semester parties like ones she'd seen advertised on the public bulletin board in the campus center. "Celebrate Christmas Break," they said. "Come dressed as your favorite elf/reindeer." She and Fenn could do that, all of it.

She could keep searching for her mother. The video had led nowhere, but there still might be other records, somewhere. Talia would help her, she was sure of it. Talia would protest and worry, but then she would help. She and her mother could live happily ever after.

The third option was crazy. It involved chasing dreams. It involved trying to reawaken the memories of a shattered old man. The third option shouldn't even be an option. It shouldn't even be one of her choices, because it had nothing to do with her. It had to do with Warren. And a man named Ned, whom she had never met.

Sleep wasn't coming. She slid out from under Fenn's arm, holding her breath and easing her legs off the bed one centimeter at a time. He stirred but didn't wake, and after a few moments, she tiptoed to the door.

In the hallway, she heard the low sound of the television. She headed into the living room to turn it off, but while she was looking for the remote, the fluffy comforter at the end of the couch suddenly moved. Gamb had fallen asleep there.

"Are you just getting home?" he yawned, unburrowing himself and stretching his arms over his head.

"I couldn't sleep."

Gamb fished the remote out from underneath his blanket. "Do you want to stay up with me and watch bad television?"

"I don't know if I'll be great company," she hedged.

"Bad television doesn't require great company. It just requires a warm body." Gamb patted the sofa cushion next to him and, when Lona sat down, shoved half of the comforter in her direction.

"Now," Gamb continued, scrolling through the channels on the deluxe cable package he'd insisted would be a good investment. "Should we watch competitive bass fishing? Or this reality show about beauty pageants? Or – what do you think that 'Killer Gymnasts' is about?"

"I'm just the warm body. You're the driver."

Gamb settled on a Spanish melodrama set in a hospital. As far as Lona could tell, the plot was about a pretty nurse who was torn between her handsome surgeon coworker and her handsome dying patient.

"Oh, Maria," Gamb fake-translated from the screen. "Stay with me. Stay with me, I am such a beautiful man."

"I can't," Lona played along. "I must go with my surgeon, and his thick and lustrous hair."

"No, my baldness is sexy, for it means I have suffered. Stay with me. Stay, and I will give you some of my Jello."

"Is it strawberry? I only eat straw—"

"You know what? Jello sounds good." Gamb paused the movie. "I'm hungry. I'm going to go find some snacks." He shrugged off the blanket and darted into the kitchen. Lona could hear cupboard doors opening and closing. On the screen, the handsome surgeon was frozen in space, discussing the contents of a clipboard with another colleague wearing a white lab coat.

"Maria," Gamb called from the kitchen. "I know you said you only eat strawberry Jello. Do you eat popcorn? I will win your heart with popcorn."

Lona opened her mouth, but nothing would come out. She couldn't stop staring at the screen. At the doctors. At what they were wearing.

Of course. In the Path program, Monitors like Talia wore black pants and shirts, blending in with the darkness of the control room and the bay. Touchers wore street clothes. Sweaters and jeans and comfortable shoes. Path doctors wore white. When they came to test Pathers on their motor skills and intellectual development, they wore long white lab coats that made them seem enormous to Lona when she was a child. Long white lab coats, and plastic nametags.

Why else would Warren have been there? How else would this be tied at all to Lona?

"Maria?" Gamb called again. "Lona? I'm just making popcorn, okay? Do you want anything else?"

The scientist from her dream. Ned. He didn't just work in a random lab. Lona was dreaming of the history of the Julian Path.

15

The prisoner had begun to think of itself as an It. There was a time when the prisoner had another name, but the prisoner had had so many names since then, it was barely worth remembering.

The room was familiar. Everything was laid out as it should be. The bed along the wall, the window beside the bed, the poster over the desk, curled around the edges. Could it be the same poster? No. Not even they could find the same poster. This must have been a reproduction.

And maybe the room wasn't familiar, anyway. Maybe it was false déjà vu, an implanted memory. They would know something about memories. If it wasn't familiar before, though, it certainly was now. Spending twenty-four hours in a space makes it feel very familiar. It was twelve foot lengths to cross one corner of the narrow end to the other; fourteen foot lengths to cross the width.

The window had security bars over it, but through the bars it was possible to see grass, a fence, beyond that an alley, maybe. The bars did not look strong. With the right tool or even the right leverage, it might have been possible to pry off the bars, but first one would have to break through the glass. It wasn't possible to break through the glass. The prisoner had tried.

The prisoner had also tried: yelling. Passing notes under the door. Eating the food. Refusing the food. Hoarding the food. Assaulting the person who came with the food, a man with a smushed-looking face, like his features took up too little space. He hadn't been happy about that. He'd said he was some kind of doctor; he seemed to think that should gain automatic respect.

None of these things made any difference, but it was useful to keep lists. Useful to approach things with the scientific method. Construct a hypothesis: *I could escape through the window, if I hurled this chair against the glass.* Test the hypothesis: *I can't.*

There was a clock and that was helpful. Dinner was served at six, with a standard deviation of eleven minutes on either side. The sun set at five fifteen now, but it was getting earlier, which must mean that it was getting later in the year. Deeper into winter.

The boy with the flaming hair came at random intervals, not tied to any particular time. Sometimes he brought the food, but more often he just wanted to talk. The others deferred to him. They left when he entered, and they gave him space, and when he talked to them, they looked down. He was beautiful. His hair was the color of bonfires in some light, of candlelight in others. His skin was pale; his movements were graceful and fluid. When he walked, he gave off the impression of a lit match floating across a smooth surface.

Today he came after sunset but before breakfast. He knocked first, he always did. Knocking, smiling, sinking to the floor on his knees as easily as if there had been a chair there. The surest sign of confidence from this man-boy was the fact that he placed himself in such a subservient position.

"How are you feeling today?" he asked. Such careful pleasantries.

The prisoner said nothing.

Hypothesis: *If I say nothing, he will be forced to give me more information.*

"I heard they took away your pen yesterday," the boy continued. They had. He was right. They didn't take it away so much as it had been removed still sticking out of the hand it had been stabbed in. They should have known better. The prisoner had a history with pens. "How did it feel, when you stabbed Anders?"

News: The man with the smushed face's name was Anders.

"Did it make you feel pleased?" he continued. "How much did he bleed, and what did you think when it got on your clothes?"

The prisoner looked away. Those discussions were unnecessarily stomach-churning.

"I'm sure it feels impossible to be without a means of communicating ideas – especially for someone in your profession." The boy sighed. "But I'm sure you understand that I can't really give you another one."

He shifted slightly, reaching into his pocket and pulling out a crayon. It was new and sharp, a dusty coal color. "Outer Space," the paper wrapping read. The name of this color was Outer Space. "I thought that this could be a replacement."

The boy placed the crayon on the floor, equidistant between the two of them. A sign of respect. He would not make the prisoner lose dignity by crawling and grabbing for the crayon.

"I hoped that you could use this to continue with your work," he said. "And when it's done, I can bring you another one. And after a while, maybe we can create a workspace for you."

A better workspace. A life outside of these four walls. The prisoner's heart jumped and then thudded back again. This was a ploy. Obviously. This was a way of engendering gratefulness. How long had the prisoner been in this room? Days? Weeks? Long enough to forget memories, and original identities. Long enough to be known as the prisoner.

"Sometimes I can't tell," the boy said thoughtfully. When he turned his head toward the window, the light caught it and made his hair glow. "Sometimes I can't tell how much it is that you don't remember and how much it is that you're just refusing to say." He reached down to the crayon, to Outer Space, and, with his graceful fingers, rolled it a few inches away from him, disrupting the equilibrium, conceding the middle ground. "I really hope this will all be over very soon," he said. "I hate to keep you here like this – not when we should all be on the same side. We need your help, and you can leave as soon as you give it."

Hypothesis: *That was a lie.*

The flamehaired boy rose to his feet. He brushed the knees of his pants – a gesture that seemed less human than humanesque – as if he had studied humans and had learned they behaved in such a manner.

"In the meantime," he said. "You must think we're very, very cruel."

16

The library was busy on a Saturday morning – little kids there for a story hour, and students Lona's age working on research projects. Lona walked past all of them to the reason she'd come to this particular branch, several miles from her usual one.

FEDERAL REFERENCE DESK, the sign said, in all capital letters.

Lona cleared her throat. The girl at the desk had dark red lipstick and an eyebrow piercing, chunky, trendy-looking glasses, and apparently no interest in being helpful.

"Excuse me?" Lona said finally.

"What's up?" the girl asked, but she didn't look up when she said it. She couldn't be much older than Lona.

"I'm hoping you can help me find some records."

"Yeah. This is kind of the place for that. Were there any particular records you had in mind?" The girl finally made eye contact. She had a large chest, painted fingernails. There was something in her voice that reminded Lona of Genevieve. The standoffishness. The coolness – like she was waiting to be impressed. Lona handed her the index card that she'd carefully filled out, using the instructions on the government website.

"Which records do you want?" The girl moved the computer's mouse lazily over the keypad. On her lap, underneath the desk, Lona spotted an opened comic book. The girl dutifully poised her fingers over her keyboard. Her nails were painted the same deep red color as her lips.

"The *Julian Path* records." She resisted the urge to poke at where the information was printed in capital letters on her index card. "I filled that in on box four, right under my name and address. I'm trying to find all of the employees of the Julian Path. Especially any of them who worked in the lab."

"I *know* that. But *which* Julian Path?"

"What do you mean, which Julian Path?"

The girl rolled her eyes. "A couple of years after the paperwork was filed for the Julian Path, a bunch of other patents and copyrights and paperwork were also filed, using the same codes." She pivoted her computer screen so Lona could see – a spreadsheet filled with letter and number combinations – and skimmed her index finger down one of the columns with exaggerated patience.

"See? These are all the same. They're all filed under the umbrella grouping of Julian Path documentation, but some of them are labeled 'Julian Side Path', or this one is labeled 'Julian Alternate Route'. And if I click on *this* one, it takes me to a grouping of records about Julian Path Expansion, which was apparently a proposed initiative to bring the music portion of Julian's education to schools where arts funding had been cut. And if I click on *this* one, it takes me to the documents for the visioneer technology that was licensed out to the entertainment industry. And this one is called 'The Julian Compact'. And if

I click on *it*—"

"I unders*tand.*"

The girl frowned, clicking again on whatever link she was trying to open, but apparently failing. "Well," she said finally. "If I click on 'The Julian Compact', I apparently just get an 'access denied' notification." She looked irritated by the firewall, though Lona couldn't tell whether it was because her access had been denied, or because her smug rant to Lona had been interrupted.

"But you see what I'm saying. Unless you can be more specific about which set of records you're looking for, I'll have to click through each of these individually, and I really don't—"

"The original one," Lona blurted out. It had to be the original one she wanted, didn't it? Because that one was the one Warren had developed. "Can you just give me the employment records for the plain, original Julian Path?"

"Kind of a purist, huh?"

"A purist?"

The girl looked down pointedly toward Lona's feet. "Your shoes. I saw your shoes when you came in. I knew some costume shops sold Path slippers this Halloween, but yours are the most realistic ones I've seen."

They looked realistic because they were real. When Lona left the house this morning, her boots were still wet from the night before, so she'd grabbed what was closest – the thin, flexible slippers designed to be worn while living in pods.

"These aren't from a costume shop," she replied automatically, but luckily, the girl wasn't paying attention.

"Which years do you want?" the girl interrupted. "And which sector?"

"All of them?"

"*All* of them?"

She didn't know how to narrow down the years. Her dream hadn't come with a time stamp. Sectors – she supposed she could estimate sectors. Warren's old company had developed technology for sectors all over the country, but she knew that most of the research had been conducted here, near his home. "All of the years," she told the girl. "But just this sector. Sector 14." Her tongue tripped for a minute over the title. Sector 14 had also been her sector. It was how she got her name and her whole identity.

"I never thought any of the costumes were very good, anyway," the girl said. "Just a bunch of people trying to be clever with whatever's in the news. In ten years, they're all going to look back at pictures and be like, what was I supposed to be that year?" She spun her chair around to the printer behind her and plucked out a paper that had just come out of it.

"Here's what I have." She laid the page on the countertop, pulling out a pen and circling what looked like an address at the top. Even without reading the page, Lona was disappointed. This couldn't be what she was looking for. Hundreds of people must have worked for the Path. There was no way the information she was looking for could have fitted on this one sheet of paper.

"I thought I could see everyone who worked there? The names of all those employees."

"You can. Just not right now. You have to fill out a government information request."

"A what?"

She tapped the sheet. "That's the office you can contact to

85

get what you're looking for, and here's how you describe what you're looking for when you contact them."

"Will it take a long time?"

The girl snickered. "No, of course not. The government is well known for being efficient."

17

Lona woke up. She squeezed her eyes together, keeping them shut, trying to trick her brain into thinking that seeing the red insides of her eyelids meant she was still sleeping. It was too late, though. Lona always woke up. For three days, she had been trying to sleep, concertedly, desperately. But chasing this dream felt like chasing a sheet of paper down the sidewalk. It waited for her until she was almost close enough to touch it, and then it floated away. And always at the same place. Always when the Architect was smirking, when he was about to say something that might actually matter.

It wasn't good for her – she slept without resting and woke up jumpy. The circles under her eyes had grown dark and bruising, and yesterday at the café where she stopped for lunch, she followed a stranger out of the restaurant and halfway to his car because she thought for a minute that he looked like dream Warren. "You look like someone I know," she'd babbled when he spotted her, and she chastised herself as she ran back into the restaurant. *Warren is in the hospital*, she'd reminded herself. *Warren doesn't look now like he looked in your dream Path*.

She threw off the covers. The bedside clock said 4:07. Almost an hour. She'd wasted almost an hour on a nap that had given her nothing. At least while she slept the mail would have been delivered. She slipped on her boots by the front door.

"Are you heading out?" Fenn looked up from the pile of papers surrounding him on the living room couch. She jumped at the sound of his voice.

"Just . . . mail."

She knew immediately that there was nothing inside the mailbox, just an empty expanse of cold aluminum. Still, she swept her hand all the way to the back to make sure.

"Anything?" Fenn asked, when she got back inside.

"Nothing."

"Were you sleeping again?"

"Just a nap."

"Maybe you're getting sick. Do you have a sore throat? Chills?"

"I don't think so."

He was so tender with her. So patient with her erratic behavior, now that he thought he knew the cause. He stood and brushed the back of his hand over her forehead, then her cheek. She couldn't lie to him while he was touching her. She ducked out of his grip and thumbed through some of the papers on the table.

"What are you working on?" she asked.

"College stuff."

"But – we're in. If we want to be. Right? Why are you working on this? We've already been accepted."

"We still have to finish the applications. As a formality." Lona looked at the pages of notes, covered in Fenn's neat handwriting. "I don't want to turn in something that makes them regret admitting me," he explained sheepishly. "Overkill?"

"No. Of course not." It was very Fenn-like, though, to take such pleasure in something like college applications, and she couldn't help the smile pulling on the corner of her mouth.

"You make fun of me now," he teased, "but you're glad I'm like this when it's time to plan you a birthday or Christmas. Then my alarming planning skills are useful."

Christmas. The reference startled her. What day was it? Lona counted backwards. Her birthday had been seven days ago. That meant Christmas was in three, and she hadn't even realized it. She'd been too preoccupied with men who haunted her dreams.

"Is there anything you want, by the way?" he asked.

It took a minute to realize he was still talking about presents. "I thought you were a master planner. I thought you'd already know what to get me. All of your presents are probably already wrapped and hidden under your socks."

"I do know." His voice was suddenly serious, and he blushed, looking down at his hands. "I mean, I know the things I'd like to get you. But if there's something you really want – maybe I've been knocking myself out putting together scrap books and really all you want for Christmas is a nice pair of gloves?"

"This house *is* kind of drafty. What are you getting Gamb and Ilyf?"

"No idea. Ilyf probably already has access to all the nuclear war codes and anything else she could possibly want."

"Maybe that's an argument to get her something really nice."

"Stay on her good side?" Fenn said. "Go do some recon. Tell

me if she gives you any ideas."

She wandered upstairs to Ilyf's study, which used to be Genevieve's room. It had sat empty for three months after Neve died. For the first few weeks, when the door was opened, the scent of gardenias would drift out, sharp and pungent at first and then more subtly, like a scent memory. When the smell was gone altogether, Ilyf had quietly moved in her computer and work. She hadn't bothered to check with anyone else in the house. It was kinder that way. Fenn would have felt too guilty to consent, but everyone knew it was time to move on.

"I'm supposed to see if there's anything you want for Christmas." Lona leaned on the doorframe. With some of Ilyf's projects, it was better to wait for an invitation. Ilyf's job seemed grownup and important and kept her locked away for days and weeks at a time.

"A solution to this problem." She minimized the window on her screen, beckoning Lona inside. "Can you get me that? And then a nap. Or bubble bath. Just get me some bubble bath."

"What are you working on?"

Ilyf sighed, leaning one elbow onto her desk, trying to figure out how to explain something Lona knew was far beyond her own comprehension level. "Picture a fun house full of mirrors," Ilyf began finally. "Only not all of the mirrors reflect back at you. Some of them look like they reflect back at you, but really you can walk through them. And then picture—" She cut herself off. "You know what? Most of this would take me an hour to explain. Basically, I'm trying to save a bunch of junk from a server in California that they think has irreparably crashed."

"But it hasn't?"

"The content is just hiding. Now I'm trying to find it."

Lona nodded as if she understood. There was a row of empty glasses on the windowsill by Ilyf's desk. Lona started to stack them, slowly, taking more time than she needed to.

"Ilyf. Can you find other hidden content?"

Ilyf looked confused. "That's what I do every day."

She put another glass on the top of her stack, then piled them all on a TV tray she found sitting on the floor. "No. I mean . . . If I wanted to find a list of people who had worked for a program, but the program didn't exist anymore, but I knew that the information existed – could you find it?"

Ilyf placed her hands in her lap and swiveled until she was facing Lona. "What are you doing, Lona?"

"Can you help me?"

"Did you ask Talia?"

"It's for Talia." The lie slid off her tongue like an eel. Easy and slippery. "It's – Talia has lost track of some of the people she used to work with. And I know she misses them. I thought this could be a Christmas present. If I could find the old records from the Julian Path."

Ilyf frowned. "It would be easier if she just looked for them online, right? I mean, they're going to be on some kind of social network. You don't really need my help for that."

"She doesn't know their last names." She hurried on, before Ilyf could think about the logic of caring enough about someone that you would track them down years later, while not even remembering their last name. "Do you think you could do it? I mean, would it even be possible? Maybe through some kind of database of records?"

Ilyf was already entering something into the keyboard. A few seconds later, a familiar table appeared on Ilyf's computer – the same one the reference librarian in the records hall showed Lona a few days ago.

"This is – wow." Ilyf's face lit up at the wall of information that appeared on her screen. "Did you know there were all of these different offshoots to the Julian Path? Sub-programs, it looks like – or maybe experimental projects that weren't ever put into action?"

Lona tried to stay patient as Ilyf clicked through the files she'd already seen. "This one's weird," Ilyf said. "This one has a wall built up." She'd landed on the Julian Compact, the same file that the librarian had commented on, the one that resulted in a blocky gray text box.

"You can't get in that one," Lona said, willing her to stop wasting time and move on.

"How do you know?"

"Because. It says. Access Denied, right there."

"It *says* that. But things often *say* that and don't really *mean* it." She typed in a few more things, and then frowned. "Oh, wait. Hmm."

Ilyf had done something that made the gray box disappear. But now it was replaced by another box, a narrow strip with a blinking cursor. "It's asking for a password. Eight digits." Her fingers flew over the keyboard.

"What are you doing?"

"One, two, three, four, five, six, seven, eight. Sequential numbers. Still the most common combination people use for passwords. Idiotically." The blank space was replaced with a red stop sign. Ilyf paused, drumming her index fingers against her desk. "People also use dates. Anniversaries. Foundings. I could try the date the Julian Act was passed in Congress. Or I could build—"

"Ilyf."

"What?"

"Please. Can we just find the names I was looking for?"

"Aren't you curious?"

"I just – I want to focus on one thing at a time."

"But what do you think it is?"

"I don't know. It's called the Julian Compact. It's probably a bunch of boring bylaws. Like the Mayflower Compact."

"Rules for children hooked up to machines?"

"Can we focus?"

Ilyf frowned. Lona saw she minimized the window instead of closing it entirely. That was fine. Ilyf could go back again later, test her lock-picking skills. She went back to the original screen, where the list was that contained all of the different Julian Path programs. "Sector 14, I assume, where Talia was?"

"Yes. Can you find them?"

"I'm already finding them."

"Right now?"

"A spider is finding them. It will keep spinning its web until it traps something in it."

The metaphor made Lona feel claustrophobic, sticky. The silk of a spider web always looked innocuous. Easily brushed away. But it wasn't, of course. By definition, it wasn't. Lona hated cleaning cobwebs from corners, even with a broom. The way that a few tendrils would always manage to wind themselves between her fingers, more tightly the more frantically she tried to shake them off. The way it felt like there was no way to escape.

"What do we do while we wait?"

Ilyf shrugged. "Eat dinner, wash dishes, play this horribly dumb game Gamb has been threatening me with, go to bed, wake up, eat breakfast. I can't make it go any faster—we just have to wait until it catches something."

18

This time, when Lona went to bed, it felt different from any time in the past week. For the first time, she wasn't chasing sleep. It chased her. It consumed her. It came after her with such a voracious appetite that at the last minute she tried to open her eyes again, tried to claw her way out of the gaping, teethy maw.

She couldn't, though. She was sucked into the dream, imploding into herself. It felt like a string was wrapped around her heart, anchoring her to something deep inside her own subconscious.

"Hi, Warren. You found me."

The Architect smiled. With the corners of his mouth, tucked up like a neatly made bed, but not with his eyes. He was amused by this game of hide and seek.

"Ned. Are you doing a little spring cleaning?" He gestured to the mess on the floor. Comically, like this was a bit they had rehearsed. "Really, you could have asked for help. I would have brought a mop."

"Just looking for something. It's not important." Keep it light.

Keep your distance. He knows, but he doesn't have to know you know. Start for the door. Casually. Like you were leaving anyway. Like you're heading for the bathroom, or the drinking fountain.

"I think it is important," Warren said. "Or maybe I only think that because I have it in my pocket."

He tapped the pocket of his lab coat. A cylindrical bulge.

Ned smiled, played for time. Then he swept his hand over the desk, closing it on a ballpoint pen, wrapping fingers around the smooth white grip. He aimed it toward Warren's eye, raising his hand and jabbing it toward his face. Warren raised his arm just in time, the metal point buried itself in his forearm, blood and ink spurting out of the hole. Warren howled in agony, frozen by the pain, doubling over. Ned grabbed the object from Warren's pocket and then he ran for the door, locking it with the key dangling on the same lanyard as his I.D. badge.

"They'll stop you at the entrance," Warren shouted, banging at the window from the inside. "I've already called security."

He looked down at the object in his hands. A syringe, filled with clear liquid. Careful, careful, the liquid inside was flammable, in more ways than one.

Once Ned got to the front door, he would be done for. But the front entrance was still fifty yards away. And that was more than enough time for what he needed to do.

Ilyf woke her. It wasn't morning yet; she could tell by the inky sky outside. Ilyf was stroking her head and saying, "Shhhh. It's a bad dream, Lona. It's just a bad dream." She looked scared; Lona could feel the unsteadiness of her hand as she continued to pat Lona's hair. "It was really weird, Lona. You were shaking.

I was about to call someone. Maybe I should go get Fenn."

"I'm fine. I'm sorry I scared you. Go back to sleep."

"I just came in to tell you. It's done," Ilyf whispered. "It found what you're looking for."

The records were alphabetical, last name, first name, stacked in a tidy pile. The names were in the first column, followed by a column for sector. Page after page, beginning with Abbott, Beatrice, Sector 8 and Abraham, Yusef, Sector 4. Ilyf hadn't been able to separate out the list by sector, and there was no contact information, no job descriptions.

She hadn't expected so many names. She knew about Monitors and Coping Technicians who were employed by the Path. She knew about the Architect. But these papers probably contained the engineers who designed the equipment and the assemblymen who built it. The marketing people who sold the Julian Path and the lawyers who defended it.

It was good, Lona reminded herself, if Ilyf's net had been cast that wide. But it did make the task more daunting. Two hours later, after she'd been through the list twice, she had three names in front of her, printed painstakingly with a black felt-tip pen.

She wanted these names to mean something. She read through them over and over again. She said them out loud. They were just names, though. They meant nothing. She read through them one last time, committing them to memory.

Was one of these the Ned from her dream? It was such an oafish name, when she thought about it. Ned. A jolly name, a red-faced name, the kind of name belonging to a man who would stay too late in a bar telling bad jokes, and pretend to pull quarters out of the ears of his nephews.

But that wasn't what he was like, she reminded herself. The Ned in her dream had stabbed the Architect with a pen and watched him bleed. When Lona was this man in her dream, she felt anger pumping through her veins, thick and viscous and surging. She felt desperation. She felt like a feral animal, trapped in a cage, like she would chew her way out if she needed to.

Was one of these Neds a man who was capable of doing all of that? Had one of them passed on these feelings, like heirloom rage that came with the dream? She hoped she had finally found him. She dreaded it at the same time.

Ned Hildreth. Edward Mansaria. Edward Lowell.

19

The grandfather clock in the kitchen struck seven chimes. It had grown light while she was poring over the lists. No one else was awake yet, though Fenn probably would be soon. As soon as she thought that, she heard the sound of water running through the pipes in the walls. Fenn stepping into the shower.

She rushed downstairs, tiptoeing past the bathroom. Visiting hours at Warren's hospital didn't technically start until eight, but the staff had never minded if Lona showed up a little early – they were happy when he had visitors at all. And now, Lona thought, she might have enough information to unlock whatever was hiding in the recesses of Warren's brain. She found a packet of cookies from the pantry and a pair of Gamb's shoes that happened to fasten with Velcro. Maybe she could bribe Warren into being extra receptive today. Jog his memory with sugar and Velcro. It was worth a try. Anything was worth a try.

At the last minute, she grabbed a pen and a crumpled napkin from her pocket. *Running errands*, she wrote, afraid to get any more specific. *Be back*— Before she could decide what time to promise her return, she heard the shower turn off and the door open.

"Lona?" His voice sounded throaty and deep. She loved the way his voice sounded in the morning when it was full of sleep. "If you're out there, could you turn on the waffle iron so it heats up? I was going to make some for breakfast." She opened her mouth to respond, out of habit, but then shut it. Coming up with an explanation would only delay her, and even if she did answer him, she wasn't sure what she would say.

"Lona?" he called again, but she was already making sure her note was visible on the kitchen table – *Running errands. Be back* – and slipping out the back door.

The same man was attending the entrance that had been there last time. He stood uncomfortably at attention, like his uniform had been washed with too much starch, like the fabric was too stiff to allow his joints to bend.

"No visitors through here," he said, even as she removed her coat to be scanned. She checked the wall clock.

"No visitors? Really? It's a quarter to eight. Can't I just get in fifteen minutes—"

"No visitors."

"But you know me. I was just here." She was going to have to learn his name, clearly, and befriend him. She should have brought him a cup of coffee as a bribe. "Veronica always lets me – it's never been a problem." She piled her coat on the conveyor belt, and then jumped back when he roughly removed it and handed it back to her.

"Miss, I'm going to have to ask you to leave." His voice sounded strangled.

Behind Lona, the door flew open. Dr. Froelich, the chief

doctor at the hospital – Lona had seen him just a few times, making rounds. He was normally grandfatherly and gentle, with an easy laugh when he talked to patients or their visitors. Today his mouth was set in a hard line. He scanned his badge at the employee entrance and brushed past Lona without even a greeting.

Behind the guard, in the space beyond the security zone, a crackled announcement came over the speakers. Lona couldn't make out the words, but it made the guard whiplash his head in the direction of the noise.

"What's going on? What did that announcement say?"

He wouldn't look at her, though. He craned his neck, back in the direction of the residential wing, back to the part of the hospital Lona couldn't see.

"What's going on?" she asked again. "Can you answer me?" She could hear her voice growing strained as she demanded a response. Behind the guard, a flash of purple scrubs darted past. Lona's heart leapt at the sight of a familiar face. "Rowena!" The nurse stopped, looking around for the origin of her name. Lona waved her hand above her head. "I need to get in. Can you tell this guard that I—"

"Lona," Rowena said. Her cheeks were flushed red and she looked flustered. "What are you doing here?" As soon as the woman spoke, any reassurance Lona felt disappeared. Rowena usually greeted her with a maternal hug. This time she didn't even smile. She walked toward Lona, but looked distracted.

"Rowena, what's going on? The guard told me that I can't get in, but I just need to—"

"I'm sorry, Lona. No visitors today."

"But this will only take—" She hated this, having to call over the metal detectors and the x-ray ramp.

"No visitors at all, Lona. We're on lockdown."

An awful feeling was beginning to develop in the pit of her stomach. "Why won't anyone tell me what's happening?"

"I really can't. Go home, Lona. I'll call you when I can." Rowena turned, her tennis shoes squeaking on the linoleum.

"Rowena, wait! Can you just give Warren something for me?" Rowena paused, but didn't come any closer. Lona searched for another napkin, like the one she'd left her note on this morning. "Your pencil." She pointed to the one stuck haphazardly through Rowena's bun. "Can I borrow it? Just for a second."

Rowena hesitated, looking to both sides to see if anyone else was watching. The security guard was on the phone. Rowena plucked the pencil from her hair and handed it to Lona over the nylon partition. Lona scratched out the names as quickly as she could, before Rowena could decide to leave again, trying to make her handwriting more legible than usual. "Just read him these names," she rushed. "Tell him they're from me. Please, it's important."

Rowena paused for only a second before taking one corner of it. "I'll read them. But I don't think it will help."

"Just try it. Read them a couple of times. Over and over again. See if he recognizes them – if he makes a face, or a noise, or if he – sometimes, you know how he makes that sound? See if he makes the Nehhh sound when he hears any of the names."

Rowena looked back over her shoulder. The security guard was still on his call. She pulled Lona in, bowing her head in and muttering so softly Lona could barely see her lips move.

"You're not his legal family so you didn't hear this from me," Rowena said quietly. "Do you understand? Nod that you understand."

Lona nodded, quickly. She held her breath. The knot in her stomach was beginning to grow bigger.

"It's Warren. He's had an – an accident. He's brain dead."

"No!" Without thinking, she stumbled against the partition, trying to push the rope aside. Rowena held her back, swiftly and firmly, before the security guard could see what was going on.

"You can't."

"I want to see him."

"You *can't*, Lona. His family doesn't even know; we're trying to get hold of them."

His family, Lona thought. He doesn't have a family. He has a dead daughter and a wife who never comes to visit him. "*You* don't know, either," Rowena hissed. "Remember, you don't know because I didn't tell you. I didn't tell you *anything*."

"What kind of an accident? What happened?" A hiccup escaped Lona's lips before she could finish the sentence. She realized she had started to cry. Rowena put her arm around Lona's shoulder, briskly pulling her in and clucking softly in her ear, warm little sounds made by her front teeth and the tip of her tongue.

"I know," she crowed softly. "I know this is hard."

She thinks I'm upset because I'm sad, Lona realized. She wasn't sad. Not as sad as she should be. She was angry that the Architect was gone. She was furious with him for leaving her. Just when she thought she was getting closer to figuring something out, even the fractured, tenuous connection she had with her vision was now taken away.

It's not his fault, she reminded herself. People don't will themselves into comas. Men who are still learning to tie their shoes cannot force their brains to shut down.

"What happened?" she asked again. "The accident. Did he fall?"

"We're going to have a full investigation," Rowena said, stroking Lona's hair. "We'll find out why it happened." Her voice was shaking. It was soothing that didn't soothe.

"How what happened, Rowena? You said that he was fine until this morning."

"The aide was new," Rowena explained. "He was playing the shoe game with Warren. On and off. On and off. His shoes had laces. He left to answer a call in another room."

His shoes had laces. Lona knew how this story ended. The speaker crackled again. She still couldn't make out all of the words, but she heard Rowena being paged to the second floor.

"He was only gone for a minute, but that's all it took," Rowena said. "We're still going to figure out why he would do that. We still don't know why Warren would try to hang himself with the laces of some shoes."

20

Lona walked dumbly out into the morning light. The rest of the lot was still empty. She couldn't have been inside for more than ten minutes; on a normal day, official visiting hours wouldn't even have started yet.

"I guess I'm an ass, aren't I?"

She froze, the keys in her hand, then looked up to the source of the familiar voice, still throaty and deep and full of morning. Fenn was leaning against a lamp post on the other side of her car, hands wedged in his pockets. She slowly walked around to the passenger's side. Now she could see his bicycle, tipped on the ground.

"What are you doing here?" she choked out.

He kicked at the bicycle. "Gamb or Ilyf must have forgotten to put the keys to the other car back," he said. "They were still asleep when I left. Which is why I had to ride this bicycle in the middle of December. Which is the smallest reason that I feel like an ass."

"You're not an ass," she said automatically. She was the ass. She was the liar.

"Really? Because that's what it looks like. When I think

you might be going off to do something with your parents, and I don't think you should have to do everything alone, so I chase after you on a bicycle because I want to be so *helpful* and *supportive*, and then we end up here. In the mental hospital where the Architect lives. So either it's some amazing coincidence that you had to stop in this parking lot to – what – *ask for directions*? Or I'm an asshole. For believing you." Her stomach clenched at the sight of his burning eyes. "If there's another explanation, it would be great to hear it."

She opened and closed her mouth. The times she'd rehearsed this confession, it never looked like this. In her mind, she'd always carefully chosen the circumstances – she'd told him the truth in his bed, in the warm kitchen, on the porch swing. She'd never imagined having to talk about this in a cold, empty parking lot.

"But you can't tell me, right? You still can't tell me anything?"

Lona remained silent.

"I'm going home, Lona." His shoulders slumped and he started back for his bike. His fingers were red and chapped from his ride.

"Fenn, don't."

"I don't *want* to be here, Lona." He spun back around. "I don't want to act like a crazy person, following you around, or wondering where you are, or sitting in front of a mental hospital – a mental hospital, Lona?" His shoulders jerked up and down. She saw his breath curl out of his mouth, a puff of heat against the cold. He lifted his palms to the air and glanced around at their surroundings. *I don't want to feel like I'm crazy. But here I am standing in the parking lot of a mental hospital.*

"You're visiting him, aren't you?" he asked. He accused. "Aren't you?"

"Yes," she admitted. "Yes, okay?" She grabbed his sleeve to make sure he didn't leave again. "But I can explain. I can explain why."

"Explain, then." His voice was blade-sharp and vicious. "Go ahead, Lona. Explain."

But now her mouth was filled with sand and half-formed rationales. *The Architect is in a coma. I know he's in a coma because I tried to visit him. I often visit him because I'm still trying to figure out my past. I'm trying to figure out my past because I think it might be connected to a strange man's memories.* It was like she was singing a version of that children's song: *I know an old lady who swallowed a fly.* The song could go on and on, listing what the old lady swallowed to catch whatever had gone down her intestinal track before it: spiders. Birds. Donkeys.

But in the end it kept coming back to the same refrain: *She swallowed the spider to catch the fly. I don't know why she swallowed the fly. I guess she'll die.* A chain reaction of events set off by the actions of one crazy woman, taking poisons no one else understood.

"What *is* it, Lona? Why are you visiting the man who ruined our lives? You're a masochist? You miss the Path? You're completely messed up?"

His words bit. Weren't they the questions she'd asked herself every time she came to visit Warren? Weren't they her deepest fears? All along she'd been telling herself that she came to visit Warren in spite of his connection to her past, but what if she came *because* of it?

She took a heavy step closer to Fenn, leaning her forehead against his chest. He didn't push her away but his body was wooden and unyielding. She stared down at his shoes. Brown. Scuffed. It was always easier for her to be honest when she didn't have to look at him. Back in the Path, their conversations happened side by side in the Calisthenics room, rather than face to face. She still preferred talking to Fenn this way, when what she had to say was difficult.

Fenn sighed. "Sometimes I wonder if it was fair, for us to be together so soon after." He didn't need to say what "after" meant. There was only one "after" in both of their lives. "I was Off Path for months before you," he continued, "so I had plenty of time to figure out what I wanted. Or actually, to figure out that what I'd always wanted was you."

He didn't blush when he said that. It was one of her favorite things about Fenn. He displayed his feelings like gifts. "But you didn't have that, and maybe it's harder for you to—" His voice was shaking.

"Fenn. That's not it." She finally found her voice. "At all. I *was* visiting the Architect. But I won't need to come back again."

She told him. Everything. She told him about the first visit here, and the children's books and the hatred she felt that had slowly melted, collapsing into itself until it had become pity. She told him about the way her body ripped itself out of the dream on the night before her birthday. About how, when she was in the dream and a man named Ned, she could feel the cold plastic of the syringe in her hand.

She told him what sleep had become to her: something she dreaded and looked forward to, something she needed and feared, every night hoping that she would be allotted another few seconds of the vision, that she would spot some new clue.

Telling him what had happened made what had happened seem real, finally. All of it was real. Her dream was real, and her fear was real, and the sweaty slip of paper she'd passed through the barricade to Rowena was real. The shoelaces were real. By the time she told him about the shoelaces, her face was wet with tears. The front of Fenn's shirt was spattered from where she'd cried on him.

"Lona. Why would you do that?" She couldn't tell if he was furious or terrified. At least he was talking. "I still don't understand why you ever started visiting to begin with."

"Because," she tried. "Because I *need* something. I don't know what it is. I don't know if it's because he's the only connection to the whole life I had before, or because I'm completely messed up, or – I don't know what I need, Fenn, but somehow I felt like he could give it to me."

"He's *dangerous*, Lona."

"He wears diapers. He's less dangerous than Gabriel."

"No, he's the one who created Gabriel. And me, and Ilyf, and Endl, and Byde – do I need to list every Pather who has ever died, gone crazy or barely escaped the system that this man in diapers invented? Do I need to remind you about Harm?"

"You don't," she said. "I'm sorry. I'm sorry I didn't tell you before."

He was quiet. It seemed like he was quiet for an eternity, and then she felt him yield. Just a little, and slowly, but eventually she felt his body begin to soften until finally he lifted his arms and wrapped them around her, gently tracing the line of her spine.

"What do you want to do now?" he said finally.

What was she going to do now? She hadn't had time to think about it, between discovering what had happened to Warren and finding Fenn at her car. "Now, I guess, I start at the beginning," she improvised. "I find them on my own. And call them, or visit them, or – I guess that's what I have to do now. I retrace some steps."

His hands clasped more tightly around her waist. "You want to keep going?"

"Of course I want to keep going." It was the only course of action, especially now, when she'd already told Fenn, when she had already ripped off that Band-Aid. She couldn't have the end of the story be, *so I guess I'll just give up*.

"Lona, how is this going to work? You're going to track down some men from an outdated directory and then pretend you're, what, doing a survey about the Path?"

"No, of course not that," she protested, although she realized that she hadn't thought through how the next step would work. "I'll figure out something else to tell them. Or maybe I won't have to tell them anything. Maybe once I see them, I'll just know. Or they'll know. Maybe they will have been expecting me."

"*Expecting* you," Fenn repeated mirthlessly. "Said the spider to the fly."

The phrase gave her chills. "Then I'll meet them in a public place," she said stubbornly. "Or I'll bring my phone and keep my thumb on the emergency button, ready to dial if one of them pulls out an ax. I'll be careful in every way a human can possibly be careful."

"It won't be careful enough," he said.

But he hadn't asked her not to go. And he hadn't said that it was the stupidest thing he had ever heard of. And he hadn't gotten back on his bicycle and ridden away, leaving her alone in the middle of an empty parking lot.

Fenn sighed, backing away from her so he could look in her eyes. "Okay. Which one should we start with?"

He'd inserted the word so casually, it took her a moment to hear it. "Which one should. . ."

"Do you just want to go alphabetically?" he asked. "Or do you have a reason to feel more strongly about one of them over the others?"

It was so much more than she had hoped for. "We? Are you . . . are you saying you're going to come with me?"

He ran the tips of his fingers from her cheekbone down to her jaw. "What did you think I was going to say, Lona? 'Good luck with everything, I'll see you when you get back?' Would you say that to me?"

"No." Of course she wouldn't. If Fenn asked her to help him, she wouldn't have to think before saying yes. Saying yes would be instinctive.

"Then I'm not saying that to you. Next discussion." He nodded once, definitively, sealing that matter closed. "Just me, though. Not Gamb and Ilyf. Let's not pull them into this."

She nodded back, and she didn't protest when he pulled her closer in to him, when he buried his face in her neck and inhaled, drawing strength from her skin. But she could feel his body shudder with fear, and she could hear the way he was trying to control his breath.

"You don't have to," she said.

"Of course I do."

Fenn had said that she would have immediately agreed to help him, and he was right. But that wasn't the right comparison to make. She wasn't Fenn, and Fenn wasn't her. If he had asked her, she wouldn't have hesitated before saying yes.

He never would have asked.

21

The flamehaired boy wanted to talk about Hannibal. The Carthaginian general. Hannibal Barca, the man whose last name meant Thunderbolt, the man who wrested control of Italy from the Romans, thousands and thousands of years ago.

"Did you know that he was raised in war?" the flamehaired boy asked. "Did you know that when he was a child, he asked his father, Hamilcar, to take him to Iberian Peninsula, to learn techniques of warfare and domination? His father took him to the sacrificial temple and held him over the open flames, making him swear that he would never be a friend to Rome. That's how Hannibal became one of the greatest generals of all time. He was trained to fear nothing. He was bred for leadership. From childhood."

His collections of facts had a lovingly curated quality, the sense that they had been repeatedly groomed, taken out to admire. Knowledge gathered by someone who had read stacks of biographies, meticulously dog-earing the pages.

"That's interesting. I didn't know that. It sounds like you know a lot about Hannibal."

Hypothesis: *If I attempt to befriend the flamehaired boy, he will let me go.*

"I think that's why he was so successful. The childhood exposure. The fact that he was raised to think of battle as a normal state of being, and to think of peace as an exception."

Today the boy sat in a chair. On a chair, rather. He kneeled on the chair, feet tucked under himself. He'd brought the chair in with him, set it across from the one that was always near the desk, as if he wanted to make the area pleasant for a conversation. It was thoughtful of him. He'd brought crackers, too, with slices of cheese. He hadn't eaten any himself, though. Just placed the plate on the desk, with two white paper napkins.

The prisoner took one now, a cracker-cheese combination. The crackers were buttery and flaky, the kind that came in a cylindrical tube of waxed paper. The cheese was neon orange, cut into uneven squares. These were the sorts of snacks that a teenage boy would pick out. How old was the boy? He couldn't have been more than fifteen or sixteen. Despite his interest in ancient warfare. Despite his old, glowing eyes.

"But there have been lots of generals who didn't have childhoods like that," the prisoner said. "It seems that you have a confirmation bias – using an outcome as evidence, instead of letting the evidence guide your findings. Perhaps Hannibal is the exception rather than the rule."

"I'd *like* to use the evidence," he said coldly. "But a means of getting the evidence hasn't been made available."

"No, I suppose not. It's a little impossible to get in Hannibal Barca's head right now and ask him whether his father holding him over an open pit of flames is what made him one of the best generals in the history of the world." This was said in a

114

teasing voice. This was meant to deflect the flamehaired boy from the conversation he wanted to have.

"No." His eyes were blue and glittering, like ice. "But there are other leaders whose heads are more readily accessible. There are other generals whose lives have been recorded since birth."

Of course there were. LifeCapture had been standard for more than a generation now. If that's what the boy was talking about. He leaned forward now, over the plate. His skin was hot. It was possible to tell that even from a distance. His skin radiated warmth like something removed from an oven.

"There are some people who do very well inhabiting the lives of others," he said. "There are some people who exhibit undesirable characteristics when they're left on their own. They need . . . help. They need the structure. It doesn't hurt them. It's good for them."

What a stark difference, the heat of his skin and the ice of his eyes. One would melt the other, eventually. Wouldn't it? Hypothesis: *This boy will destroy himself.*

"I'm not sure what you want from me," the prisoner said. "I'm not sure I can help you."

"I think you can."

"I might be able to find someone else who *could* help you, if you let me go."

"You're the only one who can help me," he said quietly. "You're my only chance."

"Was it like that for you?" the prisoner asked. "Are you someone who knows what it's like to feel tempted by behavior that's . . . undesirable?"

"The Julian Path saved my life, Ned," he said.

The prisoner stiffened at the name. It wasn't fair for the flamehaired boy to use that name. It was too personal. It made all of this too hard.

"It wasn't the right path for me, but it still saved my life," he continued. "It taught me to be good. I still try to be good. I try very, very hard."

22

The building in front of them was square and brick. The bricks looked shabby – sooty and crumbled – but the brass sign near the front door was new. "Josephine Kennedy House," it said, next to a doorbell grimy from fingerprints. Two men sat on the stoop. She could smell their cigarettes from the property line.

"It didn't say it was an apartment building," Lona said, momentarily confused by their surroundings. The building wasn't a big one – there couldn't be more than a dozen units inside – but the fact that it wasn't a single family house meant having to knock on more doors to find Ned Hildreth.

The smoke from the man on the left came out of his mouth in a slender snake. The man on the right expelled smoke in big, meaty coughs. Clouds of nicotine appeared above his head like thought bubbles. *Was one of them the man she was looking for?* The one on the left looked too slender, she decided. The Ned of her dream had a rotund belly – it was one of the few physical characteristics she'd been able to discern. *But he could have lost weight*, she reminded herself.

It was possible that one of them was the right man and she wouldn't know it until it was too late. Until they were alone in a room and he was making weapons made out of pens and stabbing them in her arm.

"What if we shouldn't have come here?" she asked Fenn. "What if this is the worst idea I've ever had?"

Fenn swallowed. She knew he wanted to turn back. "Lona, will you ever be happy if we don't go in?" She didn't answer. Fenn traced the length of her arm with the backs of his fingers. Gently, softly, shoulder to hand. It felt good. It felt good, to not lie anymore. It felt good, to be moving toward something – to be moving at all instead of feeling trapped and defenseless. When he reached her hand, he led her up the steps.

The lobby inside was small, painted a butter yellow that had gone gray in spots. The carpet was clean but worn. Off to the right side, a man sat behind a folding card table, reading a thick book. The Bible. He had a pewter cross dangling from his neck.

"Can I help you guys?" he asked. He was forty, forty-five maybe, with flat muscles and a graying ponytail. He reminded Lona of Julian, not only physically, but in the earnest, slightly lost facial expression.

"We're here to see one of your residents?" Fenn said. "Ned Hildreth?"

"Okay, cool, hold on a second." The man reached into a plastic crate on the floor and started flipping through manila folders. "Here he is. Hildreth, Ned. He's on level three. And level three means—" The man trailed off as he pulled another sheet of paper from the carton, running his index finger down the margin as he scanned the words. Lona was confused. Level three? This was a two-story building. She could tell that from outside.

"Sorry," the man apologized. "This is only my second day here. I don't want to screw the rules up. You can't get off level one unless you follow the rules. And – yep!" His index finger stopped in the middle of the paper. "Level three means he's allowed to have visitors, as long as he doesn't have them in his room, which is totally not a problem because his schedule says he's on kitchen duty after Just Kidding's Tuesday lunch shift."

"Just Kidding?" Fenn cocked his head to the side.

"Josephine Kennedy," Lona guessed. "That must be what residents call it?" she asked the man at the desk. "It's a halfway house?"

"A half-full house is what I like to call it," the attendant said. "We try to keep optimistic about everything, and we try not to take ourselves too seriously. That's where Just Kidding comes from. We accept the fact that life is sometimes God's little joke on all of us."

Fenn managed a smile, but Lona couldn't. Now that they were so close to meeting the first candidate, she couldn't think of anything but carrying on.

"Kitchen duty?" she said. "Can you just point us where to go?"

"Sure. End of the hall, last door on the right.

In the end, they hadn't chosen Ned Hildreth as their first visit for alphabetical reasons, but because he was the only one Ilyf could find, after Lona carried on the false narrative of Talia's Christmas present. Or, rather, the only one they could be sure of – his name was unique enough that he was the only person with it in their geographical area. Edward Lowell had turned up dozens of matches – sorting through the pile would take more time. Edward Mansaria couldn't be found at all. It was as if he existed only in the records for the Julian Path.

"Are you ready?" Fenn asked when they reached the end of the hall. He moved his hand over so the backs of his fingers brushed the backs of hers – a light touch just so she would know he was standing beside her.

She nodded, and they opened the door.

Ned Hildreth reminded Lona of bread. The unbaked kind. His skin was smooth and porcelain-pale; he had dimples in the backs of his elbows that looked like the indentations made by dipping fingers into yeasty dough. He was drying dishes, methodically. He had a procedure. Plates received three long swipes with a terrycloth towel; cups received an efficient circular swab.

Fenn cleared his throat, but the man didn't hear him over the dishes clanking. "Excuse me," he said finally. "Excuse me. We're looking for Ned Hildreth?"

He turned. He had dimples in his cheeks that matched the ones in his elbows. "You found him," he said. He stacked the last plate in the cupboard, using his dishtowel to begin wiping off the counter, spraying it first with something that smelled like bleach and overripe oranges. His countertop cleaning method was as neat and thorough as his dish drying; he'd folded the cloth into crisp squares. When each square became dirty, he tucked it back, producing another clean area of the cloth.

Fenn raised his eyebrows and mouthed something. *Is it him?*

She didn't know if it was him. It was exactly as she'd feared. Nothing about this man seemed familiar. *But nothing about him seems unfamiliar, either. Talk to him*, she instructed herself. That was what she and Fenn had decided. If she didn't immediately

120

know from looking at him, she should keep him talking, wait for some pang of recognition.

"Mr. Hildreth?" she asked. "We were hoping we could ask you a few questions."

"What about?" He paused, mid-swipe.

His eyes were wide and brown, slightly bugged out, like raisins on a gingerbread man half-baked in the oven. She stared into them, searching for a flicker of recognition. There was nothing. He didn't know her. Or if he did, he did an excellent job of hiding it. "What did you want to talk to me about?" he asked again.

"About your name, actually," Fenn broke in. "Your last name is really unusual. There are only a few of you in the state."

"And?"

"And we're part of a genealogy club at the historical society," Fenn continued. At least Fenn was able to remember the plan, even if she couldn't. "All of us have been assigned to research a name on an old gravestone at the cemetery and see if we can track down their descendants. We were assigned William Hildreth."

"I don't know him."

"Well, you wouldn't," she broke in. "Because he died in 1932. But we thought he might be a great-great grandfather or something."

"Look." He finished with the counter, shaking the towel out over a garbage can. "I've never heard of him so I don't know how I can tell you whether I'm related to him."

"Maybe you can just tell us about yourself, then," she coaxed him. "Just some basic biographical stuff, so if we find someone else who might be a descendant, we can figure out if you might be related to them."

"Yeah, I'd rather not." He looked around for something. "No offense. I just feel like the government has enough information on me already. And I really should get back to my—"

"Are you looking for this?" Fenn produced a broom that was tucked behind the refrigerator and started to sweep the floor with it, corralling bits of dust into a small pile. "Why don't I help you finish cleaning up while you talk to my friend? The information we need is so basic. Probably nothing that the government doesn't already have. Like, where were you born, Mr. Hildreth?"

He looked like he was weighing the cost of answering the question against the benefit of having someone help him with his work. Eventually, he shrugged, wiping down the front of the refrigerator. "Here. Two exits over. In Gaithersburg."

"And your parents' names?"

"Jerry and Ann. They're dead." Lona dutifully transcribed the information in her notebook, the way she would have if their ruse was true.

"And they were born where?"

"Here, too."

"What kind of work do you do, Mr. Hildreth?"

He raised his eyebrows. "What does that have to do with my ancestors?"

"It's not a secret, is it?"

"It's not something that strangers need to know, either."

"You're right," she admitted. "What you do for a living doesn't really have anything to do with our project. It's sort of an extra credit question. Maybe there are patterns? Like, if you were a doctor, and it turned out that William Hildreth was a doctor, then that would be interesting."

"Was he a doctor?"

"I don't know, it was just a for-instance."

"If you don't know if he was, then how can you compare it to what I am?"

"We're planning to do more research about him."

Ned Hildreth grunted. "I'm sort of between jobs right now."

She couldn't tell if the answer was honest or deliberately evasive. Either way, she felt like they were circling.

"What did you do before?"

"I worked for a small government agency," he said. "It's not in operation anymore."

A sharp rap on the doorframe made Lona jump. It was one of the men from the stoop, the cloudy cigarette smoker. "Hey man." His eyes darted back and forth between Fenn and Lona, before deciding to ignore them. "I'm supposed to come get you for group. It's almost three."

Mr. Hildreth nodded. "I'm coming down. Two minutes."

Mr. Hildreth began loading the cleaning supplies into a crate on the ground. He took the broom from Fenn; Lona watched as the tendons in his hands tightened just a little before he relinquished his grip. "Well," Mr. Hildreth said. "You heard. I'm supposed to go down now. I guess you guys can find your way—"

"Mr. Hildreth, was the government program called the Julian Path?"

The air in the room. It was charged. She could feel it as soon as the words left her mouth. It felt like electricity in here.

Fenn's eyes widened in horror at what she'd said. But she had to. They were going nowhere.

"Who are you?" Mr. Hildreth said. His gingerbread man eyes narrowed into slits. "Why are you here?"

"I know that it was the Julian Path." She pushed on, despite the warning in Fenn's eyes, despite the frantic warnings of her own subconscious that this was a terrible idea. "I just need to ask you some questions about—"

"Get out of here." He took a step toward her, an unsteady one. His shin knocked a bucket; water sloshed to the ground as he righted himself, spilling over the floor he'd just worked so hard to clean. "Get out of here now."

"Lona. Maybe we should go." Fenn reached toward her, beckoning toward the door. "I think we've made Mr. Hildreth upset." She ignored him. They couldn't leave now, because Ned Hildreth was upset. That was a reason to stay.

"Mr. Hildreth, do I look familiar to you?" she persisted. "Do you know who I am?"

He stopped in his tracks. Lona saw a bulb flicker behind his eyes. *He knows.*

"This is one of those shows," he hissed. *Those shows.* She didn't know what he was talking about, but the idea made him furious. "This is one of those cheap shows where you come in and try to trap someone into saying they did something wrong."

"No!" Lona started.

"Lying now?" He snarled. His lip curled into a snarl. He took a step closer to her, and then another one. Instinctively, she stepped back to get away. "You come and ask me questions about my personal life but you don't tell me who you are. I already talked to the investigators when they shut that program down. I already told them I left a long time before those kids died. *I didn't know anything was wrong.*"

"I'm not saying you did," she said, but his raisin-colored eyes had gone black. The broom looked like a twig in his doughy hands. Her heel stopped against something. The wall of cupboards by the sink. Now she was trapped in the corner – the only path out was through him.

"I was a janitor," he said. "That's what I did. I cleaned the floor in the room with the pods. I washed the windows. I was just a janitor. I didn't know. I didn't know!"

She tried stepping to one side, to clear a path to the open space of the kitchen, but he saw her move and mirrored it, blocking off the path with his body and stepping another foot closer. He could grab her from here, if he wanted. She shrunk back, leaning against the stove.

Behind him, a metallic clinking and a flicker of motion. Fenn. Fenn had a piece of silverware from the drying rack wrapped in his fist. He was creeping closer, raising his arm above his head.

No. She willed him to read her mind. *No, Fenn, don't try anything. It would only upset him more. No, Fenn, you'll get hurt.*

Ned Hildreth must have seen the warning in her eyes. He whirled around, and saw the shiny object in Fenn's hand. It was a kitchen knife, Lona realized. That's what Fenn had to defend himself. A dull, useless butter knife.

"Stop!" she yelled as Ned swung the broom handle toward Fenn's face. The wooden handle sliced through the air, and passed just centimeters away from Fenn's cheekbone. She moaned with relief, but it was shortlived; she saw that Ned was already moving his arm back again. He wouldn't miss this time.

She moved toward him without thinking, crashing into the freshly scrubbed kitchen table. Her shoulder hit him in his rib cage, hard enough to make him gasp for breath, flail his arms.

She saw the broom handle come in slow motion, frame by frame. It cracked against her skull and there was something runny and wet running down her temple.

"Ned, we're heading up now. It's really time to—" The cigarette man was back. He froze in the doorway when he saw the scene in front of him, the blood and the chaos and the splintered wooden pieces of broom spread out on the neatly swept floor. "Paul!" he yelled. "Paul, get up here now!"

The man with the cross appeared seconds later. He and the cigarette man had Mr. Hildreth between them.

"They're trying to set me up," he wailed. "They're trying to say I did something."

"We're not," Lona said. "He attacked us out of nowhere." *Out of nowhere?* She felt guilty as soon as she said it.

The cigarette man shook his head back and forth in a stunned apology. "I'm sorry – I don't know what happened. Ned's a good guy. I promise. You can report him to the counselor if you want," he said. "I can go get her."

"No." Lona struggled to her feet. "We don't want to report him. Things just got – we're leaving now."

"I didn't know," Ned was babbling. "When I found out about those kids, that's when I started drinking. That's when I got in the accident. The Julian Path is why I'm fucking here."

"Hey, it's cool, man." The man with the cross wrapped his

arms around Ned Hildreth, who was shaking like a baby. He stroked his hair, making hushing noises. "It's cool," he said again and again. "It's cool. It's cool. It's cool."

23

She was still panting when they reached the car. It hurt to twist her body. She could reach for the seatbelt, but not pull it over her chest and across her lap. Her head was a dull nexus of pain, but her shoulder was what really hurt. She must have wrenched it when she crashed into the table. A spot of blood seeped through her shirt, right near the neckline; something slivered and brown poked through the fabric. She pulled on it. A splinter. A shard. A thorn in her side, buried a quarter of an inch below the skin, the tip a rusty red.

"Fenn, will you help—" She broke off when she saw the state he was in. The keys in his hand jingled as he tried to steady them enough to fit in the ignition. His curls were plastered to the back of his neck with sweat, even while the temperature outside was freezing.

"Are you okay?"

He tried the keys again. He wasn't okay. He was even less okay than she was. With her good hand, the one that didn't send pain missiles up her shoulder, she reached over to help him.

"Here—"

"No." He blocked her hand with his forearm. "I can *do* it."

"Your hands are—"

"Leave me alone, Lona. I can do it." She shrunk back at the harshness. He couldn't do it. His shaking was getting worse, not better, and she didn't like the fragile edge of his voice. She took more time than she needed to buckle her seatbelt now, focusing intently on the metallic click, on tightening the strap securely against her waist. Maybe Fenn just needed to have a minute to steady himself. She tried to give him the privacy he needed to pull himself together.

"Shit. Shit." He'd dropped the keys under the dashboard; he scrambled blindly to find them. Lona saw them by the heel of his right shoe. She undid her carefully buckled safety belt and leaned over to pick them up.

"How about I drive?" she said.

"I'm fine." He reached for the keys.

"You're hurt."

"I can do it."

"Fenn. I'm going to drive."

He didn't agree, but when she got out of her side and walked over to the driver's, he stepped out without protest. Her shoulder was manageable as long as she didn't raise it above her head. It was freezing in here. Lona moved to turn the heat on, but it was already on the highest setting. She turned on the radio instead. All-day Christmas carols, cloying and warming. After a few blocks, she'd started to feel better, but Fenn was still silent, rigid, staring out the windshield.

"Fenn. Are you feeling okay?"

"I'm fine."

"You're not."

"We're done now, right?" he asked.

"Done?" Done with what? With the visit? She couldn't wait to get home, strip off her bloody top and stand under the hot stream of a shower.

"We're not going to visit those other two men."

Done with everything. That's what he meant. With their whole search.

"Fenn. I know that was . . . awful. But it was our first try. We'll be better the next time. We'll do more research. We'll have a better story." She tried to sound positive, upbeat. How could he want to be done with everything?

"I don't want to make a better story, Lona. I want our first try to be our last try. We were wrong to come here."

Lona pulled the car over to the side of the road. She couldn't drive and focus on this conversation. "We were wrong to come here because he was the wrong person," she insisted. "He was just a janitor. When we find the right person, he won't freak out like that."

"No, you're right. When we find the right person, he might freak out in worse ways."

She changed tactics. "Fenn, I know it was bad. But we can't give up. If we'd just given up six months ago, when we were trying to find out what happened to the Pathers who died – if we'd given up, then we wouldn't even be here."

"But we *are* here," he shot back. "We're alive. Only for some reason, you want us to throw away that fucking miracle of a gift and instead risk our lives again."

She was angry and she was confused. She never would have given up on that search, when it was important to Fenn and his friends. She never would have "been done". She knew none of this made sense to him. There was no logic to her yearning. There were no organized lists, no topic sentences, no neatly constructed tables of pros and cons. There was only the fact that she felt that this was the thing she was supposed to do. It was almost how she felt about Fenn. She couldn't have explained why they were supposed to be together, or the reason that his skin felt like home. But it did.

"I know it's hard for you to understand this – this dream," she began.

"I know how terrible dreams can be," he said bitterly. "Don't you think I know that? In *my* dreams you die and die, over and over again. In every way. On the floor in the remmersing room. In the river, after jumping off a bridge, like Byde. Sometimes it's you who stepped in front of the train, not Czin. Sometimes I can't get there in time to stop it, but I can get there in time to see it. To watch as you stop breathing, until you're completely gone." His eyes were dark and dead. She knew he dreamed about her dying. She hadn't known it had been so constant, so relentless. She hadn't known that his dreams were graphic documentaries about all of the bloody ways her life could be over.

"Do you know that when I grabbed that knife, I was thinking about how I could saw through his neck with it?" Fenn asked. "Or his eyes – I was thinking about how I could pop his eyes out of his sockets like pats of margarine."

Her stomach heaved, both at the image and at the perverse precision with which Fenn described it. "But you didn't," she whispered. "You didn't end up having to."

131

"But I wanted to." His voice had become a rasp. A familiar one – one she hadn't heard in months and hoped she never would again. This was the voice of the broken Fenn. The one who had appeared when they both first left the Julian Path, who thrashed in his sleep. She didn't know that Fenn still existed. She thought he'd been fixed. Repaired. Painted up shiny and new. "I wanted to. I thought that he deserved that, for hurting you. And that's not the worst part." He turned back from the window, and when he looked at her, his eyes were so intent that she found herself wishing he would look back away. She didn't want to know the worst part.

"The worst part is that I was wondering if the knife would be too dull when I was done. If I would need to get a new spoon or if that one would be sharp enough to use on myself. Because if something happened to you, I already know that I wouldn't want to be alive. Especially not as a person who had killed. I already know that."

He laid one hand on hers. Usually they were warm and she could feel his heat seeping into her skin. Today they were colder than hers. "So can you promise me, Lona?" His voice broke over her name. "Can you promise me that we're done?"

"I promise we're done," she whispered. "I promise."

24

The lights were off when they got home, and the driveway was empty. A white square of paper was taped to the door, lined with Ilyf's handwriting. *Tried your phones. No answer. Left without you. See you at Talia's.* At the bottom, a postscript from Gamb. *Ilyf's pronouns have all been kidnapped. If you see them, bring them with you.*

Talia's. For the weekly dinner. "We don't have to go," Fenn said. "We can say we had car trouble, or I felt sick. Make up some excuse. We can just stay here alone." She leaned back against his chest. Staying here was tempting. Especially with that last word. Alone.

"We can't. We're supposed to be celebrating Christmas tonight. Gabriel will be disappointed if we don't show up. And Talia will be pissed." If they stayed here alone, they would just end up talking again about what had happened that afternoon. His hands would end up shaking; they would both end up in nightmares. They needed to be around people.

She stood in the shower, with the temperature turned as high as her skin could stand it, massaging her tender shoulder. She stayed until the hot water had almost run out, and when she finally emerged, the bathroom was cloudy with steam. Standing outside the shower, she encountered a problem. Moving her left arm too high still sent shocks of pain up her side. She'd managed to wash her hair using only her right, but couldn't manage the fine work of detangling her hair with just one hand. Or even the work of pulling it into a ponytail, she realized, as she considered just letting it air dry.

"Fenn?" she called out the door. "I need a little help."

He appeared seconds later in a clean shirt, his dark curls damp after his own shower. Lona blushed. It always embarrassed her, to be with Fenn when their skin was wet. It reminded her of the first time they'd kissed, when he took her to the swimming pool, and did somersaults in the water, and confessed he'd been in love with her since he was two, and, so softly she thought she would die, put his lips against hers.

"Oh. You're not dressed." He sounded embarrassed, too.

She held up the comb. "I can't move my arm enough."

"So. . ." He was blushing.

"So can you help me?"

He slid behind her, pressed close to fit in the small aisle between Lona and the bathtub. Fenn was tall enough that she could see the reflection of his eyes, over her head. His eyebrows knit in concentration as he worked through the wet tangles. She could see his forearms, too. She loved his forearms – the bones of his wrist, the soft hairs that became visible when he rolled his sleeves up.

"What are you thinking about?" he asked her when their eyes met in the mirror.

"Your arms. What are you thinking about?"

"Your, um, arms."

"Liar," she said. The expression on his face had been too wicked for him to be thinking about her arms.

"I'm not lying. I'm thinking about your poor, sore arm, because if I remind myself that you're hurt, it's easier to stop myself from thinking about other parts of your body that are not sore, and that I could kiss."

"What parts of my body do you want to kiss?" Her skin flushed warm, all over her body.

"There are no parts of your body that I do not want to kiss."

He wasn't smiling anymore. She watched in the mirror as he reached around her shoulders, drawing a line on her skin just millimeters above the terrycloth of the towel. "Here." When he reached the other end, he continued a path up her bare shoulder, around the back of her neck. "Here." He moved down to the other side, stopping an inch before the wound, where a bruise was already beginning to form. He leaned over and pressed his lips very, very gently against the tender skin. "But I'll start with there."

She shivered. The kiss on her shoulder had traveled through her body down to the pit of her stomach, and now she was imagining his lips tracing the path that his fingers had just made.

"Do you think you can put a shirt on by yourself?"

Using her good hand to keep the towel in place, Lona experimentally tried lifting her left arm above her head, but only made it halfway before the pain made her eyes sting with tears.

"Wait," Fenn instructed. "I'll get something that you won't have to lift your arms for." When he returned, he had something

135

soft and flannel in his hand. One of his shirts – it buttoned down the front and wouldn't need to go over her head. It smelled like him. Grass and prairies.

"I'll help you." He held out one sleeve so her hand could easily reach it. "I'll close my eyes."

"If you close your eyes so you can't see anything, your hands might go off track instead."

"I wouldn't try anything."

"I'm teasing, Fenn. I can't do this without your help."

Fenn obediently closed his eyes. She let go of the towel wrapped around her chest, and she saw him swallow when he heard it hit the floor. Carefully, she eased her bad arm into a soft, flannel sleeve, then the good one. The shirt felt warm against her wet body, brushing against the tops of her thighs.

"Okay now?" he asked, and his voice was low, his eyes still closed.

"The sleeves are on. It's just the buttons now. Those are kind of a two-handed job."

"Guide me."

She led his hands past the open front of the shirt, acutely aware of the fact that the only thing between her nakedness and Fenn's eyes were his own eyelids, and placed his hands on the first button. His knuckles grazed against the hollow of her throat, and against her sternum as he fastened the second. "I'm sorry," he whispered. "It's harder to do this with my eyes closed." His hands were shaking, almost as badly as they had been in the car.

"You won't break me." His hands continued down until all of the buttons were fastened. "You're done," she whispered, as his hands lingered near the lowest button. "All dressed now."

He exhaled a breath Lona hadn't realized he was holding, then opened his eyes and kissed her again.

Forty minutes later they arrived at Talia's house, Lona wearing an odd assortment of clothes: Fenn's shirt, a stretchy skirt, thick wool socks and shoes that Fenn had tied for her.

Gamb answered the door, wearing Gabriel like a cape, the younger boy's arms wrapped around his neck. "We're being a two-headed monster," he explained. "Everyone else is done with dinner, but I think Talia put some stuff in the fridge for you. And there's a surprise guest."

"Who is it?" Fenn asked.

Gamb rolled his eyes. "Lona, did you want to explain to Fenn what 'surprise' means?" He cocked his head toward the kitchen. "Surprise guest – did you want to announce yourself?"

"Surprise!" A disembodied voice called, and Lona broke into a smile. It was as familiar as Fenn's, as familiar as her own.

"Julian!" She ran through the house to Talia's dining room, throwing her good arm around Julian's neck, jostling the glass of wine sitting in front of him.

He'd cut his hair since she'd last seen him – it was shorter now, still a light brown shot through with gray. He looked healthier, too. He'd put on some weight, which made him look younger. This should have made her happy, but instead gave her a brief pang. *We were the things that made him unhealthy. He looks healthy now because he finally got away from all of us.*

No, she tried to correct herself. The Pathers hadn't made Julian unhappy. The Path had.

"Lona Seventeen Always," he whispered, enveloping her in a hug. "Happy belated birthday."

"Julian, what are you—" She gulped back the sob that was rising in the back of her throat. *Why was she getting upset?* Why was she getting upset *now*, after everything else that had happened today? "Why are you here?"

"I came by your house first and caught Gamb and Ilyf on their way out the door."

"No, I mean, what are you doing here at all? I thought you were in, I don't know, Paris or Prague or something."

"Munich. Or just outside of it, actually. Did you know my ancestors emigrated from a town on the German-Austrian border? I've been sort of tracking my past."

"Find anything interesting?"

"German is a really hard language to learn."

It was the sort of answer Lona herself would have given. A non-answer, a deflection. Talia, who had been standing by the sink, came over with a paper towel to mop up the spilled wine. She moved uneasily around Julian. It must be so strange for her. It had been for Lona, initially. And Talia had worked in the Julian Path for almost nineteen years. She knew Julian's face almost as well as any Pather.

"What about you?" Julian asked. "Been doing anything interesting?"

How to answer that, in front of Talia and everyone else? "She's applying to colllllege." Gamb swooped into the kitchen, finishing another lap with Gabriel. "It's very fancy."

"You are? That's great."

It was. It *was* great. It was exactly what she was supposed to be doing. "Just a tiny college," she said. "It's actually not fancy at all."

They stayed late at Talia's, listening to Julian talk about the places he'd been. The burly man who had efficiently pummeled him at a Turkish bath in Istanbul, the pizzeria in Naples with the cracked tile floors that had been using the same brick oven since 1873.

Ilyf and Gamb had brought egg nog, and Talia had made pecan pies, and because the only Christmas celebrations all of them knew were the ones that Julian and his family had celebrated, those were the ones they did: taking turns reading *The Night Before Christmas* to Gabriel, opening presents that Gamb passed out, one by one, wearing a Santa hat. Lona gave Gabriel one of Warren's favorite books. She'd bought it before Warren had hurt himself. She tried not to think about that when Gabriel tore off the paper.

Fenn gave her a small box, wrapped in dark red foil with silver snowflakes. She knew it was jewelry before opening it, by the tinkling, sliding sound the contents made when she shifted the box from side to side. He must have taken Ilyf's advice this time around. Inside was a chain – almost silver-colored, though she could instinctively tell that it wasn't silver – and dangling from it, an L, a cursive one that reminded her of motion or water.

"It's titanium," Fenn explained. "The saleslady told me that titanium is stronger than gold. Or even than steel. It seemed more like you, somehow."

"I'll put it on for you," Ilyf volunteered, gathering Lona's hair away from her neck and fastening the clasp. She liked the weight of it, resting gently on her collarbone, reminding her of the touch of Fenn's fingers.

"I love it. I won't ever take it off."

Fenn had now managed to give her two gifts that grounded her to her past, that reminded her of who she was. The book of photographs, and this, the first initial of her name. So what if the name wasn't the one her mother had originally intended, she thought, remembering her birthday wish from just nine days ago. That one didn't matter. What mattered was everything she did have, and what she did have was plenty. Or enough, at least. What she had was enough.

Wasn't it?

25

"I'm not tired. Anyone else feel like staying up? Midnight hike through the woods?"

Julian extended the invitation generally, but he looked at Lona when he said it. It was well after midnight; they'd just gotten home and carried presents into the house. Lona could barely keep her eyes open. The aspirin she'd taken for her shoulder before coming to Talia's had completely worn off. She wanted to pass out, not go on a midnight hike, but she also wanted to see Julian, so she put on a warmer hat and followed him out the door.

He led her down the steep path to the creek at the edge of the property. This was where she'd first met him, six months ago, when both of them had completely different lives.

"Is it strange, to still live here?" he asked, when they got down to the creek and the flat, mossy rock. "After everything?"

"Sometimes. Sometimes it feels like we're living on ghosts. But we're used to that."

"I wasn't sure if I should come back."

"I'm glad you did." She and Julian knew all of each other's worst secrets. She couldn't disappoint him and she didn't have to hide.

He skimmed a stone over the flat ice of the creek. It had been frozen over for weeks, but still no snow. "I wanted to ask you about the others," he said, as he watched the rock form spider cracks in the ice. Lona knew that Julian didn't mean Fenn or Gamb and Ilyf.

"About the Strays, you mean."

"Do you hear from them at all? From Affl or Ezbrn, or any of them?"

She shook her head in the darkness. "I know they've all been placed with families. But the therapist they made us all see – she said it was better if we didn't keep in contact. It was too hard for them to develop individual personalities if we were all spending time together."

"Do you think they're okay, though?"

"No offense, Julian, but why do you care? You weren't disappointed about getting away from the Strays six months ago." Her description of that time period was benevolent. Julian had walked out and left her alone to manage all of them.

He winced. "Six months ago, I was kind of a mess, Lona. After everything that happened, I just needed to get away. At first I was just running – running, like, without direction. Like a chicken with my head sliced off. Put half a globe between me and the rest of my life."

"Now?"

"Now I'm trying to run to something. Or back to something. But it's hard."

"What makes it hard?"

"Because even if I retrace my steps, I can't run backwards, you know? I can't erase the steps I've already taken. So I figure

142

all I can do is make the best of where those steps have taken me. Apologize to the people I can, fix what I can."

"That sounds very . . . evolved. Did they make you see a therapist, too?"

He laughed. "I saw enough of them when I was twenty-two, I guess. Remember that they decided I was a very wise and special young man." He paused to throw another rock. This one reached the middle of the creek, where the ice had stopped.

"I tried to find Harm," he said.

"You did? Why?"

"Because he was the one I felt most guilty leaving." He saw the words had hurt her, and hastily backtracked. "What I did to you was worse – abandoning you, leaving you in charge. But I knew that you were going to be okay. I knew you were determined enough to be okay on your own, that I didn't need to worry. I don't think Harm was."

But you did need to worry, she wanted to say. Because since Julian had left, she'd been putting herself in danger, and Fenn. Harm didn't need Julian like she did. The beautiful boy with ugly impulses. Harm just needed a straitjacket.

"You couldn't find him, though?"

"I doubt he was placed with a regular family. His needs were too—" He stopped himself. "I just wondered. Those are the things I wonder about."

She didn't like thinking about the fact that Harm hadn't been given the same do-over that she had. He was the closest of the others to her age – less than a year younger. But instead of looking at colleges or celebrating Christmas with friends, he was – *what was he doing?* She picked up a rock and aimed it for the hole Julian's last stone had cut through the ice.

"I also tried to go see Warren."

Her stone went wild, skittering across the ice. Panic rose in her chest. She wasn't used to anyone besides her referring to him by his given name instead of as the Architect. What had he seen, when he tried to see Warren? Lona had called the hospital every day. No improvement, Rowena told her. None at all.

"I know," Julian said softly. "I stopped by this morning. They told me what happened. And they said that before it happened, he'd only had one visitor. It was you, wasn't it?"

"Why did you want to see him?" Lona countered.

Julian sighed. "You forget that I had a history with him. A long time ago, when his team chose me. I thought we were friends. I owe him for – well, it won't make sense if I say it now, given everything that happened. But I actually owe him for some very good things in my life."

He'd known Warren before. A long time ago, before the Julian Path even was the Julian Path. *Was it possible he'd known Ned?*

But she'd promised Fenn she wouldn't. She couldn't break that promise. Instead she just said, "I'm sorry you had to find out that way. I would have told you, if I'd known how to reach you. And if I'd known you wanted to know."

"It bothers me and it doesn't. I lost him when he remmersed himself. I lost him when he betrayed the program. How many different ways can you keep losing the same person?"

26

Christmas Day was lazy. They picked at leftovers from Talia's without even bothering to microwave them, stayed in their pajamas until noon, watched the holiday parades on television, talked about going into the city but never quite made it.

Julian was scheduled to leave on the 27th for a wedding of some old friends. In the meantime, it was nice to have him for a few days.

Lona didn't have the dream again. That was intentional. She'd done everything she could think of to chase it away. To keep her promise to Fenn. She staved off sleep with endless cups of coffee and slabs of sugary peanut brittle from Talia's mother. She exhausted her body by suggesting another hike through the woods, insisting that they keep going long after everyone else wanted to turn back. She threw herself into the college application that Fenn had been soldiering through on his own, refining the essay questions again and again.

"Finish it tomorrow," Fenn suggested, as she hunched over the coffee table in a sea of computer printouts while Fenn, Gamb and Julian played a board game in the next room. "You were the one who reminded me that the application was just a formality."

"And you were the one who told me that you wanted to get it right anyway." She read over the selection of essay questions again, the letters going blurry in front of her eyes. *Good.* All she had to do was get too tired to dream. The farther away the dream receded, the closer the rest of her life could be.

This is what was real, she tried to convince herself. The crisp rustling of these papers, the smell of peanut brittle from the kitchen, the clicking from Ilyf's keyboard upstairs, the weight of Fenn's necklace against her collarbone. The dream wasn't. Just because the dream seemed real didn't mean it was real. She'd had a bad dream and she'd invented a story around it.

"This question," she called into the kitchen. "The one that asks you to describe a challenge you've overcome. I don't really know how to answer it."

"Easy," Gamb said. "There was this one time when a crazy wackadoo who ran the government program that I was an experimental subject of tried to kill all of my friends so we wouldn't expose his conspiracy, but it was okay because I managed to save myself in the end and all he did was erase all his own memories." He turned back to the board. "That's two hundred dollars, Fenn. And I'm going to build a hotel on Illinois Avenue."

"The more accurately I answer that question, the more insane I look," she said.

"Skip that question," Fenn offered. "I did. Just choose one of the others."

She rubbed her eyes and scanned the options. Fenn was right – the instructions said she only had to choose three out of six.

Describe your relationship with the family member you consider to be your greatest influence. She wasn't going to choose that. It felt like cheating to describe any of Julian's family members, and she didn't know any of her own.

"Learning is what happens inside the classroom. Education is what happens outside." Evaluate this quote and, using supporting examples, discuss whether or not you agree with it. Ugh, she would tackle that if there were no other options, but she'd prefer not to. She had no idea what it meant, much less whether she agreed with it.

Describe how attending this college would influence the course of your life.

It would more than influence it. It would completely change it. It would be the first opportunity she'd ever had to make new friends – on her own, not because of anything to do with Julian. The first time she could create a block of memories that had nothing to do with him. It would be a fresh start.

"Did you find one?" She jumped at Fenn's voice, just a few feet behind her. "I didn't mean to scare you," he apologized. "Did you choose a question?"

"I think so." She looked back into the kitchen. "Game over?"

"I donated all of my money to Julian for the cause."

"The cause?"

"Of beating Gamb. Do you need any help?"

"Actually, no." She gestured to the pad of paper she'd started to make some notes on after reading the last question. "I think I have an idea of what I'm going to say."

"I got a message from Jessa." He read the confusion on her face and explained. "Jessa. The tour guide? From the campus visit?"

"Right, sorry." She hadn't realized he was in touch with Jessa, and was briefly annoyed. "I didn't know you talked to her."

"Only a little," he said. "She was really nice about waiting with me after my interview when you – after my interview."

When I abandoned you with no warning, Lona filled in. "What did it say?"

"She's organizing a New Year's Eve lunch thing and invited us."

"Invited *you*, I bet. She liked you."

"No, us. Actually, everyone in the area who is applying for early decision. Just to give us all a chance to meet the other people who might be our classmates." He shrugged. "But we don't have to, of course. I know you've been—"

"No, I want to."

He looked surprised. "You do?"

"I think it sounds great."

"I'll tell her both of us will come."

"And did you see?" She sifted through the papers until she found what she was looking for: a residential life brochure made of thick, slippery paper. "Jessa didn't show us this part of campus, but one of the residential options is called the Green House. It's a coop – the residents cook meals together and stuff – and it's co-ed. So that might be good, because it's like what we're used to here. Except that maybe we *should* be living in a regular dorm, to get the full experience of college? I bet we'd meet more people if we were eating in the dining hall every day."

Fenn was looking at her with a dazed kind of half-smile. "What?" she asked.

"I'm glad you're back."

"I didn't—" She was about to say she hadn't gone anywhere, but she knew what he meant. "I'm glad, too."

"She *liked* me, huh?" He wiggled his eyebrows playfully.

"Unfortunately for her."

"She really did seem nice."

"Gamb is single."

He reached out to the hem of her shirt, running his fingers along the fabric. The gesture left Lona short of breath – she was never going to be able to watch Fenn even fold laundry without thinking of the way he'd helped her get dressed in the bathroom. His lips were very close to hers now. "Do you think she's worthy of Gamb?"

"I'll ask her at the lunch." Lona gasped as he kissed her neck, just under her earlobe. "I'll ask whether she can play the musical birthday hat."

"I wish you could stay longer, Julian," Ilyf said, but the sentence was cracked open in the middle with a giant yawn. She'd been up all night again, trying to save a system that had crashed in Singapore, Lona thought, or maybe Malaysia. Now she had bags under her eyes and her hair was smushed flat on one side of her head from where she'd fallen asleep at her desk.

"Me too." Julian tossed his duffel bag in the back of his van. "Who gets married the week between Christmas and New Year's, anyway? It seems rude to your guests. But they're my last single friends. And really the only people who haven't let me slip off their radar screen for the past twenty years. So I owe it to them, I guess. Right?"

Lona knew what a big deal it was for Julian to be going to the wedding at all – for him to be trying so hard to stay in contact with people. With her. She didn't like to see him go, but it was better this way – for their relationship to be easy. Unforced. Julian was like that saying: If you love something, let it go. It was better not to hold on to him too tightly.

"You don't have any old friends?" Gamb sounded appalled. "Are you at least bringing a date?"

Julian shook his head. "I haven't really had one of those in almost twenty years either. A relationship. At least not the kind that got to the point where I would bring her to a wedding."

"You were a player!" Gamb screeched, at the same time Ilyf said, "Who was the woman twenty years ago?"

"Let Julian go," Lona interrupted. "You're scaring him."

Lona waited until the others had gone inside, sticking her hands in the pockets of the parka she'd thrown on top of her sweat pants.

"Well," she said finally. "Bye."

"Well, bye." He awkwardly patted her arm, then laughed. "I guess we're not the most eloquent at goodbyes."

"Better than last time." Their last goodbye was in the remmersing room, and there had been blood.

"Not a high bar. But maybe we'll keep getting better." That meant there would be a next time. A next goodbye and a next hello. Lona watched his car pull out of the driveway and disappear over the gravel road. Behind her, the front door opened and closed.

"Fenn wants to know if you want blueberries or bananas in your pancakes," Ilyf asked. "Or neither."

"Bananas." She didn't turn around.

"Julian get off okay?" Ilyf leaned against Lona for warmth, yawning again into Lona's sleeve.

"Yeah. You should go to bed. You're barely standing."

"I think I will after breakfast. Last night was crazy work, but then also just lots of waiting around, but I couldn't close my eyes in case someone called me." She wrapped her bathrobe more tightly around her body and started to pad back to the house. She was wearing slippers. Big fuzzy ones that looked like grizzly bears, that made claw prints on the ground.

"I almost forgot, in my delusional state," Ilyf said. "I never asked you how it went a couple days ago. With the guy you were trying to track down? Ed or Ned?"

"Oh. It went fine." Lona's skin prickled at the mention of the name she'd done so well to not mention.

"Was he the one you were looking for, then?"

"No. He wasn't."

"But you said it went fine."

"It did. I mean – I realized you were right, Ilyf. If Talia really wanted to keep in touch with this guy, she would have done it. It's stupid."

"So you're not looking anymore? Since Christmas is over, and it was going to be a present, are you done looking?"

What was Ilyf getting at? Lona had just said she wasn't looking anymore. Why couldn't she drop it now, before Lona started thinking too hard about the dream again? "No. I'm not. Why?"

Ilyf shrugged. "While I was trying to keep myself awake for work last night, I had time to do some research on my own. I found one of the others. I found Ned Lowell."

27

"Can I ask you a question?"

Hypothesis: *Flattering the flamehaired boy by asking for information will make him feel important. Will make him feel inclined to offer assistance. Tit for tat.*

He looked surprised but pleased. "I wish you would ask me a question."

"Have I been in this room before?"

"Do you remember having been in this room before?"

It was annoying how he did that – answered a question with a question, refused to give up a nibble of information without asking for a bite in return. "It feels familiar." There. That was an answer that didn't give away too much.

"What feels familiar about it?"

"Have I been here before?"

"It's been a long time. But you remember it?"

"I might." It was difficult, actually, to put into words exactly what felt familiar. The dimensions. The position of the door. The hinges of the closet. Hazy but familiar. "I might remember it."

"What's your earliest memory?" the boy asked.

The prisoner didn't answer. The goal was to get information

from the boy with the red hair, not to divulge personal information. The prisoner didn't have enough personal information to spare. Nickels worth, not dollars. The currency was too dear to spend recklessly.

"I have two earliest memories," the boy continued, forgiving the silence. "I have my first memory as Julian. He was three, maybe, or four. We were on a merry-go-round at the park with some other kids we'd just met that day. One of the girls wasn't fast enough. She couldn't jump on when it started spinning. She held on because she was too scared to let go, and soon her knees were dragging in the gravel, bloody and red like raw meat."

The prisoner's stomach turned at the image. Today the boy had brought pâté, it looked like, or some other meat paste, smeared on small, square pieces of toast. Now the pâté just looked like knees.

"As soon as Julian saw, he made them stop the merry-go-round. He gave the girl a tissue from his pocket. All the grownups said he was such a good boy. So empathetic." The boy smiled. "That's how Julian learned what empathy meant. That's how I learned, too."

"That's a nice first memory," the prisoner said. "Actually, it's not, it's grotesque, but I can see how it would be an important first memory. It's young, too. Most people don't fully remember things that happened before kindergarten."

"I also have a first memory as myself," he said. "I was just a few weeks old. I was hungry and my mother didn't want to feed me. She told my father that she didn't like the way I looked at her. She said she could tell I had evil in me. So I bit her. I bit her hard on the breast."

Bile rose in the back of the prisoner's throat, tart and acidic. "That's impossible. It's impossible for you to remember something that far back, from when you were only a few weeks old. Your consciousness hadn't developed enough to retain memories then. You only think you remember that. Maybe you remember a story someone told you about yourself."

"Is it impossible?" the boy said lightly. "I don't think so. I think with the right tools, we can remember back and back and back. But the right tools are so important, don't you think?"

"I'm not sure what you're talking about."

"I can remember Julian's memories. And he was older than twenty before I was born."

He was gaining control of the conversation. The prisoner wasn't even sure how it had happened. He'd taken the question, about whether the room was familiar, and he'd spun it back so they were talking about something completely different.

"Soccer," the prisoner managed.

"Soccer?"

"My first memory is playing soccer with my father in the yard of the apartment complex we lived in until I was five. The ball came up to my knees. There were grass stains on my shorts. The dog kept getting in the way because she wanted to play, too, until finally my dad put her inside and she left nose prints on the sliding glass door."

"That's a nice memory. That's a nice, all-American memory. Even more American if you were playing baseball or football."

"My dad didn't like football or baseball."

The boy leaned in close, resting his elbows on his knees like a child at a library story hour. "That's your earliest memory. What's your *latest* memory?"

"My latest memory is you asking me what my latest memory is. And now it's me telling you that my latest memory is you asking me what my latest memory is. Latest memories are whatever just happened. As soon as you articulate them, they're not your latest memory any longer."

"But that's not what I meant. I meant, what is your latest memory before you came here? Before this room?"

That was the problem, though. That's how the prisoner had become the prisoner. All prior memories before this room had been chopped up, remixed, blended together. The ingredients might be there, but it was impossible to reconstitute them into whatever they had been before.

"I don't have memories of before this room. Did you do that to me?"

"You did that to yourself."

"I don't think so. Why would I?"

The boy sighed. "I don't think we'll have to wait much longer. I think everything will work. I have faith. In the meantime, maybe you're ready to meet the others."

"The others?" The prisoner was confused. What others? It was as if a page in the manuscript of their conversation had gone missing.

"The others," he smiled. "You didn't think we had you in here alone, did you?"

28

"Can I help you?"

The man who answered the door was portly, with a wide neck disappearing into a neat pink polo shirt. "My wife usually handles all of our charity things, if that's what you're here for." He didn't say it rudely – just as if there was a certain way things happened in this house, and he was well-trained to the procedure.

"I'm not selling anything," Lona assured him. "I'm just – I'm sorry, are you Mr. Lowell?"

The street was wide and quiet. The houses were split levels, whitey-beige, only differentiated by the colors of shutters. The shutter colors unfurled in a pattern. Blue ones, then green, then brick red, then gray, then blue, then green. *Like my name*, Lona thought. Her name also seemed unique, until you understood how it worked. She was Lona because she was born December 15. If she had been born one day earlier she would have been Lnna, and if the Lowells had bought the house one door down, their shutters would have been green.

Behind Lona, the sound of tires whirring on pavement. A kid on a scooter, small with floppy hair. "Hey, Mr. Lowell," the boy called. "Can I use your driveway to make circles? My dad's car is in the way in ours."

The man looked over Lona's shoulder. "If your mom says it's okay, Zeke."

He turned back to Lona. "Can I help you?" he asked again. She hesitated. She'd done exactly what she promised Fenn she wouldn't do. Her stomach plunged when she thought of how she had left him at home with another lie. *Going shopping*, she'd said. *Thinking about starting college makes me want to update my wardrobe. That's nice to offer, but you don't need to come. I'd prefer to go alone.*

Why was she here? Why would she do this to Fenn? She should turn back now, before anything went further.

"I'm sorry – what did you say you wanted?" the man asked.

"You're Mr. Lowell. Mr. Edward Lowell?"

He flinched, quickly, like the name caused him pain. "Ned," he said.

Her heart raced. "Do you go by Ned?"

"No, I mean, you want my brother Ned, but he's dead. I'm Thomas. Ned left me and Marlene his house, you know, since he didn't have any other living relatives."

Died. One of the men she was trying to find was unfindable. The other was dead. She pushed back her disappointment long enough to find her manners. "I'm really sorry. Do you mind if I ask how—"

"Last year. Pancreatic cancer. He didn't suffer long."

Last year. If Ned Lowell had died last year, he couldn't have had anything to do with her dreams. Unless he'd time-released them. Path knew how to do that – the drugs that had nearly killed Fenn took almost a year to leave his system. But what were the chances of this man setting up such an elaborate plot just to invade the dreams of a teenage girl he'd never met?

Thomas cocked his head at her, in a way that reminded her of a dog, one of the bounding, friendly breeds like a Labrador or golden retriever. "You didn't know him, did you?"

"No. I didn't. I just—"

"I didn't think so. You're too young to be a friend. Obviously. I just wondered." He shook his head. "Sorry – why don't you come in?" She started to protest, but he beckoned her in with both hands. "Please. Mar's out of town with the kids, but she left a bunch of stuff in the cupboards if you're hungry. I always get sort of lonely when she's away."

The interior of the house was orderly and precise – tasseled pillows neatly centered on a floral sofa, a matching straight-backed chair. Thomas Lowell gestured for Lona to sit there while he settled himself into the only comfortable-looking piece of furniture in the room: a tattered recliner with stuffing poking out on the side. He took a sip of the soda sitting next to him on an end table, but apparently had already forgotten about his promise of a stocked pantry.

"I like getting a chance to talk about Ned," he said. "We weren't close when we were growing up. I thought he was kind of a weenie – hanging out with the chemistry club and those guys when he could have gotten a position on the wrestling team. I mean, he didn't have the natural skill for it, but I would have helped him out. He was the smart one, I was the jock. That's what people were always saying about us."

"That's . . . interesting."

"Not that I was a dummy. I went to college. It just happened to be on an athletic scholarship. And that's where I met Marlene, anyway."

Lona scanned the room. The magazines on the coffee table were all neatly spaced and alphabetized, something she couldn't imagine Thomas Lowell having done. It must have been his vacationing wife. Thomas was lonely; he would have invited the postman in to chat, filling up hour after hour with tepid cola.

"So, Lona, was it?" he asked. She nodded. "Lona, why were you looking for my brother?"

What could she say? She'd planned on saying she was updating his current address for a college alumni directory, but that wouldn't work now. Current Address: six feet underground. She stalled for time. "I'm sorry – did you say Ned was a member of the chemistry club?"

"He always knew what he wanted to do. He used to ask for – what do you call them? – Bunsen burners for Christmas. He loved running the lab for that Joshua Program thing."

"The Joshua Program?" she repeated.

"The Johnny Plot?"

"Do you mean Julian Path?"

Her heartbeat had grown very slow. She could hear every beat thudding against her sternum. The pumping blood whooshing from her chest sounded like a seashell.

Ned Lowell ran the lab. That was his job. He ran the lab of the Julian Path.

"Yep. That's it." He nodded. "So is that why you wanted to talk to him? The Julian Path?"

She listened for notes of caution in his voice, for the wariness that made Ned Hildreth's conversation go so horribly wrong. But she heard none. Thomas Lowell seemed perfectly nice. Bland. The pleasant consistency of pudding. "Yes," she said. "Sort of. He was—" She swallowed, wishing that he'd thought to offer her a drink. "He was working on a project that my professor was thinking of including in a new textbook. About modern discovery. I'm her research assistant – she asked me to help track Ned down and ask him a little more about – about the lab environment. You know, how creativity develops."

"For a textbook?"

"For a pull-out box, maybe. One that highlights different inventors."

"Huh." Thomas leaned against the sofa, cradling his can of soda. "Ned would have liked that. He was super into his work." He shrugged, equivocating. "At least, from what I could understand of it. That is, he was in the beginning."

"Toward the end he wasn't? Into it?"

"It sounded like office politics. High-grade office politics. Put a bunch of PhDs in a work environment together – it's not like their IQs keep them from arguing. They just use bigger words to do it. Anyway, Ned was really worried about his boss misusing some of his work, or not giving him the credit. I can't exactly remember. And of course, he'd gotten really fat, too – stress will do that to you. That's why Marlene makes me come to spinning class with her two days a week."

"He'd recently gained weight?" Lona had a flashback to the beachball tummy from the dream, to the ungainly way it had felt to move with that stomach, like it wasn't weight that the body was used to. She strained to remember anything else she could about the physical appearance of the person in her dream. *Scrambling on the floor. Reddish bangs falling in front of his eyes.* "Did he have light hair, like you?" Thomas's hair was graying, but she could see that it had once been strawberry blonde.

"Right and right. To both things. A little darker than mine." Lona tried to keep steady, but she was trembling with excitement. Ned Lowell had worked in a lab. He had been unhappy in his job. He felt his work wasn't being respected.

This was the man she was looking for. This was the man whose dreams she was living. She knew it. "What weren't they giving him credit for? Did he say? What he was working on?"

Thomas looked at her strangely. "Well, you'd know better than me, wouldn't you? Aren't you working on a project about his work?"

Calm down, she warned herself, but now her knees were shaking too. "Of course. Yes. I just meant – I wondered if he ever talked about it with you."

"Sorry, he really didn't." Thomas shrugged. "Wish I could help."

"But you know it had something to do with office politics. Something that was making him unhappy. And you're sure this is while he was working for the Julian Path?"

"It would have to be – it's the only job he ever had. Sorry I don't know more. So I guess you're not going to be able to do the box, huh?"

"I guess not. But it was nice to talk with you anyway."

"Yeah." Thomas nodded, and then his eyes brightened again. "Hey, if you were just looking for personal biography stuff, my parents left me everything from when we were kids. I have

161

some of his science fair ribbons in the basement. I could bring those up."

"That would be nice."

She had found him. She wasn't crazy – she hadn't invented the nighttime play that had plagued her dreams for the past weeks. The man in her head was real. He was real. When she told Fenn, he would see that this was important; he would understand why she had to keep doing this.

"And I guess you could always go talk to Zinny about Ned, if you could find her. She might be able to tell you some things."

"Zinny?"

"Zinny Croft," he explained. "Zinedine or Zineria or something – I only met her a couple times, but I think that was her name. She and Ned ran the lab together. If anyone could tell you what he was working on, it would probably be her."

29

The shape of him looked angry. Fenn sat on the porch, rigid and perpendicular. Waiting.

"Where were you?" No preliminaries. No smile.

"I told you I was going shopping," she faltered.

"I assumed you were going shopping to buy something for the lunch," he said. "But you never showed up."

The lunch. Crap. The lunch for admitted students. That was today. That's where she was supposed to have been, with the students who were supposed to become her future friends. She'd forgotten. As soon as Ilyf had given her Ned Lowell's address, she'd forgotten.

"Did you have a good time?" she asked.

"I bought you a shirt from the campus bookstore." He gestured to a pile of dark fabric sitting next to him. "And I saved you a piece of panettone. It's an Italian dessert thing. There's a penny baked in – the person who gets it is supposed to have a lucky year. Nobody got it, though. This is the last piece. I had to fight for it so you could be the lucky one." He was staring down at his folded hands instead of looking at her, but she knew that his eyes would be hard.

The lucky one. She was the lucky one. She didn't need a penny to remind her of that. Or maybe she did. Because she kept doing things to mess it up. "Thank you." She took the container from him. The cake inside smelled like citrus. "I'm sorry I missed it. I'm really sorry, Fenn."

"Should we finish the applications now?"

"The applications?"

"College applications? Remember? The essays you were so interested in working hard on three days ago? Early admission? Postmarked January 1?"

He kept talking like that – an angry question mark after every phrase. She knew which applications Fenn was talking about. She just didn't know how she could think about them right now. How she could sit quietly at a desk with a ballpoint pen.

He sighed deeply, dropping his head into his hands for a minute before looking back up at her. "Come inside, Lona. Let's not argue today. We'll make a fire and finish the applications. It really is just a formality – today at lunch, a dean told me that I could even start this semester, after the winter break. Let's just do them and get them out of the way."

He stood and reached for her hand, but she couldn't come with him. Her feet felt frozen to the spot she was standing in. "I found him, Fenn."

He furrowed his eyebrows. "You found – what?"

"I found him. From my dream. It's Edward Lowell. He died last year, but before that, he worked in a lab on the Julian Path." She knew she should sound more contrite, but she couldn't keep the excitement out of her voice. Not when she'd found the nexus of where her dream world met reality, and where

164

her present met her past.

Fenn didn't respond. Not at all, not a word. She hadn't expected him to erupt with joy, but she thought he might offer some encouragement – or acknowledgment, at least. He knew how important this was and he couldn't say *anything*?

"He was angry with Warr— the Architect," she said, more loudly. "He was worried about the Architect stealing something he'd worked on. His brother said everyone called him Ned."

"You went there," Fenn said slowly. "You went after him even though it was incredibly stupid and dangerous."

"But I came back fine. I came back totally safe, and until thirty seconds ago, you thought the worst thing that had happened was me getting lost in the mall."

"It was stupid," he said again. "It was *shockingly* dumb."

"But I *found* something."

"You went there even after you promised me you wouldn't."

His voice was low and terrible. But instead of making her feel bad, it made her angry. She needed his support, not a lecture. "I promised under duress, Fenn," she spat. "I promised because you basically made me feel like I would be a terrible person if I didn't promise."

"So were you trying to catch me on a technicality?" Fenn yelled. "Make a promise you had no intention of keeping so you could go off and do whatever you wanted anyway?"

"No. I was trying to excuse you from having to participate in something you clearly disagreed with."

"By sneaking around," he said.

"I didn't know I was supposed to ask *permission* before leaving!"

"That's not what I meant."

They were both screaming now. Her body was burning with frustration that she had to justify any of this. That *Fenn*, who was supposed to love her more than anybody, didn't get this.

"You can't stop me from wanting to know this, Fenn. You can't just cover it up with – with sweatshirts from some university. You can't—" She was on the verge of sobbing now. She forced her voice louder, so that it would come out as angry rather than sad. "You can't just magically make me become *normal*."

"Is that what you think?" Fenn asked. "You think that I'm trying to make you into some definition I have of normal?"

"I don't know what you're trying to do. It seems like you're trying to resist doing *anything*."

"I'm just trying to resist the idiot things."

"So you think I'm an idiot now?"

The screen door behind Fenn suddenly banged open. Gamb, hands awkwardly jammed in pockets, was looking like he might try to slink away unnoticed. "Helloooo," he said, when he realized it was too late. Fenn folded his arms in front of his chest and looked away.

"Ilyf sent me out here to tell you that the ball is dropping," Gamb said. "But I'll just tell her that no one wants to watch that stupid ball thing anyway." He practically sprinted back inside.

When the door closed behind Gamb, Lona became aware of the cold penetrating through her clothes. Something wet landed on the tip of her nose. A snowflake. The first snowfall of the season was blanketing the yard in white.

The fire that had fueled her argument with Fenn slowly left

her body. It was replaced with the cold wet of melted snow, numbing her toes. And with sadness. They couldn't keep having different variations of this conversation. It was too awful. It hurt both of them too much.

On the porch, Fenn leaned against the railing. He looked empty and wounded. Her first instinct was to un-hurt him. To explain she hadn't meant what she said. But she *had* meant what she said.

"I think," she began. "I think that you want us *both* to be normal. That you have this whole, perfect normal life planned out."

"I don't think it's a bad thing, to want to move on. I don't think it's a bad thing to let the past recede into the distance instead of letting it strangle you."

Strangle her. Is that what he thought of what she was doing? Was he right? Was her past stealing its hands around her throat, luring her closer until, by the time she wanted to escape she wouldn't be able to?

"It's not a bad thing." she allowed. "Unless I can't do it. Fenn, I can't move on, and I don't even know if I want to. What I want is to finish this."

"You're following a dream, Lona. Not a fantasy – a literal dream. You're forcing clues to fit together in this – I don't know, this pre-constructed idea that it all means something. You've found a random guy named Edward – not at all an uncommon name – and you've convinced yourself that he's this man you're supposed to find."

"He worked in the *lab*, Fenn."

"Have you ever stopped to think about how little this makes

167

sense? Why a dead man would take the time to implant anything into your dreams to begin with? Have you ever thought that maybe—"

That maybe this was all in her head. That's how he was going to finish the sentence.

"Lona." His voice was broken. She had to steel herself the way she always did when she heard him say her name like this, like it was the most important word he would ever say. "Why does this matter to you so much?"

When Fenn and Lona had been on the Julian Path together, their lives were inextricably bound. They didn't have two lives so much as they had one. That's how Fenn had always felt to her. Someone she loved as effortlessly as breathing, who she knew as easily as she knew herself. She was being unfair to him. It wasn't his fault that he didn't want her to continue on her search any more than it was her fault that she wanted him to abandon everything else and come with her. It was nobody's fault. It was just that now they were two people instead of one.

Suddenly the numbness in her feet was comforting. It was halfway up her calves. If she stayed still long enough it might eventually reach the sharp pang that had begun in her heart, a cold and benevolent anesthesia.

"Come inside, Lona," he said. When she didn't move, he walked down to her, through the snow. His skin was much warmer than hers; when he wrapped his arms around her, she could feel heat transferring from his body to hers, or maybe it was the other way around. Maybe she was giving him the cold. Either way, this was as it was supposed to be – both of them using each other to reach an equilibrium. His mouth was even warmer than his skin. His lips on hers felt achingly tender, their heartbeats still matched and so did their breathing. For a moment she let herself accept the familiarity of this safeness. Fenn moaned, softly, at the feeling of her lips.

"What does tonight taste like?" he whispered. "It's snowing now – is it peppermint?"

She tried to play the game. She tried to think of what this night would taste like, sound like, feel like, look like – but everything was gray. It didn't taste like anything at all.

"I think you should go," she said when her head was buried in his shirt and she didn't have to look at his face.

"Come in with me."

"No." She didn't accept the hand he'd extended toward her. "I don't mean go inside. I mean that if the university is offering you a place for next semester, you should take it."

Fenn's hand slowly fell to his side. "This was just an argument. We don't have to talk about it any more tonight."

"But we're going to talk about it tomorrow night. And if not tomorrow, then next week. We're going to keep doing this for as long as the thing I want more than anything is to understand my dream and the thing you want more than anything is to move on."

"The thing I want more than anything is you."

"Please don't," she said, and when he reached out to her, she said "Don't," again.

It had to be this way. Because sooner or later, one of them would cave. Either she would feel too bad about worrying him, or he would feel too bad about curtailing her. One of them would win the selfless war and neither of them would be happy.

"Please go," she said. "Go inside now, and go to school next week. It's what I want."

"But you don't want to come with me?"

"I want you to go alone."

"You want to break up."

The words were a knife in her stomach. Break up. She couldn't make herself agree to that out loud. She couldn't even comprehend that. Fenn interrupted her silence with a sharp noise, a yelp of pain. "Then I guess," he said, "I guess that's what I want, too."

From inside the house she could hear music, coming from the television. Bawdy lyrics, sung by a crowd. *Should old acquaintance be forgot, and never brought to mind.*

A song about remembering friendships, even in the face of change and progress. It only came on once a year. Julian's family used to sing it around a piano. Of course. Lona had been so wrapped up in everything else that it hadn't even registered what Gamb meant when he talked about the ball dropping. It was New Year's Eve.

30

When he left, she didn't come out of her room to see him off. She knew she should, she just couldn't. "I've already said goodbye," she told Gamb, when he pressured her. And it was true. What else could she and Fenn say to each other that they hadn't said a few days ago? And more importantly, how could she open her mouth again and not try to take it all back?

Instead she heard Fenn outside of her bedroom, just before Ilyf took him to the train station. She knew his footsteps. She knew the balance of his weight, and she knew, when she heard the softest noise against her door, that it was Fenn's fingertips pressing against the wood.

Ilyf and Gamb had a party the night before he left. A small one. A sad one. It seemed the most counterintuitive thing in the world, to celebrate Fenn leaving. "It's not a party," Ilyf rationalized to Lona. "It's a dinner that a few friends are holding for another friend because he's moving on and they're happy for his success. You should come." Her message was clear. *Don't let you and Fenn ruin our whole group's friendship.*

But Lona couldn't bring herself to sit in a restaurant and watch Fenn open goodbye presents, and be reminded in a dozen ways of all of the reasons she wanted to be with him. It would hurt too much to see his face.

Instead she spent that night in bed. And the day after that – sleeping, reading, listlessly finishing backlogged homework assignments that were too easy and didn't seem important anyway. She cancelled a dinner with Talia, claiming she had the flu. She was sure Talia could tell that her throat was raw from crying and not from coughing – Ilyf must have told her what happened – but she let it slide. "Just this once," Talia said. "And I'm calling you every day."

Now there was a knock at her door. A rapping that turned into a pounding. "Go away, Gamb."

"I can't hear you—"

"Go *away*, Gamb."

"I think it's because this door is closed. I think if the door were open, I could hear you better."

"Go—"

"Unless the problem is that I'm not knocking loudly enough. Maybe that's the problem."

She scooted off her bed long enough to undo the lock on the handle before diving back under the comforter.

Gamb's face appeared seconds later, peering around the door. "Redecorating?" he asked, sitting on the edge of her bed, gesturing to the tissues piled on her desk and nightstand.

She didn't answer, keeping her eyes on the physics problem set open in front of her.

"Lona, the stuff with you and Fenn is not really any of my business. Even I'm not too oblivious to realize that." He grinned. "Fortunately, I *am* too oblivious to let the fact that it's none of my business prevent me from making it my business."

"What do you want, Gamb?"

"To drop off your mail." He waved a couple of envelopes. She nodded toward her desk and he shoved aside an empty tissue box to leave them. "To see if you're alive."

"I'm alive."

"To see if you're wasting away into a sad, malnourished ghost figure."

She picked up a box of granola bars from the floor and rattled it in his face.

"To see if I can make you laugh. A little tiny bit? A chuckle? A chucklette?"

That was too much to ask. She would show him she was still breathing and eating, but asking for a smile was too much.

Gamb sighed. "You're not talking to him at all? Not even to ask about his dorm, or his orientation or his asthmatic R.A.?" The asthmatic resident advisor was such a specific, personal detail that Lona knew immediately that Gamb must have heard from Fenn since he left for school. *Of course he had.* Why wouldn't he? But it hurt that Fenn hadn't contacted her. Even if she'd asked him not to. Even if she would have been mad if he had.

She didn't want Gamb to see her cry. *Recite the periodic table of elements*, she instructed herself, but she stopped before she got to the metals. Iron would have undone her. Fe. Fenn.

"You dared him to leave, you know."

"What are you talking about? We broke up. He left. There was no daring."

"He never would have, until you told him you wanted him

to. Then what was he supposed to do – *make* you be in a relationship with him? You made him leave so you could be the one who didn't leave."

"You have no idea what you're talking about." She turned away from Gamb and drew her knees up to her chest, staring determinedly out the window. She was done talking.

After a few minutes of silence, Gamb sighed and heaved himself off the bed. He stopped when he got to the door. "Can I just say one more thing? And I think it's actually a smart thing, so can you listen? You and Fenn broke up because you're on this mission. This – I don't really understand it, obviously, because neither of you talk about it – but this *thing* you feel like you have to do, and he feels like he has to . . . not do."

"Yes. Sort of. Yes."

"Then why aren't you doing it, Lona? I mean – if the reason you're not with Fenn anymore is because you feel like you have to be out Wonder Woman-ing this mystery, then you should be doing that. Not crying in your room."

She was silent for a long time. "Yeah."

"Ye— wait. Yeah?"

"Yeah, Gamb. You're right, okay? You're right."

She had broken up with Fenn – she still hated that phrase. Broken up. Like they had shattered and couldn't be repaired – so that she could do the things she felt she needed to do without being responsible for Fenn's feelings. And all she had to show for it was two empty tissue boxes and a ragged hole in her heart.

"So you'll go? You'll go and do . . . whatever?"

"I think so." He looked at her expectantly. "Not now, Gamb. Not right this very minute. But I'll go."

174

Once he left, she picked up the mail he'd left on the desk. There was a yellow envelope that looked official; at first she thought it might be the belated government information request, but when she looked at the return address she saw it was from Warren's hospital. She opened it and a stack of magic marker drawings fluttered out, along with a note from Rowena.

Lona –

We had to move Warren to another facility for patients in vegetative states. His wife told us to throw out his art projects, but I thought you might like them. I hope you're doing okay. You can come by and visit me any time; we miss seeing your face around here.

Rowena had affixed little sticky notes to every drawing, explaining what the assignment was. For "Draw your favorite animal", Warren had scribbled something indeterminate with four legs, entirely in purple. For "Draw your favorite thing to do", he'd made a stick figure next to a bunch of square things, which Lona thought were supposed to be books.

The last sticky note said, "Draw a sad memory." This time there were two stick figures, both of whom had frowning faces. An attendant must have helped Warren write a caption; there was writing in black ink peeking out from under the sticky note. She peeled it back:

Ned Broke the Rules.

31

It was starting to feel familiar. The stories. Standing on stoops of unfamiliar buildings, not sure who would answer the door. She'd done this twice now. It shouldn't make her as nervous as it still did.

Zinny Croft lived in a blue, two-story house in an older neighborhood with giant trees and crumbling sidewalks. Lona heard someone running a vacuum cleaner inside, layered over the fainter noise of someone talking on public radio. Both noises stopped when Lona rang the doorbell; a few minutes later, a woman with cropped white hair opened the door.

"Can I help you?" Shiny red globes hung from her ears and bobbled when she talked.

No stories this time, Lona had decided. No invented extra credit or ancestral research projects. She just needed Zinny to tell her anything she could about Edward Lowell.

"My name is Lona. I'm looking for Zinedine Croft. Or Zineria? I was hoping to talk with her about the Julian Path."

The woman's smile contracted. Just a little. A twitch, a spasm. The door swayed slightly as she leaned on it for balance. The wreath hanging on it smelled like pine needles, and from the inside of the house there was a different kind of pine smell. An air freshener, or an artificial cleaner, maybe. Something that smelled sweeter than the real thing.

"I wondered if someone might come one day," Zinedine said. "Yes. You can talk to me. Would you like to come inside?"

The vacuum cleaner sat in the center of a half-finished carpet. One side had neat vertical stripes marching up and down the beige; the other side was covered in footprints. Zinedine gestured to a sofa seat in the middle of the vacuumed zone. Lona tried to tiptoe along the perimeter, not mess up the pattern. Bowls of mixed nuts and foil-wrapped chocolates sat on the coffee table.

"You're getting ready for a party," Lona said. "I'm sorry. I can come back?"

"It's just for my husband's students. He always holds the first class of the semester at our house. An Epiphany reception – we invite them over to eat up our leftover Christmas candy – but they won't start arriving for another hour." Lona felt a twinge at the mention of college students. *Fenn's not coming to this party*, she reminded herself. *Fenn goes to school two hours away*.

Zinedine perched just on the edge of the chair, hands folded in her lap. *She knows something. She knows why I'm here.* The thought made Lona's throat too dry to speak. "May I have something to drink?"

"Of course," Zinedine said, but she didn't move.

"I could get something myself – if you just told me where the kitchen is."

Zinedine leapt from the chair. "No – I'm so sorry. I don't know what I was doing – what would you like to drink?" She backed around a dividing wall into what Lona presumed was the kitchen. "We have almost everything, for the party. Soda? Juice? I was going to make some punch, but Jeremy's not back from the grocery store yet."

"Just water."

She heard cupboards banging in the kitchen, several, as if Zinedine had forgotten where she kept the glasses. She finally returned with water in a cut-glass tumbler, but then almost as quickly hurried out of the room again. "Ice," she muttered. "Of course you'll want ice."

The ice she brought back to the living room stuck to the paper towel she'd wrapped it in for transport. Zinedine shook the napkin over Lona's glass, vigorously, dashing one of the cubes against the coffee table where it broke, splintering into the mixed nuts. Zinedine yelped. "Oh, dammit. Dammit, dammit, dammit."

With shaky hands, Zinedine plucked the ice slivers out of the nut bowl, wrapping them back in the paper towel. "It's so silly," Zinedine said. "It's just a little ice. Like I said, I always wondered if someone would come – I suppose you think you're prepared, but then the time comes and you're throwing ice around the living room. Do you – would you mind if I had a drink?"

Lona shook her head. Zinedine opened the wooden china closet behind the sofa, taking out a dusty bottle and pouring amber liquid into a small glass. "I really don't even know if this is any good. Someone left it at our house after a party. I don't usually—" She tipped her head back and emptied the glass, coughed, and returned to her chair across from Lona.

"I really can come back another time," Lona said. "Maybe – you said your husband would be home soon?" This woman didn't make Lona nervous in the same way Ned Hildreth had, but there was still something off.

"No, of course not. I'm fine. I was being ridiculous. Now tell me about your business with my daughter."

"Your – I'm sorry. What?"

"Zinedine Croft. My daughter." The woman raised her eyebrows. "You're here because you have information about – oh, I see. You don't have information. You're here because – why are you here?"

"I'm here because I'm looking for – I'm sorry, I guess I'm confused. But you told me that *you* were Zinny."

The woman shook her head. "No, I'm sure I wouldn't have. I said that you could talk to me about Zinny."

"Mrs. Croft. I don't want to be rude. But I'm here because I'm looking for something I think your daughter knows. Something she might remember from a long time ago. It would be easier to explain it directly to her, if you have her address."

"Her address?"

"Or a phone number?"

"Lona? You said your name was Lona?"

"Yes."

"I'm Magdalena. Maggie. You can call me that. You don't need to call me Mrs. Croft."

"It's nice to meet you." Lona awkwardly extended her hand. This was all going backwards.

"Lona. I would love to give you Zinny's address, but I don't have it myself. Zinny has been missing for more than fifteen years."

179

"Has been . . . missing for. . ." The words came out slowly, as Lona tried to process them. Missing. Edward Lowell's lab partner was missing. The one person left who could help her understand what was happening was missing.

From the rear of the house, Lona heard a loud grinding sound. It must be the garage door. Footsteps came in through the back, stamping as someone shook the snow off their boots.

"Woman, I have procured with my own hands four jugs of the finest cider, on sale two-for-one at the Safeway when I use my manly coupon book—"

The man who entered the room wore a plaid shirt under his parka, and a hat over hair the color and texture of a clump of steel wool. He broke off when he entered the room and saw Lona.

"The first guest!" he said heartily. "But unless I'm even more senile than I think I am, you're not one of my students."

"Jeremy, she's here about Zinedine," Maggie said.

His smile disappeared. He let the plastic grocery bags drop to his sides. "Why did you let her in?"

"Don't be rude."

"Haven't we been through enough?"

"Jeremy—"

"I need a drink."

He brushed past his wife to pick up the same glass bottle Maggie had poured a glass from a few minutes before.

"Jeremy," she said again.

"I think I'll have it outside." He'd left his boots by the back door, but he walked out the front in stocking feet, carrying the bottle with him. The door was still cracked; Lona shivered

180

at the cold wind that blew inside. Maggie peered anxiously after her husband, then gently closed the door, wrapping her cardigan more closely around her body.

"I'm sorry about that," Maggie said awkwardly. "Men are always so much more emotional. Women have to be strong. Not that I don't miss Zinny every day. But I think it's harder for him."

"Mrs. Croft. Maggie. I'm so sorry. I didn't mean to upset you."

"It's not your fault," the woman sighed. "I should have known better than to get my hopes up. I don't suppose there's anything I could help you with?"

"I don't think so. Not unless your daughter talked about her coworkers often? Or, I guess, just her work in general."

Maggie shook her head. "Not that we would have understood it. Jeremy is a literature professor and I'm a retired piano teacher." She brightened. "We kept her room like it was. Do you want to see?"

Lona hesitated. Did she want to see? She'd already patiently looked through Ned Lowell's useless old science trophies, and she couldn't imagine Zinedine Croft's bedroom would be much different. She felt deflated. Here she was at the end of the road, and it was another dead end.

"It will only take a minute." Maggie looked so hopeful at the thought of sharing her daughter's childhood with someone else that Lona acquiesced – she could force herself to do this if it would please Maggie.

In the hallway there were pictures of Jeremy and Maggie at Halloween parties, or with their arms circled around each other's waists at the Eiffel tower. There were also empty ovals

181

where Lona could tell pictures used to hang. She bet they would have been of Zinny.

Maggie opened the door at the top of the stairs. The room inside was painted a pale yellow. A rocking chair sat in the corner, the back covered with a star-patterned patchwork quilt, and along the sides were a birch dresser and a baby's crib. Lona was confused. Maggie said that they'd kept their daughter's room like it was when she left, but this was a room for an infant.

"I suggested to Zinny that we do pale green in here," Maggie said. "Jeremy was the one who wanted yellow. Of course, he always won with her, from the very beginning." She smiled. "Even before the beginning. Even with her name."

"Her . . . name?" Lona asked politely.

"There's a photo of her that I really like – I was just looking at it the other day. Now where did I. . ." Maggie opened the bottom drawer of the bureau, which Lona could see was filled with photographs. Everything that had been on the walls.

"Her name?" Lona asked again. "You said Mr. Croft always won, even with her name?"

"Zinedine. After that Algerian soccer player. He's not one of those men who wants a boy so badly he gives his daughter a male name – he just thought it would work for a girl, too. She always liked it – she came up with her own nickname, sort of mocking the masculinity."

"What nickname?" Lona's throat had gone dry. She already knew what nickname.

"Ned." Maggie laughed. "From the middle of her name. Some people called her Zinny, but she liked Ned – I think she mostly liked seeing the expression on people's faces when they were expecting to meet a man and instead they met her." She picked up a photograph. "Oh! Here's the one I was looking for."

She showed it to Lona, and Lona suddenly couldn't hear anything else in the room because the blood rushing through her ears was so loud. She swayed in place, catching her balance on the crib, leaning against the smooth, polished birch of the railing. The wood was how she knew she was awake right now, that these events weren't a dream.

She had thought that Ned was a man, because his name was Ned, and because his clothing was unisex, and because his hair was short, and because of the way Ned's stomach protruded in the way only men seem to gain weight. Slender legs. Beer belly. Except, of course, she only assumed that because of the context clues. It wasn't only men who gained weight that way.

"She was pregnant?" Lona took the photograph. Zinedine had a sand-colored pixie cut, streaked through with highlights of red, and fine, pointed features – nose, chin, even ears – and she was laughing at something happening off-camera. Her right hand supported her belly, which, underneath her lab coat was a round bowling ball. Her left hand rested on top of it.

"Jeremy and I weren't thrilled. She might have had her PhD, but she was so young. And, we're not exactly prudes, but just from a logistical standpoint – it made me nervous that she was planning to raise a baby all on her own."

"The father?" Lona asked.

"Never met him. That is, *we* never met him. Zinedine did, of course. She said we would like him. She said she was going to bring him around for dinner, if we could promise to hold off on asking them anything about marriage. He would have – that was the impression that I got. He would have gotten married; she was the one who thought they hadn't been dating long enough."

"But you didn't meet him."

"She disappeared. Ran off with him. The father that we never met. And then had a miscarriage, which was, of course, tragic. And then she never wrote us again." Maggie sighed, taking the picture back from Lona, using the hem of her shirt to wipe a thin layer of dust off the top of the frame.

"This picture is . . . how old?" Lona asked. Underneath the reddish hair were clear blue eyes and a sharp nose.

"Let's see. Zinny was twenty-four. So that would make it seventeen years?"

Lona felt stupid for not realizing it sooner, like the person in the group who can't see the funny-shaped cloud everyone else is talking about. It was so obvious. The person in her dream was Zinedine, and Zinedine was also her mother.

32

"Lona? Lona?" Maggie's face swam above her own. She felt something soft under her rear. Carpet. She'd slid down to the ground, still grasping the smooth birch rungs of the crib. "Wait here," Maggie instructed.

Dimly, Lona heard her rush downstairs, and return a few seconds later with a damp washcloth and one of the bowls of candy from the coffee table. She pressed the cloth against Lona's cheek and, when she seemed satisfied that Lona could hold it there herself, tore the foil off a piece of candy.

"Open," she said. Lona obediently put the chocolate in her mouth. It melted quickly; inside was mint liquid, running down the back of her throat. Maggie handed her another piece. Peanut butter. Only after the third – mint again – when Lona's teeth were beginning to ache from the sweetness, did Maggie stop unwrapping chocolates and sit back on her heels.

"Better?"

Lona nodded.

"I know how young girls can get. Running from one thing to the other, living out of vending machines, and never having proper food."

"I'm better." She started to stand, but Maggie gently pushed her back down again. Maggie. Zinedine's mother. Her grandmother, she realized. She was in the same room with someone who shared her blood. It was too much. She needed to get out of here. She felt like Jeremy, needing to escape from the house. Jeremy. Her grandfather.

"My car," she mumbled. "It's outside. I feel better. I can drive myself."

"I don't think so, honey. You're in no state to drive anywhere."

"I need to go."

"I'll drive you wherever you need to go, and Jeremy can follow behind in our car to bring me back." She groaned and slapped her forehead. "Except for that stupid party. The students will be here any second, if they're not late. Which they will be."

More strangers. More chaos. She couldn't handle that right now. "I was just lightheaded. I feel better. The food is helping."

Maggie shook her head, her mouth set in a firm line. "I'm going to make you a sandwich so you have something besides sugar in your system. We'll get you set up in the guest bedroom. You can lie down for a while, and when the students leave, Jeremy and I will drive you home. Okay?" She ended the sentence with a question mark, but Lona could tell that it hadn't really been a query. She was being ordered to bed. She couldn't remember anyone speaking like that to her before, with that kind of maternal concern. To Julian, maybe, but not to her.

The room Maggie led her to had a double bed, a treadmill, a few dusty shelves of books. Lona felt relieved by the impersonality. It was less overwhelming to be in here than in Zinedine's room. Maggie left and returned with a cheese sandwich, a peeled orange and a cup of something hot on a tray. "Just leave it outside the door when you're done," she instructed, promising to return in a couple of hours. "Do I need to call anyone for you? Your mother?"

Lona shook her head no. *But I do need you to call my mother. That's the problem. You don't know how to.*

Where had her mother gone? How had Lona ended up in the Julian Path? How did her memories get in Lona's head? Why had they only arrived a few weeks ago? There was another question on the outskirts of Lona's consciousness. She tried to bar it from entering, but it got too big: *Was her mother dead?*

After Maggie left she forced herself to sit down. The bed was soft. Downstairs she could hear the sounds of a party beginning and cresting. Clinking silverware. The tinkling sounds of shattered glass, an exclamation of apology, the murmur of Maggie reassuring the student that it was fine, accidents happen, they'd had those glasses for decades and she would love an excuse to replace them.

Had the glasses for decades. Had Zinedine drunk out of them? What about the plate for Lona's sandwich? Had she eaten off that? Had Maggie made Zinedine sandwiches in her school lunch? It was easier to think of her that way: Zinedine. Much easier than thinking of her as "mom".

Her mother had worked for the Julian Path. Her mother had known Warren. Her mother had taken something from him. Her mother had taken something from him and stabbed him in the arm with a pen, while she was pregnant with Lona. What had led up to that? And what followed that? Why did her dream always end with the fluorescent lights in the wide hallway?

This room smelled clean, like laundry detergent, like verbena flowers and sweet basil. She knew that smell. She had a scent memory of that smell. Her mother's lab coat in the dream had been that smell. Her mother felt almost close enough to touch.

Her head was light. Her fingers were numb. She didn't fall asleep this time. She knew it because she was still sitting, not lying down. She didn't fall asleep, but the vision came after her anyway.

Warren grabbed at her sleeve, but too late. She slid out the door of the lab. It locked from the outside. Through the window she could see Warren search his pants pockets. Keys. Of course he would have keys. Run.

The hallway was wide and bright. It burned her eyes, after the dimness of the lab. There was a minute, maybe, just one minute, before Warren found his way out, or before the people Warren said were outside would come inside.

The main entrance was at the end of the hallway. The main entrance is what she would use if she were trying to escape. But she wasn't trying to escape. Not anymore.

The bright hallway gleamed. It must have been recently washed; she could see a yellow caution sign a few feet away, a stick figure man slipping on the floor. She tried the first door, on her left, marked "Janitors' Closet". Locked. The one next to it was a private office, and it was locked too. In the middle of the hallway, she was completely exposed.

A stairwell. The stairwell would be unlocked. The stairwell was the third door down. She pressed down the lever handle. The steps inside were concrete, covered in peeling rubber treads. The fluorescent bulb hanging overhead emitted a low droning hum. With her dwindling minute of remaining time, she could run up the stairs or down them. Which had the better chance for survival? She hesitated for less than a second before making her decision. Escaping wasn't important. Capture was inevitable.

She crouched against the door she'd just come through, using her body to block the entrance, buying a second of delay if someone tried to come in now. She pulled out the syringe from where she'd dropped it in her pocket. She pulled up her shirt, running her hand over the place where she had last felt the baby kick, the spot where the baby seemed to nestle more than any other place. And then she jabbed the needle in.

33

"What is this place? Who are these people?"

"You sound so melodramatic," the flamehaired boy said. "It's what I told you. I told you I would bring you to the others."

It was true; that's exactly what he'd said. Still, she hadn't imagined this. She'd imagined other prisoners, other scientists who had information the boy wanted. But the room he led her to – down a hallway, down some stairs, down another hallway – wasn't a holding cell. It was big, dimly lit, with rows of bulky things.

Pods. Her brain supplied her with the word. The bulky things were called pods. In the pods were men and women, eyes shaded with black goggles. Strong-looking men and women – their muscles flexed, in response to whatever was on their screens. Immediately next to her was a pod containing a young woman with a French braid.

"Katie," Harm explained. "Anders says Katie is the most advanced volunteer here." She saw Anders now, a few rows down, observing her. "We're excited for the two of you to work together."

Her, work with Katie? *On what? Why?* "What are they

doing?" she asked. "What Path do you have them on?"

"Do you want to see?"

Of course she wanted to see.

She heard a grunt of disapproval. She turned – Anders had managed to sneak up behind her. He still had a Band-Aid covering the meaty part where his thumb joined his index finger. When he saw her looking at it, he glared and folded his other hand over the wound.

"Is there a problem, Anders?" the boy asked.

"I don't think you're supposed to let her do that."

"Do that *what*?"

"I don't think you're supposed to let her do that. Sir."

"They told me to figure this out. They put me in charge here."

"Of almost everything. They put me in charge of watching you."

"Are you threatening me?" the boy said lightly.

"Of course not. But I think you might want to remember where you came from. And think about whether you want to go back there."

Something had just happened, between Anders and the flamehaired boy. She didn't know what, but when the boy turned back to her, his eyes looked scared.

"You can come over here to this one," he said to her, a little too loudly. "Here on the end."

He guided her toward the empty pod, handing her a pair of visioneers. "These aren't quite the right size," he apologized as she put them on. "You won't be wearing them for long. You're just getting a taste."

"A taste of what?" she started to ask, but then suddenly the boy was gone. And the pod was gone. And the room was gone.

Suddenly she was . . . where? Somewhere hot. Somewhere where, when she opened her mouth, sand particles flew in. Except *she* hadn't opened her mouth. She had a body, but she didn't have any control over it, not over how it was moving, or what it was seeing. The eyes that she didn't control looked down. The hands at the end of its arm were dark-skinned, thick like sausages, a gold wedding band on the fourth finger.

"You have the coordinates?" the body asked. Its voice was deep and controlled.

"I do, sir." The other speaker was a young man, gap-toothed, in khaki fatigues. "But we don't know if they're insurgents or just kids. I think they're just kids. Here." The young man passed over a pair of binoculars. Through them: two boys. Black hair, one in blue jeans, one in striped pants. Sitting on a low wall, playing with a kitten. One boy was fourteen, maybe, the other couldn't be older than twelve. The kitten was tiny, white with brown markings, batting at a skinny piece of fabric the younger boy swung over its head. He raised it a few inches higher and the kitten's tiny claws sunk into the boy's pants as it scampered up him like a tree. The boy giggled and pulled something out of his pocket. Kibble, or a treat.

"You have evidence?"

"Boys meeting their description were spotted near two explosive devices, but we can't be sure they were the same boys. They're awfully young."

"You can't be too careful."

And then something exploded. Something bright and white that filled the air with dust. She had thrown the exploding thing. It was a grenade that had come from her hands. She had thrown it, and when the dust settled, the boys were gone. The wall was gone.

In the binoculars, she could make out a leg. Stripes. The boy with striped pants must have fallen off the wall. She moved her binoculars to see the rest of the boy. The leg wasn't attached to anything. It sat in the dirt, trailing bloody octopus tentacles.

The kitten stumbled into the screen. She couldn't hear it from this distance, but she could see its tiny mouth open in a mew, its pink tongue as it wailed, looking for its owner. The kitten picked its way between fallen rocks, and then curled up in the middle of a pile of dust, next to a head that stared back at her with one unblinking eye.

She screamed. She screamed and screamed, and the dust went in her mouth, but no one could tell she was screaming. The gap-toothed boy was saying, "Nicely done, sir," and she had to get out, but the legs refused to take her anywhere. The legs wouldn't let her leave. She was going to explode. "Get me out," she yelled. "Get me out."

She was trapped in this body, and the body wouldn't look away from the eye. "Please." Her voice was hoarse from the yelling. "Get me—"

The visioneers slid up her face, the rubber scraping against her skin.

"Do you need a drink of water?" The boy stood next to her, holding the visioneers. She coughed. Her clothing was plastered to her body, cold with sweat running down her chest.

"I was screaming at you to end the Path," she yelled.

"You weren't screaming. You didn't make any noise at all."

193

"What was that? Where did you put me?" she shrieked. *What happened to the boy in the striped pants? Don't tell me. Tell me. Don't.*

"Let's go sit down," he said.

She tumbled out of the pod, not waiting for the levers to properly release, catching her sleeve on one of the claws designed to cradle her arms.

"Tell me what I saw!"

"Shhhh."

She couldn't be quiet. She could still feel the weight of the explosive device in her hand before she threw it.

The boy led her to a little room. It had a wooden veneer table and a vending machine. He produced money from his pocket and bought her a soda.

"No," she protested. He set it down on the table anyway. He'd bought her ginger ale. He'd known she would want something to settle her stomach. "What I just saw. What do you call that?"

"We call that the Hannibal Project."

"That man who I was wasn't Hannibal."

"No. Of course not. As we've already discussed, nobody has access to Hannibal Barca's memories. That was Corey Ducett, the most decorated soldier in the Red War." He waved his hand before she could ask. "Small Central Asian conflict. Not historically important, except that Corey Ducett revolutionized urban warfare." He glanced at the prisoner. "He was safe, in case you were wondering. He survived the Red War. He didn't die for a long time after that."

"Where did he die?"

"In a prison. His methods weren't appreciated in their time."

"Are they all – are all of the people in there watching Corey Ducett?"

"No. Almost none of them. He's just one of the standards. He's part of the curriculum."

Why had he brought her down here? Was it a threat? If she couldn't give him the information he wanted, would he make her sit through that simulation again?

"That affected you," the boy said. "That made you upset. Why? You've been in lots of pods before."

"For *good*," she almost yelled. "For programs experimenting on perfect lives. For research about improving the human experience."

"Perfect means something different in different human experiences."

"Why did you *show* me this?" She didn't understand. *What could he hope to accomplish by bringing her here?* Unless. Her stomach filled with dread. "I helped design this, didn't I? That's one of the memories I can't remember. I helped design the Hannibal Project."

"No. You didn't. Don't worry about that."

"I didn't? Then why am I here? Why do you think I can help you?"

"After the design for the Julian Path was finished, you dedicated yourself completely to one project. It was much more advanced than anything we have here. You worked on it alone."

"What was it?"

He hesitated. She could see him debating whether or not to tell her in his head. He wanted her to remember the program on her own – that had always seemed to be important to him. But he was rattled by the conversation with Anders earlier. He was afraid she wasn't moving fast enough. He didn't want to go back to where he'd come from, wherever that was.

"Doesn't any of this sound familiar to you?"

"It was an advanced project that I was working on alone?"

"Yes," he said.

"And I kept all of my research private, so no one else could replicate it?"

"Yes."

"Can we go back up to my room now?"

"I thought you wanted to get out. I thought you'd been saying that for days, that you wanted to get out."

She had been saying that for days. But she'd just had the tiniest flicker of a memory. Less than a flicker. Like a candle that had been extinguished minutes ago, but still glowed orange at the wick. It was barely anything, but it was more than she'd had before. And if the memory was accurate, then she wanted to go back up to the room, because she wasn't sure she should ever be allowed to leave.

34

Breath came flooding back into Lona's lungs almost as if she'd been under water; she put her hand to her heart and sucked oxygen in big gulps. She was still sitting on the bed.

How much time had passed? How long was she stranded in that non-sleeping nightmare? A red light blinked at her from inside the television cabinet; she stumbled across the room to open the door wider. Almost midnight. *Without even sleeping.* Her throat swelled with panic. *The dream had sucked her in without even putting her to sleep first.*

It must be this house – this house where Zinedine had lived, which still smelled like her laundry. It had reeled Lona in too close. She had to get out of here before Zinedine's dream Path came after her again.

She found her shoes by the side of the bed. They were slip-on ankle boots; she pulled them on as quietly as possible, glad that she'd worn shoes with no laces. Shoes with no laces. It made her think of Warren. The one in her dream, the one in reality, the one from today, the one from the past before she was born. Her head ached, and no matter how hard she tried, she couldn't stop herself from replaying what happened beyond the door of the lab: *my mother stabbed me through her belly with a needle.*

That part of the vision was perfectly clear. The vicious satisfaction Zinedine had felt when she slid the needle into her flesh. No wonder Lona had been immediately placed in the Julian Path after she was born. Her mother couldn't have found a better way to demonstrate that Lona was unwanted.

The house felt quiet and still, with no sounds coming from either of the other bedrooms. Downstairs, the kitchen sink was piled with dishes and there was a half-eaten cake on the counter. She felt a momentary stab of guilt, leaving without saying goodbye. She would find an excuse to come back later. She would ask Maggie a million questions then. But for now she just needed to get away from this house.

Her coat was neatly folded over a stool by the front door. She picked it up and was just about to ease the lock open when –

"I think your car keys are on the floor there. I heard something clunk out of your pocket earlier." Jeremy. She hadn't seen him sitting there on the couch, a dozen chocolate wrappers dotting the coffee table. He unwrapped another and looked at it suspiciously. "I don't like the weird jelly ones." He bit into the candy and smiled. "Peanut butter is my favorite."

He pushed the dish toward her and raised his eyebrows. She shook her head in refusal. "Don't worry about leaving, if you need to," he said. "I'll tell Maggie that you got off all right and that you didn't appear to be on the verge of fainting or anything. She knocked on the door earlier but you didn't answer, so she assumed you'd fallen asleep."

"I'm sorry to leave without saying goodbye, or thank you,

or anything."

He waved her away. "It's no bother. We're the ones who should apologize. You come here looking for information about Ned's old research partner, and suddenly I'm storming off into the snow in my socks."

"I wasn't . . . very clear when I knocked on the door. I know Maggie got the impression that I had information about your daughter." She swallowed, hard. She'd almost said *about my mother*. "It must have been shocking."

Jeremy grunted. "Do you like olives?"

"Excuse me?"

"Maggie's going to know I was up snacking if I eat all of the chocolates. I need to diversify." He nodded at the sofa cushion next to him and then disappeared into the kitchen. Lona left her coat on, but sat where he'd gestured. When Jeremy returned, he was carrying a tray of pickles and olives covered in plastic wrap and a plate full of grapes. He peeled back the plastic and popped an olive in his mouth.

"Maggie is—" He shook his head like he was reconsidering his phrasing. "Maggie and I have different ideas of what happened to our daughter."

"Different ideas?" She tried to keep her voice as noncommittal as it would be if Zinedine were a stranger, as if this was neighborhood gossip rather than the story of her life.

"Maggie thinks there's something . . . nefarious about the fact that we haven't seen Ned in as long as we have. She's got a whole conspiracy figured out – abusive husband, or undercover CIA mission, or, I don't know, space aliens."

"You don't think the same thing?"

199

"I wish I thought the same thing." He corrected himself. "No, I don't wish that. Maggie worries all the time because she believes Ned was taken away from us. I don't worry as much as I just feel hurt. And angry."

"You think that she's not missing?"

"If she were really missing, would she send us postcards?"

The olive in Lona's mouth suddenly felt eyeball slimy. She forced herself to chew it. It slid down her throat in a lump. "She writes you?"

"She does. She did. She wrote that we weren't supportive enough about her decision to have the baby before the miscarriage, and that she needed to start over, away from us. She said she was going to take a research position in Finland. Or Estonia. Somewhere cold. Then the correspondence slowed. Her emails started bouncing back. It wasn't a mysterious disappearance like Maggie tells herself it was. It was just her cutting us off. Nothing mysterious about it."

Except that she hadn't gone to Finland. Or if she had, she hadn't gone there because she'd miscarried Lona. Because Lona had been placed in the Julian Path when she was just two hours old. "Do *you* know who the baby's father was? Was he a researcher, too?"

She'd never imagined finding her father. She'd always assumed that if she could find any parent, it would be her mother, who would have at least had to be present for her birth.

"I always thought it was that lab partner – part of what upset me so much that you'd come looking for him. She worked fourteen-hour days. I didn't see how she could have been seeing anyone who wasn't with the Julian Path."

Was Edward Lowell her father? Had Thomas been her uncle? Had she met all of her living relatives, without knowing it, in the past week? She'd gone from having nobody to having everybody. Or to having pieces of them. Fragmented memories that had haunted her dreams.

"I never told Maggie this," Jeremy began again. He had placed an olive on a napkin, hole-side down, standing on its end, and balanced another one on top. Now he was trying to stack a third one on top, an olive snowman. "Because I love my wife and I don't think that revealing this information would ultimately do any good, and mostly because I'm a coward. But a couple of days before she disappeared, Ned and I had a pretty bad fight. I told her what a mistake I thought it was, for her to have this baby. I told her she was going to set herself back in her career – end up in some dead-end staff researcher job with a pharmaceutical company or something, instead of doing the brilliant work she was supposed to do. I told her it wasn't fair for her to expect her mother and me to pick up the slack."

The olive snowman tumbled to the ground. The head rolled off the table and under the sofa. Jeremy grunted as he sank to the floor, patting the carpet in search of it. "I know it was a terrible fight to have, terrible things to say. I was just worried about her. I'm sure when she lost the baby, she thought I'd wished for it."

He located the olive, dotted in lint, and stacked it on the coffee table. "So that's the other reason I think she ran away. Because I basically invited her to."

Lona didn't know what to say. For the briefest of minutes, she thought about telling him everything. But he'd kept his secret for seventeen years, because he thought it would hurt Maggie, not help. Would knowing what she knew help or hurt him?

"Do you want a drink?" Jeremy stood up again, started for the kitchen. "We have so much leftover cider. I told them it was mulled specially for the party, based on a fifteenth-century wassail recipe, but they all drank soda instead. It doesn't give me a lot of confidence in the class."

She stood up after him. "No, thanks. I should be getting home. I have roommates – they'll be worried." She thought, for the first time in almost twelve hours, about Ilyf and Gamb.

"Well." He brushed his palms together, shaking off the crumbs, and extended his hand to Lona. "Thanks for being my midnight snacking partner. If I get in trouble tomorrow for eating all the food, I'll tell Maggie it was your fault."

"I'll come back again," she promised. "Don't tell her it was me who ate all the chocolate, or I won't be welcome."

"Oh, you'll be welcome any time. More than welcome, in fact. Leave your phone number and we'll do it again. It was nice to have someone to fuss over and put to bed, even if it was in the spare room." His hand was still there, extended a few feet from Lona. Instead of taking it, she found herself flinging her arms around him, pressing her cheek against his scratchy cardigan.

35

Ilyf's light was still on when she got home. Lona waited to hear a cry of relief, or a scream of anger. Some outburst over how sick to death worried Ilyf and Gamb had been. The stony glare Ilyf gave her when she opened the door to Ilyf's office was even worse.

"That was a crappy thing to do." She folded her arms in front of her chest. "You were gone for hours."

"I'm sorry. I got . . . distracted."

"I got scared."

"I should have called."

The conversation was interrupted by a deep, pig-like snuffling. Gamb had fallen asleep, still in his clothes and shoes, sprawled across the futon along the wall of Ilyf's office.

"He came in to help me stay awake," Ilyf explained. "He fell asleep in ten minutes." Gamb snored again, and then, in his sleep, chortled loudly. "He's like a human sound machine. I don't know why I told him he could come with me."

"With you?"

"To New York. Company headquarters – they want to actually meet me face to face and Gamb asked if he could take advantage of the free hotel room. Didn't I tell you this?"

She probably had, and Lona would have remembered if she hadn't been so absorbed in her own life. "You probably did."

"Anyway. Gamb really wanted to go. Said he'd never been to New York. At least, not as himself, only as Julian. We're leaving tomorrow."

"Fun."

"If by fun you mean horrible," Ilyf said, but she was looking affectionately in Gamb's direction. "What do you think he dreams about?"

"I don't know. Unicorns and whoopee cushions?"

"Probably. I don't dream at all."

"Really?" Lona was surprised. She wished she could have Gamb's dreams instead of her own. But if the alternative was to go to sleep and see nothing but blackness, she wasn't sure which one she would choose.

"I haven't. Ever. I don't know if it's because my brain is too logical, that I like to solve problems, not invent false realities. Or if it's because of Julian. Maybe I would have dreamed if I'd had a different path." She shrugged and gestured to her screen. "Maybe that's what this project is. Maybe it explains why some of us dream and some of us don't—" Gamb snored again. "And why some of us can finish all three boxes of cereal but instead of throwing them away, leave them on top of the refrigerator so the next person doesn't know we're out until they try to have breakfast."

Lona smiled, but she was looking at the screen Ilyf had just gestured to. It didn't have the familiar coding that usually ran across Ilyf's monitor. It had the empty blinking box. Ilyf was looking at the Julian Compact again. Lona had forgotten about it until now, but Ilyf probably hadn't. Ilyf was so good at unlocking things. It had probably nagged at her for days that she couldn't unlock this file.

"No luck?"

"I think it's numeric. Only because the prompt asks for the eight security *digits* – and if it accepted letters too, then it would have asked for security *characters* instead. But beyond that, no. Usually I could run a program that would try out passwords automatically – go through numerical combinations starting with eight zeros and moving all the way up to eight nines. But this system only gives you ten tries before it locks you out for good."

"How many have you tried so far?" Lona asked.

Ilyf looked embarrassed. "Six. I tried sequential numbers, then sequential numbers in reverse order, then the date of the Julian Path's founding. Then I thought that maybe it was a date, but a less obscure one. So I tried Christmas and Independence Day and – what was the other one? Anyway. I've tried six. I'm sorry for using so many up."

Lona shrugged. "You don't have to apologize. This is your mystery, not mine." She had enough mysteries already. She had a whole family of mysteries. *She had a whole family*. She thought about telling Ilyf everything that had happened that day. About Zinedine, who also went by Zinny, who also went by Ned. Who stabbed herself in the stomach when she was pregnant and who then disappeared. Ilyf would probably be better at coming up with a plan than Lona would on her own, with her orderly mind and obsessive work ethic.

But if she was going to tell anyone, she wanted it to be Fenn first. She always told Fenn first. She had for her entire life. She felt now for her phone in her pocket. While she was driving home from Maggie's, in a moment of either weakness or strength, she'd dialed his number. It had gone straight to voicemail, but that had been before midnight, when the library still would have been open. She bet that's where he was. It would be just like Fenn to cap off his first week of classes by studying at the library.

"Why do you think it's locked, though?" Ilyf was still staring at the screen, moving her cursor back and forth in the empty space, as if she could will the right digits into existence. "The other programs are all kinds of weird things. But none of them are locked up."

"Maybe that's just where they keep all of the proprietary technology or something boring like that," Lona said. She was having a hard time focusing on the conversation. She really was desperate to call Fenn. Now it was after midnight; the library would be closing and his phone would be turned back on. She could picture him walking back to his dorm, his curly hair wild, the way it got when he'd been studying and running his fingers through it. She could picture him opening the door to the boys' dorm they'd toured, and then – and then she didn't know. She had no idea what his room looked like, whether he'd hung anything on the walls, if he had a view of the green or the pond or the street. She had no idea what the campus tasted like to him today. The realization suddenly filled her with emptiness. She pulled her phone out again. Zero missed calls.

"Ilyf, why didn't you try my phone if you were worried?

I'm not showing any missed calls."

Ilyf looked embarrassed. She slid her hands under her legs and sat on them. "I promised Fenn I wouldn't."

"You promised – what?" Ilyf had talked to Fenn? About her? "When did he call?"

"Tonight." Ilyf still looked uncomfortable. "A couple hours before you got home. We didn't only talk about you. But since we were already on the phone, I told him we were taking care of you – that we were making sure you were eating and stuff. And I mentioned that you'd been out for a really long time, and I was starting to get worried, and I was going to call you if you were too much later. And he told me not to."

"He told you not to?"

"Not to call, and not to worry. He said you'd made it clear what you wanted."

"Oh."

This is what she'd asked for. This was Fenn giving her everything she wanted. But she couldn't help but feel stunned. She could have been in danger, and he'd told Ilyf not to worry about her. He didn't even worry himself. "What else did you talk about?" She tried to sound neutral. "Did he sound okay?"

"He did, actually." Ilyf wrinkled her nose. "Are you sure you want to hear about this?"

"Of course I do. We're still friends."

"Okay. He sounded good. He was with, um, people. They were out getting pizza. We didn't talk long – the restaurant was loud."

Lona knew exactly what pizza place it would have been. She and Fenn had passed it on their way to campus. It had scuffed wooden tables and a mural on the wall. Students had been inside, laughing; Fenn had reached out and taken her hand.

She still needed to call him, though. Despite what Ilyf had just told her, she couldn't believe that he wouldn't want to know what had happened to her today. This was bigger than their argument – this was what could end their argument.

"I'm going to – I'll just be—"

"Go." Ilyf waved her out of the room and immediately turned back to her computer.

In the kitchen, she dialed his number again. The phone rang this time; he'd turned it back on. She held her breath – three rings, and then a click. He'd picked up.

"Fenn?" she said, before he could say anything. "Fenn, are you there?"

"It's Lona," she heard him say. What was he talking about? Of course it was her. But why was he saying it like that, in the third person?

"Fenn?" she said again. The connection must be bad. He didn't respond to his name.

"Hello?" he said. And then, "I can't hear her – all I can hear is static."

She could hear him fine, though. He must have left the restaurant. There was none of the background noise Ilyf had described. There was only one other voice. A girl's, a familiar one.

"Can we go home now, Fenn?" the girl asked. "It's late. We've been driving around for hours."

"Okay. Just let me call her back once. It's probably better if I don't tell her what we're doing, though. Can you stay quiet?

208

I'm glad you're here with me tonight. I needed—"

The phone went staticky on Lona's end too, his words dissolving into crackles. The girl's voice. It had been Jessa's, Lona was almost sure of it.

She leaned against the doorframe, trying to keep from throwing up. Apple-cheeked Jessa, pinchable Jessa, the tour guide, who arranged New Year's Eve lunches and who was so very helpful to Fenn. Who was cute and friendly and deliciously normal. What were they doing that required driving alone, and why was it better for Lona not to know about it?

Nothing was open now. The pizza place would have been closed. There was no reason for Fenn to be out driving around with a strange girl. *Not strange to him*, she reminded herself, forcing the words like vinegar in a wound. *Not strange to him anymore.*

Her hand vibrated. She looked down. Fenn was calling her back. She could pick it up and yell at him. She could pick it up and cry. Or ask him what Jessa's hair smelled like, or whether she knew the taste game, or if she had seen his dorm room. Before she could figure out what to say, her phone went to voicemail.

"Lona, it's Fenn." She winced at the familiarity of his voice in the message. As if she would ever need him to identify himself by name. "I saw that you called, and—"

She pressed the delete key. It was painful enough to hear him. She didn't need to subject herself to hearing him lie.

36

"Do you think I'm a bad person?"

The flamehaired boy spoke so softly she wasn't sure she'd heard him correctly at first. They were back in the room. He'd taken her there as soon as she'd asked, and he'd remembered to bring the ginger ale, and he'd sat it carefully on the desk. He looked away from her when he said it, which was unusual. He never looked away. He always looked too close, if anything. His looks usually felt too much like peering.

She didn't know how to answer his question. The smart thing to do was to tell him no. Of course he was a good person, of course he was. He was a good person, and he probably knew that the right thing to do was let her go.

Hypothesis: *He didn't want to hear the smart thing. He wanted to hear the truth*.

"I woke up in this room weeks ago for reasons I didn't understand, and you kept me here without explaining anything. That doesn't seem like something a good person would do," she said flatly. "And you scare me. And that doesn't seem like an emotion a good person would make me feel. But those are both circumstantial fragments of evidence. I'm a scientist.

We don't deal with circumstantial evidence. I don't have any proof either way."

He nodded morosely. For once he looked exactly as young as he was. Like a dejected teenager. Like he could have been upset about a rejection from the basketball team, or a homecoming date. Like she should pat him on the shoulder. Not quite that. But almost.

"I'm more interested in why you asked me that question," she said carefully. The question felt like playing therapist. She was nobody's therapist.

"Downstairs," he said. "Downstairs you remembered something you did and it made you feel bad."

"Yes," she agreed. "Because the thing that I did was a bad thing. So it made me feel bad." When a response didn't come, she pressed on. "Are you saying that you don't feel bad when you do bad things? Do you . . . feel good?"

He sighed, and briefly rested his head in his hands, his palms flat on his forehead. "I don't feel good," he said. "But I don't feel bad, either. Sometimes it's hard for me to feel at all. Sometimes I think that's why I do the things that I do. Because I want to see how they make other people feel. Because I hope they'll help me feel something, too."

"I remember that my mother used to knit." She didn't know why she was telling him this.

The boy cocked his head to the side. "Pardon?"

"Badly. Not for long. She was going to make scarves one Christmas. She ran out of patience and ended up buying everyone scarves instead, then she got annoyed that the knitting needles and supplies and everything cost more than the finished ones from the department store."

She shook her head in frustration. "Why do I remember that? Why do I remember all the normal things about my childhood? Soccer, and my father, and my mother – and remember so little about where I was before I was in this room?"

"When we were downstairs, it sounded like you thought you were starting to remember."

She had been enclosed by panic downstairs. Panic, and guilt and revulsion. At what she was seeing, and at herself, for doing something bad. That particular cocktail of emotions. That's what had felt familiar, what had led her to remember something. That emotion was her last memory, before her world went soupy for years and years, before she woke up in a room with a boy whose hair looked like fire.

"I think I was remembering a feeling," she said. "I was remembering being a part of this. Not exactly what you showed me downstairs. But like you said. Another project. I remembered very small fragments of that other project."

Another memory. It ripped through her suddenly, viscerally. A very tactile memory. She remembered opening her mouth. Forming her lips to say something deeply personal and strangely joyous, in the middle of all of the chaos. "And most of all," she said. "I remember a name."

37

She let the syringe fall to the ground. It was done. It was finished. There was nothing left to do but wait for them. They would find her soon.

Her belly spasmed. She ran her hand over it. A reaction to the injection? A side effect? No. It was something else. Something stronger. Her pelvis had been tied in knots. Pain radiated around her entire mid-section. Once it was gone, she tried to stand, bracing herself on the metal handle. Before she could reach her feet, the pain was back again. Stronger this time. Larger.

It was too soon. It was too soon for this to be happening. It wasn't supposed to be this way. Her body was betraying her. The floor beneath her feet was wet. It hadn't been a second ago. This was all coming too fast. She'd thought she could wait for them to find her. She was wrong. She needed to be found, right now.

"Help!" she called. "Help me – I'm in the stairwell."

The world went fuzzy. The stairs blurred in front of her. The door nearby opened and it sounded hollow and far-off.

When the people came in, their voices were triumphant at first, because they had found her. Then their voices were angry, because she had caused them so much trouble. And then finally – though the shift probably only took seconds, it felt like an hour – their voices were scared.

"Call an ambulance," someone said. "Would somebody call a goddamn ambulance?"

A different person was slapping her on the face. Gently at first, then harder. She could feel it, the sharp sting on her cheek.

The ambulance must have arrived, because she was on a stretcher. It was covered in white cloth that was scratchy. They put a brace on her head. An orange one, made of foam. It made it impossible to turn her neck.

They wheeled her outside and it was cold. A snowflake fell in her eye. From the narrow vantage point of the orange foam brace, she could see an evergreen tree as they passed it, and she could see that it was strung through with tiny, colorful lights. These were the wrong holiday decorations. By the time her pelvis hurt like this there were supposed to be different decorations. There were supposed to be pink and red hearts, cut out of construction paper. There were supposed to be cupcakes with tiny cupid's arrows etched in the frosting.

February 14. That was the day she was supposed to be going through all of this. That's the day her doctor had given her. What day was today? She didn't even know. There wasn't supposed to be anything special about today.

"Please, can you get me my computer?" she gasped to the paramedic.

"We're going to take good care of you." The paramedic was young, pretty, with freckles across her nose. They were probably the same age. "You're going to be fine."

"I need my computer!" She heard how crazed her voice sounded, *how sick-desperate. "Bring it to me," she begged. "Not to those men who called you. Just to me."*

Maybe it was because she was young, because it looked like they could have been friends – maybe that's why the paramedic wrinkled her forehead and hesitated for only a second before turning and sprinting back in the direction of the building.

She was strong. She only had to stay awake for two more tasks now. She could do that.

The snowflakes burned cold on her eyelids.

Lona's body convulsed with sobs. Her face was cold. She reached up to touch it. Her skin felt warm under her fingers. Her face wasn't cold. Zinedine's face was.

She looked down. She was still wearing her coat, still holding the phone she'd pulled out to call Fenn. Just like earlier, at Zinedine's house, she hadn't fallen asleep before being sucked into the Path. She was still standing in the kitchen, though her knees felt like they were about to buckle. What was *happening* to her?

How many minutes had she lost? She checked her phone for the time. She'd lost more than twenty minutes standing there, split between realities. She was being ripped in two. She was there, on that stretcher, feeling the snow on her face. She was lying there breathing into an oxygen mask with her hand on her belly.

She knew what the password was.

Gamb was still sprawled on the futon – one leg dangling over the edge, his forearm thrown over his eyes. Ilyf's desk was empty – she must have finally gone to bed – but she hadn't shut off her computer. Lona clicked open a browser window, scrolling down to where Ilyf had bookmarked the page with the Julian Compact.

There it was. The empty prompt. Four tries remaining.

Behind her, Gamb sighed in his sleep. *If it's wrong, you still have three more tries*, she reminded herself. This wasn't her last shot. But it wouldn't be wrong. Slowly, pressing each key with deliberation, making sure her shaking fingers didn't strike the wrong ones, she typed in the numbers.

One. Two. One. Five.

Twelve fifteen. December 15, her birthday. The day that she was born, but shouldn't have been; the day that Zinedine lay on a stretcher and begged a young paramedic to get her computer so she could change one last thing.

Lona typed in the four digits of her birth year. Almost immediately after she struck the last key, the prompt disappeared, and in front of her was a brand-new document.

She laughed.

"Whattt?" Gamb stirred behind her. "Lona, are you in my bedroom?" he asked groggily.

She covered her mouth, but the giggling spilled through her fingers and then turned into hysterical chuckles. After all of her searching. All of the traipsing across the state. All of that and all she needed to do was remember her own birthday.

The only thing on the new screen was an address:

33479 Buxton Road
Laurel, Md.

38

"Is it almost over?"

He looked tired. "Is what almost over?"

"This. Whatever I'm here for. Whatever you brought me here for."

"Does it feel like it's almost over, Ned?"

Her stomach had finally begun to settle. They'd been sitting in the room, silently, for more than an hour. Dinnertime must have passed. The boy must have told them not to bring anything. Now she was getting hungry, though. The opened ginger ale sat on the desk. She picked it up and took a few sips. The ginger felt spicy in her mouth but soothing as it traveled down her throat. When she set the can down, it was half empty. She was hungrier than she thought. The boy reached into his shirt pocket and pulled out a packet of soda crackers. They didn't sell those in the vending machines. He must have brought them himself.

Did it feel like it was almost over? That depended on what "it" was. It felt like her patience was almost over. Like she had to be reaching some kind of breaking point. But it felt like everything else was just beginning. Like whatever ball of yarn was sitting in front of her hadn't even begun to unravel.

"I think the beginning is over," she said. "I always liked that quote. I think it's Winston Churchill, in World War II. 'This is not the end. It is not even the beginning of the end. But it is, perhaps, the end of the beginning.'"

"You don't ever call me by my name," he said. "Why is that?"

She was thrown by the topic change. Always keeping her on her toes, he was. "I don't know. Names feel awfully personal."

"Mine's not."

"I can use it if you want me to," she said, but she found that at that moment, she couldn't. She opened her mouth to say it and it got caught in the back of her throat. He noticed.

"You thought you remembered a name. What was it?" he asked.

"The name I remembered *is* personal."

"You're not going to tell me."

She shook her head no, and she saw a flash of anger ripple through his body before he managed to control it. He stood up abruptly, though nothing he ever really did was abrupt. The movement was still fluid and cat-like.

"We're farther along than Churchill was," he said. "I think this is the beginning of the end."

39

She had an address. It was all she could do not to immediately drive to it. *Calm down*. She needed to think this through. Maybe the address wasn't meant for her. Maybe it didn't have anything to do with her.

Of course it did. It was an address she had opened using her own birthday as a password, an idea she had divined from one of her own dreams. This address was giftwrapped especially for her.

Zinedine.

Was that it? Was that the whole purpose of the visions? To lead Lona to this address?

Maybe, she realized, she should start by figuring out what that location even was. She wasn't thinking clearly. The day had been impossibly long. When she woke up this morning she didn't know who Zinedine was, or who Maggie and Jeremy were. She didn't know what Fenn would sound like, flirting with another girl.

"I told you not to wish for that." She whipped around at the noise. It was just Gamb, smacking his lips and curling his knees in toward his chest. "Told you to wish for a million dollars."

219

"Gamb? Gamb!"

"Unhh?"

"Gamb, it's time for you to go to bed." She wedged her shoulder under his armpit, digging her heels in deep and propelling him to his own bedroom, depositing him face down on his bed.

On the way back to Ilyf's office, she passed Fenn's room. The door had been closed since he left for school; she didn't want the pain of looking inside. Gamb had kicked it open as he stumbled down the hall. Inside, the bed was stripped of sheets, the shelves were emptied of books, and in his open closet there was only one shirt, longsleeved and brown with a zippered pocket. Why had he left that? It was one of his favorites.

Because I gave it to him, she realized. They'd passed it in a store, and he'd said it looked like it would taste like caramel, and she'd bought it when he wasn't looking.

And also because, she realized, she was the one who had worn it last – it was the shirt he'd given her on Christmas Eve when she couldn't dress herself. *He left it because he knew he'd be trying to forget me.* She closed the door.

When she got back to Ilyf's desk, she rubbed the sleep out of her eyes and typed in the database Ilyf had taught her how to use when she was looking for the other addresses. It collected unpublished listings, so Lona should be able to find out who lived in Laurel, even if the address was private. It also could perform reverse searches, spitting back the owner's name even if she only had a street number. She waited.

Her answer popped up after a few seconds. The address wasn't private. The address belonged to the Pequod Corporation.

That was Warren's company, the one responsible for building so much of Path technology. Next to the listing was a birdseye view of the street, dominated by a large gray structure with a flat tar roof.

My mother wants me to go here. She wants me to find her.

What was this place? She clicked another button to change the building view from birdseye to street level. Now she was standing across a four-lane road, looking across at pixelated gray stone. She tried to move closer, but the program wouldn't. The windows appeared to be boarded. There was a sign by the main door, but she couldn't make out the letters; it was faded and weather-beaten. She could make out a symbol, but just barely. Something round. Even without being able to see more, she already knew what it was: a big orange sun, rising over a small child whose face would be tilted toward the warmth.

This was the symbol of the Julian Path. This building must be the old lab.

<Why are you up so late?> Lona started at the ping coming from her computer until she realized it was just the chat function on her email. Fenn? Her heart jumped for a second, but it wasn't Fenn. It was Julian. *<Wild party?>*

She paused, her fingers over the keyboard, trying to think of the best way to shortcut everything she was feeling. *<Crazy day>* she typed back eventually. And then, after a minute, *<Can I call you?>*

Her own phone rang a few minutes after she'd hit send.

"What's going on?" he asked as soon as she picked up. "Do you want to talk about it?"

"Are you still in Pennsylvania? How was the wedding?"

"It was a wedding. Lots of bad dancing, lots of ribbing me for being the only one there without a date. Why did you want to talk?"

"Julian," she asked. "Did you ever go to the lab that the Julian Path was developed in? The one in Laurel?"

He paused before answering. She knew it made him uncomfortable to talk about that period of time. "A few times," he said cautiously. "Why?"

"I was thinking of going there," she said.

"How did you hear about that place, Lona?"

"I'm just trying to understand my past a little better," she sidestepped. "I don't know where my ancestors came from. This is my equivalent of going to Munich."

"It's not there anymore, Lona. The building might be, but it's not like the lab would still be open."

"I know. But I can still see what it looks like. There still might be ghosts of the place."

"I wouldn't. It was in a bad neighborhood. Run down, lots of gang activity."

"Maybe it's better now," she said.

"Better after it's become abandoned?"

"I want to go anyway."

She could hear him shifting his weight, sighing into the phone. "Then I'll come with you."

She hadn't been expecting that offer, and she wasn't sure if he really meant it, anyway. Julian hadn't chosen this role, as he'd reminded her before. Julian hadn't meant to get tangled up with a bunch of government-issued kids.

"You don't have to."

"Look, it's ninety miles east for you, and about seventy-five south from where I am now. I was going to be heading back in that direction anyway. I'll meet you in the middle."

"Are you sure? I know you kind of want to be done with all of that. With everything related to the Path."

"What are the chances of me ever actually being done with that? Okay?"

"Okay."

She hung up the phone. Her skin was buzzing; it was hard to sit still. There *had* to be a reason that her dream always reverted to the same night. The same location. She knew every inch of those antiseptic halls now. She knew the precise number of paces it took to get to the stairwell. She knew which way the handles turned, and where the light switches were. In her dreams, Lona had walked those halls again and again. She was an expert on that memory. Someone wanted her to come there, and wanted to make sure she was prepared when she arrived. If Zinedine was still alive, Zinedine was in the lab.

40

The highway was nearly empty when she left the next morning. Too early for rush hour; the other cars on the road were long-haul trucks and city vehicles. It was damp out but not rainy, the kind of weather that makes the landscape look smudged, like a Monet painting. It made driving feel hypnotic, motoring through a dream. After thirty miles, she looked down and saw her phone was blinking. A text from Julian. "Leaving now. Need coffee."

When she picked it up to attempt a one-handed reply, she saw there was also a voicemail, one that must have been left early this morning while she was in the shower. *Fenn?* She thought, but of course it wouldn't be. And she couldn't allow herself to want it to be – she had to let him move on. She could have made herself believe that, if her last act before walking out the door this morning hadn't been to go into Fenn's closet and take out the brown shirt, pulling the soft material over her own T-shirt. It still smelled like grass.

The voicemail wasn't from Fenn. "Hi. Lona? It's Maggie. Maggie Croft? You came to my house yesterday?" She said it like a question, like Lona wouldn't remember passing out in her guest bedroom twelve hours ago. Lona had almost forgotten that she'd left her number with Jeremy. "I'm calling because I think you left your hat here. At my house. It's black with blue stripes and a tassel? I thought it belonged to one of Jeremy's students, but he emailed the class and nobody claimed it. Anyway, if you give me your address, I can mail it to you. Unless you want to come and pick it up. It would be nice to see you again, dear. I have a doctor's appointment at two, but otherwise I'll be around all day. Come any time."

Her stomach was rumbling. She was on track to beat Julian by at least a half an hour – there was plenty of time to stop somewhere for breakfast, but she hadn't passed a food sign for miles. The exits along this stretch of the highway were mostly industrial: tire stores and auto-repair.

After a couple of minutes, she pulled into an off-market gas station, refilling the tank and then ducking into the attached convenience store for a bag of chips or a candy bar. Inside was nicer than she thought it would be. Half of the store was occupied by a refrigerator with cold drinks and a few shelves of packaged foods, but the other half had a countertop with bar stools, and behind that, an oven that smelled like something warm and sweet.

"No fun to travel in that wet, huh?" The clerk was an older woman with bleached hair. She flicked her fingers disapprovingly toward the weather outside.

"It's not bad. It's not raining."

"Huh. Wanna muffin? Blueberry or chocolate chip. In the oven, be done in ten."

"Maybe." She checked the time again. A muffin sounded

better than the cheese curls she was holding in her hand.

"Or the scones are done now. Apricot pecan. Kinda dry. Which is all *your* fault."

"I'm sorry?"

"Make me come out in the wet looking for you and forget about the timer."

"I'm really sorry, but I don't know—"

From under the counter, Lona heard a whine. A small dog, fluffy and white. The clerk unwrapped the tray of scones, breaking off a piece to toss to the dog and putting another whole one on a plate for Lona. "Isn't that right?" the woman asked the dog. "Make momma come out in the cold and forget the scones?"

Lona slid onto the bar stool and accepted the plate. The woman was right. The scones were dry. She took a squeeze bottle of honey from the center of the counter and drenched the top.

"Daisy. Daisy, you already had your breakfast." The dog was weaving between the rungs of Lona's stool, looking for scraps. "My fault," the woman said. "The trainer always tells me feeding her table scraps makes her beg, but I do it anyway."

"Should I just ignore her, or—" The dog was dancing on its hind legs, eyes glued to Lona's plate.

"Just ignore her. Dammit, *Daisy*. You bad dog. Unless you want to give her a treat, and then you'll have a friend for life."

"Hi, Daisy," Lona said to the dog. "Hi, Dais—"

"Keep your head up, Ned."

The black and white ball in front of her was huge. It went almost

226

up to her knees, covered in pentagons and hexagons. She stuck her tongue out in concentration, balanced on her right foot and drew her left one back. The ball disappeared from in front of her.

"Warned you to keep your head up, Ned." Her dad was dribbling the ball away from her, down the length of the courtyard. "Ball won't go anywhere on its own. You don't have to worry about what the ball's doing. You have to worry about what your opponents are doing." He weaved the ball between his feet; she could barely follow the blur. Then there was another blur – a black and tan and furry one.

"Daisy!" her father shouted. "Daisy, get out of the – dammit, Daisy."

The sliding door behind him opened. Her mother, holding a book in her hand, her glasses propped on the top of her head.

"Jeremy, what are you doing?" she called. Daisy clamped the ball in her jaws and trotted it through the grass; Jeremy dived after her and missed. "Daisy, come here," Maggie ordered. "Daisy – Jeremy, she's in the Pydnowskis' garden again. Get her over here and I'll put her—"

"Did you want some more coffee?" The clerk swished the coffeepot back and forth. "Woo-hoo. Hon? Coffee?"

"What happened?" Lona gasped. The counter was swaying in front of her; she slammed her palms down, trying to keep steady.

"Someone just walk over your grave?" the clerk asked knowingly, then swished the pot again. "Coffee?"

"No. No thanks. I need to – thanks anyway." She pulled a ten-dollar bill out of her pocket and dropped it on the counter, lurching off the stool, groping blindly for the swinging door.

"Change, hon? Do you want your—"

A sheet of water hit her as she opened the door. The dampness had turned to pouring rain. She dived into the car, shaking in her wet clothes, out of anger and cold and fear.

"A gas station." She said the words out loud so she could hear them and they would be real. "You are Lona Seventeen Always. You are not in a courtyard playing soccer. You are in the parking lot of a gas station." Her teeth were chattering, and hearing the way her voice shook scared her even more.

She jumped at the sound of a knock on the car window. The woman from the counter was standing outside, wrapped in a plastic raincoat, waving a five-dollar bill. "Change?" she yelled. "Hon, are you okay?"

Lona shook her head, without rolling down the window. No, she wasn't okay. She pulled her seatbelt over her shoulder and skidded out of the parking lot, leaving the woman behind, her raincoat flapping around her knees.

This wasn't fair. This had changed the game. Lona had done everything. She had submitted completely to this Path. She had subjected herself to the same dream, over and over again – she could draw a scrupulously detailed map of that lab with her eyes closed. And now, after all of that – after all of that, why would she suddenly have a different vision? One from decades ago? One from when her mother was a child? *Why would she dream that?* Every time it seemed like she'd found solid ground, it was taken out from under her.

Her phone rang. Julian. It took her three tries to answer it, and when she finally did, she had to keep her elbow pressed against the window to steady herself enough to hold the phone.

"Where are you?" Julian asked. He sounded energized, full of coffee. "I just passed an exit for Fernwood Road, and I'm driving past this dump of a gas station with a big muffin in the window."

"That's where I am," she choked out. "I'm pulling out of that parking lot. I'll follow you."

"Lona, are you okay?" It was raining hard. She had to fight to hear him over the noise of nails hammering against the roof of her car.

"I'm fine." Her hands were shaking worse than Fenn's had been outside of the Josephine Kennedy center.

"You don't sound okay. The roads are really slippery out now – don't drive if you're—"

She thought she could already see his car, the familiar square tail lights of his rusty green van, several traffic stops ahead. The light in front of her was about to turn red, she pressed down the accelerator to make it through in time and felt the car skid to the right, hydroplaning across the blanket of water. The wheel spun in her hand and the car behind her honked; she saw the terrified faces of its passengers just inches away.

"I'm fine, Julian," she said, when she managed to get control of the car. He must have seen her in his rearview mirror; he would be angry with her for driving recklessly. "Julian?" she said again. No answer. Bad weather must have wrecked the signal. The phone rang again a split second later.

"I drive better with two hands," she testily answered the phone. "If you don't want me to get in an accident, don't call me."

"Lona?"

229

It wasn't Julian. It was Maggie Croft again. *I just saw you*, she wanted to say. *I just saw you forty years younger and achingly pretty, chasing after an unruly dog.*

"Maggie." She couldn't think of anything else to say.

"It sounds like you're driving, dear – I don't want to distract you. I just realized that when I called you earlier I forgot to give you our address. You know, in case you wanted to pick up the hat. I'll be around all day except for that doctor's appointment. We live at three-oh-one Dogwood Court, which is just off—"

"Maggie, I already have your address. Remember? I came to your house."

"Of course you have. Where is my head? I do hope you'll come by."

"Wait, though – Maggie, that's not your address."

"What?"

"Whatever you just told me. Don't you live on a street called Sycamore?"

Maggie burst out laughing. "Ever since you visited, it's like my brain keeps getting stuck in forty years ago. I hadn't thought about the past in so long – you must have jostled something. Our real address, as you know, is eight-thirty-two Sycamore."

"What was that other address?" she asked. The rain drummed on the roof of her car; she had to shout to hear herself. "Maggie? Maggie! What was that other address?"

"Oh, it's silly," Maggie clucked. "When Zinedine was born, Jeremy was still getting his PhD. We lived in married student apartments until she was in kindergarten. Dogwood Court. It's funny. I hadn't thought of that place in years. It was horrible – linoleum floors, and the neighbors were these rude people who were completely maniacal about their garden."

Lona had finally caught up to Julian at the next traffic light. He turned to his left and he saw her, shaking his head in frustration, pointing up toward the sky. *Don't drive crazy in the rain.* But then crossed his eyes and stuck his tongue out, trying to make her laugh. He must not be able to see she was on the phone.

"Lona? Are you still there?"

"I'm here."

"Do you think you'll come over? You'd be welcome to stay for dinner."

Julian jabbed his index finger toward the front of the car twice, then to the side. *Through two more traffic lights, then turn right.* He raised his eyebrows, making sure she'd understood.

"I can't come today, Maggie." Her voice sounded hollow, like it was coming from someone else, somewhere far away. "I have somewhere important to be."

She hung up the phone. The light changed. And then Julian went straight through the green light and she did a U-turn left, coming back in the direction she'd just come from, hearing the whir of her turning tires on the wet asphalt.

41

Calm. A calm had washed over her, had seeped from her toes to her scalp, like sliding into a warm pool.

She should have been scared. She had been scared almost every day since the first morning she woke up after having that dream. But she wasn't now. Every mile marker she passed, another coil of tension in her body seemed to unravel itself. Not because she was sure that what waited for her was a happy ending. But because she was sure it was an ending. Now it didn't feel peaceful so much as it felt inevitable. This was the final destination.

On the seat next to her, her phone rang. She didn't have to look to know that it would be Julian again, the seventh time he'd called. Maybe the eighth. She hadn't listened to any of the messages, which would be confused and then mad and then worried. He might offer to come and meet her. She didn't want him to, though – his company made sense when she was going to the lab. That was a place that belonged to both of them. This wasn't. This place was in her past alone.

The apartment complex was made of yellow brick. She had thought it would look abandoned, the way the old lab had in its pictures. It didn't. There were no flowers planted around the perimeter of the courtyard, the way there had been in the dream, but the grass was neatly mowed and none of the windows were broken. The building itself was shaped like a U, with three separate entrances, one on each side. In the middle, in the grassy area, there was a swingset and a cluster of picnic tables.

Zinedine had a birthday with a piñata by those picnic tables. Maggie made it out of pâpier mâché and hung it from a tree; the glue she used was too strong for the children's wiffle bat to break, and Jeremy eventually had to bust it open with a tire iron.

How did she know this? Memories that didn't belong to her, that had never appeared in one of her visions, were flooding her consciousness. As if they had always been there. As if they were just waiting for the right sensory memories to activate them again.

There were no signs – nothing identifying this as Dogwood Court. *That's because it's not anymore*, she realized. It couldn't be. The parking lot had spaces for at least fifty cars, but there were only a few others in the lot when she pulled in. And the apartments themselves – there were no bicycles on the balcony, or flower pots or hibachi grills.

For the first time in an hour, she hesitated. This still felt right, in her bones. But how was she supposed to get to the next step? Was she supposed to go in the main entrance, and walk down the hall, to the back, to Zinedine's old apartment? Was she supposed to stand in the courtyard and yell, "Mom?"

The rain had slowed to a drizzle. She parked the car in the spot closest to a bank of communal mailboxes and got out. *Where Jeremy used to park. Where he used to park and get the*

233

mail and complain when the Pydnowskis' catalogs were delivered to them instead. The mailboxes were empty now. The door had fallen off one; some kind of bird had built its nest inside. Clever bird, where it was dry and warm. Her phone rang again. She pressed ignore, and tucked it in the zippered pocket of Fenn's shirt, where her fingers brushed against something cold and metallic. *What was that?* She pulled out the object – a silver cigarette lighter. But Fenn didn't smoke. She reached in the pocket again, and this time she felt something waxy and cylindrical. A small green candle, half-melted. The lighter he'd used for Lona's birthday cake, and he'd saved a candle.

Her heart pierced. How was it possible they'd celebrated her birthday less than a month ago? She tucked it and the lighter back in the pocket, zipping it shut for safekeeping. It hurt to know they were there, but it soothed at the same time, to have a piece of him along.

Out of the corner of her eye, she saw a flicker of motion. Someone was standing behind the main entrance door along the left side of the building. Too far away to tell anything about them, except that the person's build was slender. Zinedine? Would Zinedine be waiting for her? Did she know Lona was here? She had another thought: *Could Zinedine see what she saw?*

Is that why the Path had grown so much stronger since she met Maggie and Jeremy? Was it because the closer she got to Zinedine, the wider she opened the door for Zinedine to come in?

The figure in the doorway had seen her. It was waving. She squinted.

"Lona!"

The voice knew her name.

"Lona Seventeen Always!"

The voice knew her full name. And she knew the voice.

Her phone was ringing again. She turned it off.

"Harm," she said. "It's been a long time."

42

"I knew you would figure it out."

Harm clapped his slender fingers together. "I knew it would be harder for you to figure out to come here. But it had to be harder. If you'd just gone to the old lab, we wouldn't have known if it went back far enough."

Lona stopped a few yards away. She'd forgotten how beautiful he was. Harm had always had an ethereal quality. As if he hadn't been born, but designed by ancient gods. His skin was smooth and white; his eyes were a turquoise pool, his hair was a glowing ember. He was taller since the last time she'd seen him. Six months ago, he'd been the same height as she was. Now he was half a foot taller, lanky, with sculpted muscles.

"I knew if I was patient," he continued, "and it was hard to be because I wanted to see you again, but I knew if I was patient, you would figure it out."

"You brought me here?" she sputtered.

"Technically, you brought yourself here."

Her brain was spinning. He'd said he had to know if "it" went back far enough. What was "it?" The memories? *How would he know anything about the memories? Why would Harm have anything to do with any of this at all?*

"You're even faster than I told them you would be," he said. "And I told them you were very good. How did you find it? What was the final clue?"

"A woman named Maggie Croft. She gave me the address."

"But you knew to ask for it. You would have gotten here on your own eventually."

"What are you doing here, Harm?" That was good. Ask him direct questions. Don't allow him to throw you off balance. It was all coming back, the tips and trips for how to deal with Harm. This pungent blend of attraction and revulsion and fear that came from being near him.

"Mostly, I was waiting for you. Working on some other things, too, but mostly waiting for you."

"That's nice of you to wait for me. I didn't think I'd see you again."

"I hoped I would."

What are you doing here? She screamed at him again in her head. *Why did Zinedine's memories lead back to you?*

"So do you live here now?" she asked out loud.

"Why don't you come inside?" He opened the door wider and made a grand, inviting gesture with his arm.

Obviously, she shouldn't. She should call the police. Or if not the police, Julian – Harm listened to Julian. Or if not Julian, Talia. Nobody even knew where she was.

But what would she tell anybody that she called? Harm wasn't threatening her. Harm didn't have a weapon. Harm hadn't said anything to make her believe that his invitation was anything other than that – an invitation. Not an order. Not a warning.

Obviously, the careful, serious thing to do was leave immediately.

Lona hadn't been making very careful, serious decisions lately.

So she went inside.

The foyer of the building wasn't much more than a landing: an end table, a mirror, a vase with silk flowers. There was a flight of stairs up and a flight of stairs down. The same memory connection that had told Lona about the piñata and the mailboxes now reminded her how the building was laid out: three stories of apartments – sparse, efficient, university-issued two-bedrooms – which they would reach if they took the stairs up. If they took the stairs down, they would reach an open space with concrete floors – a laundry area, shared by and accessible from any of the entrances in the U. A bank of washing machines should be clustered in the center.

There was a noise, a far-off one that sounded like whooshing, that was familiar to Lona but too out-of-context to place.

They didn't go upstairs or downstairs. Instead Harm opened the single door immediately across from the table with the flowers. The building manager's apartment. Was this where Harm lived now? The walls were off-white and empty; the furniture was sparse and impersonal: a sofa, two chairs and a stereo piled with music. Old jazz, it looked like – at least, she could see a picture of a saxophone.

"Here, sit." He gestured to the chair – a boxy, Swedish-looking thing – farthest from the entrance. She didn't like that. The only exit that she could see was the door they'd just come in through, and Harm was now sitting between her and that door. She didn't like that at all.

"Would you like something to drink?" he offered. "Or eat?"

"I'm fi—" she started to say, but he looked so disappointed by the refusal that she cut herself off. "Water. If you have any." He leapt to his feet – floated, rather. Harm never leapt; he glided – and returned with a pitcher of filtered water, a glass and a plastic bowl. The bowl was filled with lemon wedges, one of which he delicately placed on the rim of the water glass.

"I've been practicing my hosting skills," he said. "If you're a good host, your guests will feel more comfortable." He said it like he'd read it somewhere – a Miss Manners column or an old issue of *Good Housekeeping*. He set the glass precisely down in front of her. This form of hosting wasn't like Maggie and Jeremy's hosting, which was haphazard and warm, and therefore truly comforting. This was formal and labored in a way that made Lona uneasy.

"Thank you," she said.

I'm having ice water with Harm. I'm at my mother's old house, chatting with the boy whose teeth have ripped into human flesh.

Now the apartment door opened, without a knock. It was a man, with kind of a squished face, like someone had taken their thumb and forefinger and pinched his features together from top to bottom. She exhaled in relief. It was better for someone else to be here. Probably.

"Sir?" Squish-face's voice was low and nasal; she wondered if he might have a cold. "I know you have a visitor, but can you come and look at something downstairs?"

Sir. So others were here, but Harm was still in charge. He looked irritated by the interruption, pressing his lips together, widening his eyes.

"Will you be okay here while I take care of something?" he asked Lona. "Please feel free to play some music while I'm gone." Again, she felt like these quotes had been copied from an etiquette book. "Or I could bring you something to read."

"I came here to find somebody, Harm. I came here to find—" She didn't want to admit that vulnerability while Squish-face was standing with one hand on the doorknob, looking impatient. "I need you to explain what you're doing here, and then I need you to help me."

"How about I leave you something to read?"

"No." *Remain calm. Be declarative. Don't be afraid.* "How about you help me? I've been through a lot to come here, and I need you to tell me what this place is."

He was ignoring her, disappearing down a hallway that she presumed led to the bedroom and returning a second later with a white stack of papers.

"Have you, in your search to find this place, come across something called the Julian Compact?" he asked.

Blood pounded in her ears. "I found a file labeled that. It had an address. Not this address, though." *Give those to me.* She reached out for the papers but he didn't hand them over yet.

"At one point, the file had a lot of additional information. Like this." The papers rustled in his hands. "This used to be in the file."

She feared that the papers would go up in flames or dissolve into pulp before he would pass them to her, that this was somehow a trick. But he placed them on the coffee table, turning on the floor lamp next to her chair for extra light.

"I'll be back in a couple minutes," he said. "Make yourself at home."

When he opened the door to leave with Squish-face, she heard the noise she'd first noticed coming into the building. *Pods*, she thought. Pods made that noise. There are pods in here. Her hands felt icy in her lap and for a second she had to remind herself to breathe. *What was Harm doing with pods in this building?*

The document in front of her didn't look official – it wasn't printed on any special letterhead, it didn't have a watermark. It didn't even look like much of a document. There were sentences with lines through them, blank spaces marked with X's – all things that she did when she was working on the rough draft of a school paper, when she was just trying to get her ideas down on the page. Fenn was much better – he bothered to make outlines before even starting on papers; by the time he started writing them he knew exactly where he was going.

Call Fenn, she thought. *Call somebody. Tell somebody where you are.* She looked at her jacket hanging on the coat rack, with her cell phone in the pocket. That would be the smart thing to do. But Harm had said he would be back in a few minutes. What if he took the papers away when he returned?

Funding Proposal for The Julian Compact [DRAFT]

Problem:
Since the Julian Path's inception, a primary issue has been the program's reliance on cumbersome equipment. Children who

241

are on the Julian Path are, because of the affiliated technology, bound to pods and visioneers. This results in many negative repercussions. Some examples:

It is difficult to relocate on-Path children from center to center.

If a pod breaks down, the Pather's entire experience also breaks down.

Because the participants of the Julian Path are children, they are still growing. Constantly updating their pods to accommodate their changing size is both complicated technologically, and a drain on resources.

Although strides are being made in improving the safety and comfort of the pods, they are still prone to causing occasional bedsores, endangering the health and safety of the participants of the Julian Path.

Hypothesis:
It might be possible to construct another experience that serves the same function as the Julian Path, but which is not tethered to equipment and large technology.

Proposed Research:
Currently, the memory data affiliated with the Julian Path is transmitted through pods and visioneers – external media. The experimental project would size this data down to a nano-level. Instead of being streamed externally, the experiences would be transmitted internally, time released over the course of several months or even years. The "Path", as it were, would now be a portable, compact program. There are several obvious issues with this hypothesis. The first, and most obvious, is—

It went on for several increasingly technical pages. Lona read as much as she could understand. A portable program. A portable Path. *The Path is in you*, she thought. That had been one of the Julian Path's slogans, cooed into her ear every day back when she was on Path. With the Julian Compact, that would literally be true. The Julian Path would literally become a part of her, coursing through her blood, no matter what she was doing or how far she ran.

This whole time, she'd been thinking that the word "compact" referred to a covenant or agreement. It didn't – the Julian Compact referred to the fact that it was literally compact, small enough to be carried in someone's body without them ever knowing.

"Do you see now?"

She hadn't heard Harm come back in the room, but he was there, standing in front of her with his arms dangling simply by his side. "Does it all make sense?"

All of it? No. But some of it did. Her mother's memories, slithering out from a needle, pierced through flesh, passing from Zinedine's body to Lona's. Zinedine's last act before she disappeared.

43

Lona swallowed thickly. "Why wasn't this in the original file? The one that I found?"

"The person who made it tried to delete it. All we could recover was a draft."

"Did anybody ever build the Julian Compact? Did anybody ever figure out whether the technology was possible?"

"I think it's pretty obvious who built it, isn't it?"

"But why did you need *me*?" That was the part she didn't understand. Her mother might have built the Julian Compact, but that was years ago, before Lona was born. Lona didn't even know what it *was* until seconds ago. "You wanted me to come here and do what, exactly?"

"We wanted you to come here, period. We needed to see if you could. Our scientists think they've been able to replicate some of your mother's research from seventeen years ago. The problem is that they can't make the memories stick. And they can't replicate the seventeen years. There was no way to make sure that implanted information would stay as long as they needed it to, because no one had ever tried it before."

"Except on me."

"Except on you. You were the only test case."

"And that's why I'm here, instead of at Zinedine's old lab." That's what he'd meant about seeing if it had gone back far enough. "Because this is the oldest memory."

"Because remembering this place doesn't just pull you back to the beginning of your life. It pulls you back to the beginning of hers. Two generations of memories. We need Zinedine's expertise in how to make memories stick, but first we needed to make sure that she had successfully done it herself."

He made a gesture, like he was spreading those memories out over a table, to look at or sort through and put in a photo album. *That's what I am*, she thought. My whole life has been a photo album of other people's memories, other people's experiences laid out on acid-free paper.

"But why are *you* here?" she asked again. She was connected to Zinedine. Harm wasn't connected to anyone.

He shrugged. And though the gesture was meant to look casual, she had the distinct impression the question had made him tense. "I'm in charge. Mostly. I'm mostly in charge of this whole program."

"You?" she sputtered. "But you're just—"

"I'm sixteen." He jutted his chin out defiantly. "I'm the same age you were when you helped shut the Path down. Doesn't it make sense that they would turn to one of us when they wanted to build another kind of Path up again? We know what it feels like. We know what it can do. Or what it can't do," he added softly. "We know what it can't do, too."

Inside, she crumpled. Over the past three weeks, she'd convinced herself of so many things. That her mother was searching for her. That her mother wanted her. That her mother needed to be saved. That Lona was going crazy. It was none of those things. Lona wasn't the hero in this story; she was just a pawn, a way to test the success of an experiment.

Was her mother even here? Probably not. Her mother was probably in a federal prison cell somewhere, someplace with orange uniforms and plastic utensils. Her mother was probably in a three-bedroom house with a swing set in the backyard and other children who looked more like her than Lona did. Her mother was probably in Finland or Estonia, or whatever cold climate she'd told Jeremy and Maggie she was going to. Her mother was probably dead.

"What are you thinking about?" Harm asked. He'd leaned in closer, looking at her like her brain was something to be decoded. "What are you feeling?"

"Nothing."

He frowned and pushed the water glass over a few centimeters, then back again, watching the water slosh to the brink but not ever letting it spill over the side. He didn't like that answer. "You're feeling nothing?"

"I'm feeling nothing that I can put into words right now, Harm. You can't explain all of your emotions. Some of them are too complicated."

She thought he might press her on it, but instead he asked something else.

"Where did you go?"

"Excuse me?"

"Six months ago. When the Architect took you and I distracted the guards in the bay," he continued. "When I let them take me so they couldn't take you, where did you go?"

She was startled by the incongruousness of his question. "He took me to be remmersed, Harm. You know that." *He wants to know about the blood*, she thought. *He wants to know about the white room and the red walls, and Julian and Warren fighting over a gun*. She didn't want to tell him about that. She didn't want to play trauma currency, where she paid for information with bloody details. "I went to the remmersing center, and Genevieve died."

He was already cutting her off though, shaking his head impatiently. "I mean after that. I mean, where did you go next? Where have you been for the past six months?"

"I went away with Fenn," she said slowly. She still didn't know what he was asking. She never trusted Harm's questions. They always seemed too personal. "I went back and lived with Fenn and Ilyf and Gamb."

"I thought that's probably what happened. Fenn loved you. His eyes dilated when he was around you. You loved him too, but you didn't know it yet. I always wondered what that would feel like."

"To love someone and not know it yet?"

She was confused. Talking about love with Harm. It wasn't a concept she would have thought possible.

"Do you know what happened to me after you left?" said Harm. "Where I went?"

He hadn't answered her question, and now there was something hard added to his voice. Not hard. Brittle.

She *didn't* know what happened to him after she left. She had casually wondered about him. She'd had nightmares about him. But she had never, not even when she was trying so hard to unravel every other mystery, tried very hard to find out what had happened to Harm. She should have tried. She saw that now.

"I don't," she said.

"They took me for tests," he continued. "Do you know what kind of tests they took me for?"

"I don't," she whispered again.

"They weren't painful. Not most of them, at least. Some of them were. Some of them were designed to test my responses to things. To see if they were normal. Or actually, on the 'normal spectrum'. That's the term they use. 'The Normal Spectrum.' Some of those tests were painful, but when they figured out that my physical responses were all N.S., then all of their tests were mental. Pictures. Flashcards. Electrodes attached to my forehead and my heart while I watched movies or listened to recordings. I was in a room, by myself. I was lonely. I told them I was lonely, and they said I couldn't be, because loneliness was an N.S. emotion that I hadn't registered. They thought I was faking it, because I wanted to get out."

He said everything so matter-of-factly, so chronologically, like reciting a grocery list. She still couldn't ignore the brittleness behind his words, or keep from thinking about what was unsaid in his story. Where had he been kept? In a hospital bed? In restraints? When Gamb and Ilyf were singing her birthday songs and she was eating cake, or when she was babysitting Gabriel or talking about school with Talia – *when she was lying next to Fenn in the dark and his lips were traveling lazily over her collarbone* – where had Harm been then?

"Anyway," he said. "I don't know how long that was. Then some men came and asked if I wanted an assignment. They said it would involve leaving. I wanted to leave. So I said I would come. And they brought me here to be in charge of this."

"Harm, I'm sorry. I should have come looking for you. Julian did. Julian tried to find out what happened to you." *But not very hard. None of us looked very hard.*

"It's fine," he said. "I was just sharing. I've been reading a book about making small talk. It's called *The Art of Easy Conversation*. Have you heard of it?"

"I haven't."

There was a sharp rapping sound on the doorframe. The man was back again, Squish-face, still looking irritated.

"Anders?" Harm said testily. "Can I help you with something? *Again?*"

"Katie has reached the end of one of the cycles. Do you want us to start it again, or rest the subject, or start her on a different one?"

Harm rose to his feet. "I'm sorry," he apologized to Lona. "We're about to begin a new phase of testing. They can't do it without me – they don't know what signs to look for. I have to be there." The explanation made no sense to Lona.

"You want me to wait here again."

"You could." He hesitated. As if she had a choice. What would he do if she refused? She still couldn't tell what she was. His prisoner? His guest?

"Do I have a choice?"

He looked surprised. "Of course you have a choice, Lona. You came here to us and you can leave when you want to. But now that you're here, I thought I might take you to someone. Someone who I think would appreciate the company."

249

44

The apartment was the last door on the left. Lona knew where they were going as soon as they turned off the first landing. Here was the Weavers' apartment, which used to smell like garlic. Here was the Pydnowskis', which used to have a welcome mat laid out in front, a scratchy sisal one that Mrs. Pydnowski would get irritated about if anyone actually tried to use it to wipe their feet. Here was the Crofts' apartment. It used to say that, on the outside, in magnetic letters that Maggie had affixed to the door and let Zinedine arrange and play with. THE CROFTS.

The palms of Lona's hands felt damp and clammy. What if this was a trap? What if nothing was inside but an empty cell, barred windows, a waiting prison?

"Are you nervous?" Harm asked.

"No."

"But you keep swallowing. That's a sign of nervousness. I read it."

"Is it locked?" She rested her fingertips on the lever handle. *The last time I did this, I was too small to open it. I had to reach above my head to touch the handle*, she thought. And then: *I have never been here before. Those are Zinedine's memories.*

"It's only locked if you're on the inside," he explained. She didn't let herself think about how once she walked through this door, she would be on the inside.

The woman was slight, an inch or two taller than Lona, and built boyishly, straight up and down. Her hair was still red, or strawberry blonde, with a single streak of white running from her temple back through the bun her hair was gathered in. She'd grown it out of her pixie cut.

Everything else looked the same. Her eyes were blue and bright. Her hands – Lona had seen her hands more than any other part of her body. She had seen them sifting through papers on a desk, and slashing at Warren with a pen. She had seen them pushing open doors, and carefully tapping the side of a syringe to remove air bubbles. Lona could be forgiven for thinking they belonged to a man – her mother's fingers had uneven fingernails and chapped knuckles. The hands of someone for whom work was more important than beauty.

That's how she knew. The hands were what made this woman someone she'd met before. Suddenly her chest ached, like something inside it was swollen and she didn't know whether to cry or laugh.

"Mo—" She couldn't finish the word. "Mom" tasted too strange in her mouth, too foreign. "Zinedine?" she tried again. "Are you Zinedine Croft?"

The woman sat on a single bed, covered in a pink comforter. The desk was white, the lamp had gingham frills around the edges. Except for the poster of Zinedine Zidane, her mother's namesake, it looked like the room of a very young girl. She was in her mother's childhood room. Through the window – though it had bars on it – she would have seen the courtyard where Daisy the German Shepherd chased a soccer ball through the grass.

It took Zinedine several seconds to look up at her. Her reflexes seemed slow. Or, if not slow, then out of practice. Like an athlete recuperating from an injury. Lona wondered if she was drugged.

"I'm Zinedine," she said finally. She turned to look at Lona, and her eyes were cool and appraising. "But nobody calls me that anymore. Nobody has called me that for a long time." She turned back away again, her eyes fixed on the soccer poster.

Lona waited for a glimmer of recognition. She had expected – she didn't even know what she had expected. She'd spent so long wondering if this moment was even possible – if her dreams were leading her someplace real or someplace crazy – that she'd never stopped to think about what it would feel like. She didn't know whether she would feel happy or nervous, she didn't know whether she would laugh or cry. She didn't know what expectations to have, or how to tell whether reality met them.

Zinedine moved again, lifting her right arm, and Lona instinctively moved toward her – to shake her hand? To be embraced? – before realizing Zinedine was just removing something from her pocket. A crayon – a slate-colored crayon, worn down to the nub, which Zinedine peeled at with her fingers to work it back into a point. Lona looked back over her shoulder. Harm was gone. Probably part of his experiment. Probably there were hidden cameras in this room, monitoring the mother and daughter reunion, looking to see if they remembered each other, if the shared memories had created some kind of psychic bond.

"Are you going to sit?" Zinedine asked.

There should have been tears.

That's what was missing. Whatever emotions were felt in this odd reunion, there should have been *some* emotion. Her mother should have hugged her, or stroked her hair, or made a comment about her posture, the way the mother had on the college tour all those weeks ago. There should have been tears.

Her hands tightened into fists. *There should have been tears.* Why wasn't her mother looking at her? Why wasn't she searching Lona's face, the way Lona was searching hers, for similarities? There were some, a few, if she looked close. They had the same eyebrows. They had the same wrist bones, knobby and protruding. Why was her mother playing with a crayon instead of noticing those things?

She lowered herself onto the chair. A gingham-covered cushion that matched the lampshade covered the seat. "What have they called you, if they haven't called you Zinedine?" she finally asked through her teeth.

"Lots of things. I've been a lot of different people. And a lot of different blank slates in between." She blew the wax particles off the crayon and tucked it back in her pocket, covetously, a prized possession.

"You've been different people? How? Have you – have you been on a different Path?" In spite of her annoyance, her curiosity was piqued. Is that something they had in common? If her mother had worked in the lab for the Julian Path then had she made a guinea pig of herself?

Zinedine looked over Lona's shoulder, toward the door. *I'm sorry for boring you,* Lona wanted to say. *I'm sorry that it's not as interesting for you to meet your daughter as you might have liked.*

"A different path?" Her eyes finally drifted back to Lona's. "I've been on lots of different paths. For years. I've been lots of people's test tube lab rats. The months that I've been in here have been the first period of time in a long, long while that they've wanted me to be me. But you already know that, don't you?"

"Why would I know all that? *Why would I know all that?*" she repeated louder when it didn't look like Zinedine was going to answer her question.

"Is that redheaded boy coming back soon?" Zinedine asked instead. "We were talking before about something that I think was important. I think I was about to have a breakthrough."

You weren't about to have a breakthrough. I had the breakthrough. I came here. I found you. "Why would I know about all of the Paths you had been on?" she asked again. "I just met you." Was there more that Zinedine was supposed to transmit to Lona? Was she supposed to have been dreaming about other people's lives as well? How many people was Lona supposed to be able to fit inside her own head?

"Aren't you with him?" Zinedine asked. For the first time, her eyes locked on Lona's; she seemed to actually be seeing her. "The redheaded boy – don't you work with him?"

Lona shook her head slowly back and forth. "I don't work with him. I just got here. I came to see you."

"I'm sorry," Zinedine apologized. She waved her hand in front of her face, and for a moment Lona saw a hint of Maggie. It was the kind of gesture Zinedine's mother would have made, though she would have intended it to be self-deprecating and Zinedine just looked like she couldn't be bothered. "I just assumed you did – you came in with him. Have we met before? My memory is full of holes. I assumed you worked with the redhaired boy."

"I don't work with Harm. Like I said. I came to see you."

She didn't want to be the one to say any of this. She wasn't the one who was good with words. That was Fenn. She was the one who was good at acting, not talking.

"Zinedine," she said. "I'm your daughter."

Now is when the tears would come. Now is when Zinedine would rise from the bed and wrap her arms around Lona, commenting on how tall she was, asking where she'd been, talking about how many nights she'd spent dreaming of this moment.

Zinedine looked at her again, shaking her head back and forth. "No," she said, and while her voice wasn't unkind, it was firm. "No, I don't think I have a daughter."

45

"Lona?"

She didn't know how long Harm had been standing in the doorway, or how much he'd witnessed, or if he noticed how much her mother's words had hurt.

"What, Harm?"

"Would you like to come on a tour? I thought I could show you around."

Zinedine was listening; Lona could tell by the way her head was bowed low but tilted in their direction. "Are you going to show her what you showed me?" Her voice was sharp. "I don't think that's a good idea."

"No. Something new," Harm said. "Something that wasn't ready before."

Lona didn't want a tour. She also didn't want to stay in the room with this disinterested woman who was supposed to be her mother but didn't even know who she was. The fact that Zinedine seemed to *not* want her to go is what made her decision.

"Fine. Take me on the tour."

***

They walked back down the hallway in the direction they'd come from earlier. This time, Lona noticed changes she'd been too preoccupied to notice before: cracks and dust and dinginess that hadn't been in Zinedine's memories.

"The university was going to tear it down – it hadn't been used in a while," Harm explained proudly. "We got to assume control."

"That's nice."

His smile deflated at her indifference; he didn't say anything else until they were almost to the stairwell. "How did it go?" he asked. "Was it what you expected?"

"No."

"Isn't that what you warned everyone about living Off Path?" It took her a few beats to register what he was talking about. "Didn't you warn all the Pathers that nothing was going to turn out as they expected?"

Was that a warning? A threat? It was always so hard to tell what was behind Harm's words. When she'd lived with him at Julian's house six months ago, the only thing preventing her from being completely terrified of him was the sense that they were – as much as they could be – on the same side. Was that still true now? *No*, her inner voice told her, but she tried to ignore it.

When they reached the main landing, Harm kept going, down toward the basement laundry room. Except when he pushed open the door, it wasn't a laundry room anymore.

Breathe, she told herself, but the air was caught in her lungs and wouldn't go down. The washing machines had been replaced. Instead there were pods. More advanced than the ones from the Julian Path – sleeker, rounder, fewer pointed edges. They were also bigger than any she'd ever seen, because the people in them were adults. Twenty of them, maybe – the room was dim and narrow but they were organized five a row.

She shrank back; her breath was coming out more quickly than it should and she couldn't control it; she was going to start hyperventilating. What if the trials Harm had talked about involved more pods, more monitors, more losing of her own identity? What if he was going to put her in there? She wouldn't – she would refuse. She would fight, she would—

"This isn't what I wanted to show you." Harm's breath on her neck felt hot, and closer than she'd expected, but she felt relief at the words. "Follow me."

She did, past the rows of pods and through a door into some kind of break room, with a laminate table and a soda machine. Harm passed through this room, too – the basement was more labyrinthine than she ever would have expected. Through the next door was a room that was nearly empty. The light in here was fluorescent; she squinted to adjust after the dim of the laundry area. A glass partition separated the entryway from the rest of the room. On the other side was just a clean white floor and, in the middle, a plain folding chair.

A woman sat on it. She was young, maybe just a few years older than Lona, her light brown hair pulled back tightly into a French braid, and she was wearing camouflage pants and heavy black boots, and a long-sleeved tan T-shirt. A chunky black thing – a heart rate monitor? – was strapped to her arm.

"What is this?" Lona asked.

"It's the first test," Harm said. "It's the first test in the new phase."

"What is the new phase?"

He raised his eyebrows in surprise. "The Julian Compact." He raised one finger to his lips and then pointed to the girl in the chair. *Watch. It's starting.*

Anders appeared from the other door in the back. He carried a small, black case, and if he noticed Lona and Harm standing in the corner, he didn't acknowledge them. The case made a cloying, peeling sound as he unzipped it, and when Lona saw what he removed, she recoiled the way she had when she saw the rows and rows of pods. A syringe, filled with something clear, like the one she'd only seen in her dream.

Harm's eyes were glowing, just a little; he had almost imperceptibly leaned in closer to the scene in front of him. "Katie volunteered."

The girl named Katie nodded at something Anders told her, then rolled her sleeve up past her elbow, baring a taut, sinewy bicep. She took the syringe from him and, biting her lip in concentration, slowly plunged it into her own flesh.

"That's smart," Harm whispered. "If she feels like she's making it a part of her, instead of something being done to her."

Lona couldn't peel her eyes away from the girl. Her eyes had fluttered closed. *Maybe it was just a sedative*, Lona told herself. Maybe it was just something to put Katie to sleep, maybe she would start to quietly snore, maybe she would be fine, just fine, maybe all of this was still a dream, maybe Lona was trapped in Zinedine's brain and she had never woken up.

Anders walked around the glass partition, standing next to

Lona, watching the girl.

It wasn't a sedative. Katie's jaw clenched together, then dropped to her chest. Lona could see the veins popping in her neck, blue and pulsing with blood, and in her arms, too, as she clutched the sides of the chair with both hands.

"Help her," Lona whispered. Beside her, Harm and Anders were silent. "Help her!" she said louder. She moved to do it herself – to hold the girl's hand, at least, or make sure she didn't hurt herself – when a claw clamped around her bicep. Anders grunted in irritation at her distraction. "Harm, why aren't you helping her?"

A sound was coming from between Katie's teeth – enamel grinding – and it was joined by another noise, a grunting, an animalistic sound coming from deep in the back of the girl's throat. Spittle dripped down her chin, and then the frothy mixture turned pink. She'd bitten something inside her mouth and now blood was dribbling out, and there was a coughing sound too, in her throat – a full, wet sound that it took Lona a second to place.

"She's choking." She was hysterical now as she tried again to pull away. "She's not going to be able to breathe."

"You can't, Lona," Harm said softly. "She has to finish it."

Finish it how? Finish it dead? Is that what was going to happen to this girl with the long French braid, the girl who now had sweat pouring from her forehead and quivering muscles? Lona forced her eyes to stay open, even while she wanted to squeeze them shut, to cover her ears. She would watch this to the end.

But then the end didn't come, not the bloody one Lona had

feared. The horrible growling noise quieted and then stopped; her breathing went from a hiss to a shudder, and finally to a steady inhale. As the girl's eyes blinked open, Anders loosened his grip on Lona's arm, and she knew he'd left five perfect bruises. He jogged quickly over to Katie, producing a small pen light, which he shined into her pupils, and then pulling a tissue from his shirt pocket. He reached for the blood on her chin, but she took the tissue from him and did it herself.

I'm fine. Lona still couldn't hear her well, but she thought she could make out some of the words on her lips. *I can do it.*

Anders pulled out a notebook. "He's asking her some questions now," Harm explained. "This is where we keep getting stuck. The experiences while people are in the Compact are as intense as they're supposed to be, but the memories aren't sticking. People come out of it and don't remember what they saw. Anders is seeing if she can tell him certain details from the Path."

Anders stood up, looked toward Lona and Harm, and very deliberately drew one finger across his neck, shaking his head and frowning.

"It didn't work," Harm said, his voice sinking. "She still doesn't remember."

That's what the gesture had meant, but it looked like it meant something else too: *You are in trouble. I will make sure you pay.*

46

"Tell me what I just saw," Lona demanded, when Anders had led Katie away, when Harm had seated Lona at a table in the break room and given her a ginger ale. "I thought you said this was the first trial? Trial of what? What did you do to her?"

"I said it was the first trial of the new phase. We've done it before. In hospitals. We knew she was going to be fine. She volunteered. Lots of people have volunteered."

"Why would anyone volunteer for that?"

"Because, Lona," he said testily, "some people believe in causes that are bigger then themselves. Some people have a sense of duty."

"You said before – the documents that you showed me before – they were about a Path that could be injected. Whatever you did to that girl, it didn't look like she was on Path. She was having a nightmare. She would have hurt herself if it didn't stop when it did, and neither of you helped her."

"But she didn't get hurt. And we had to. The whole point of the Julian Compact is that it has to be able to function anywhere. Soldiers in a battlefield, or stock traders on a floor. If we didn't test it outside of a hospital setting, we wouldn't know whether it would be safe when we released it."

Released it? Of course. Test subjects were just test subjects. The whole point of this technology would be to sell it, to expand it, to put other people through what she'd just witnessed.

"Someone's going to find out," she said. "Someone's going to find out that you're doing this."

He looked puzzled, tilting his head to the side. He was so beautiful. "I don't understand what you mean. Of course people are going to find out. That's the point. It's – what's the word? Quaint. It's quaint for you to be worried about what the authorities are going to do when they learn about these experiments. Don't you remember how the Julian Path functioned, Lona? The authorities are the ones funding this."

"Who?"

"Government. Military. Lots of people are excited about this."

"This isn't like the Julian Path," she said weakly.

"Are you defending the Julian Path? *You?*"

Was she? She didn't know. She was the one who convinced all of the Strays that the Julian Path was wrong. She was the one whose brain refused to kneel to its will. "The Julian Path was about providing perfect lives for children, at least," she said. "It wasn't monstrous."

"This isn't monstrous." His voice had risen, but he sounded excited, not angry. "The Julian Path was about improving childhood; this is about improving all of society. If we're going to send people into war, shouldn't they be as prepared as possible? Shouldn't we arm them not only with weapons, but with experiences?"

"No!"

"Why not?"

"Because—" *Why not?* Because she'd spent sixteen years of her life hooked up to a pod, and when she saw a roomful of them down here, she felt like her head had been shoved underwater, like she was clawing for oxygen. "Because it's wrong to make people live their lives as other people."

"We're *not* making them live their lives as other people. Just a few weeks of their lives. In some cases, a few days. Katie did less than five minutes."

Harm didn't seem to understand that five minutes of memory could feel like a year. "Why do you have to inject it, then?" She couldn't stop thinking of the way the needle had looked going into Katie's arm. "Why couldn't you just put them in regular pods? Why couldn't you just give them visioneers? They sell them everywhere now."

"Why do you think, Lona? What did your experiences with the Julian Compact feel like? Were they the same as visioneers? Were they the same as the Julian Path? Think about it."

She thought. The Julian Path had been like – what was the best way to describe it? – like a three-dimensional movie, maybe. Like the most realistic movie ever made, with tastes, textures and characters that viewers would grow to love deeply over the course of many years. But still just a movie. No matter how long Lona was Julian, she could never feel exactly what he felt. She could only witness him feeling, wondering if she was experiencing the right companion emotions.

Zinedine's memories – the Julian Compact – were different. She didn't have to imagine what Zinedine was feeling. She knew it, because she felt it herself.

Maybe a movie hadn't been the right analogy. Living on the Julian Path had been like going through life coated in plastic wrap. She could experience everything, but slightly dulled. Nothing was dulled in Zinedine's dream. It ran through her blood.

"What were you showing Katie?" she asked. "It obviously wasn't anything from Julian's life."

"We were showing her what it feels like to win."

An involuntary shudder ran through her body. "That's not what it feels like to win, Harm. She was scared to death."

He pushed the already-opened soda can across the table. It scraped along the laminate in a way that reminded her of the girl's teeth gnashing together. She grabbed the drink only so she wouldn't have to hear it anymore. It wasn't ginger ale, she saw when she pulled it closer. She had assumed it was because that's what the vending machine was stocked with: ginger ale in green cans, cola in red cans, orange soda in orange cans. Harm must have brought this from somewhere else. It was apple-flavored – a brand that wasn't sold at regular supermarkets. Julian and his best friend Nick used to ride their bicycles to the bodega by Nick's house to buy it specially. This was Julian's favorite soda. Harm had brought it for her so she would have something comforting to drink after he showed her something terrifying. She picked it up and took a sip. It tasted sharper than she remembered, and slightly sour.

"Sometimes what it feels like to win isn't what you would think it would feel like."

"Can I leave now?" she begged.

"No," he said. "I'm afraid you can't. You're going to feel

dizzy soon," he said. "You'll want to lie down for a while and you might fall asleep."

As soon as he said that, she noticed the table seemed wobbly – it looked like there were two tables. She had to reach out and touch to see which was the real one, but when she did, there were two right hands floating in front of her. "What did you give me?"

"Just something to calm you down. I knew you'd be upset. Lona, I'm sorry. They told me I had to."

His words were blurry. She couldn't tell if he was really saying them, or if she only thought he was. "You said I could leave. You told me I could see my mother or I could leave."

He looked sad now, but that must have been her imagination. Harm didn't look sad. That was emotion he wasn't supposed to have. "I know," he said. "I wish I could have told the truth."

47

Everything was swirly, like a kaleidoscope. Faces floated in front of her, in pieces – eyes and noses and flaming red hair. Zinedine was there, putting her cool hand against Lona's sticky cheek, and Fenn was there too, stroking her wrist. Except Fenn couldn't have been there, so that made her wonder if Zinedine was there either, or if she'd concocted everything.

"She has a fever," Zinedine said sharply. *"If it lasts much longer, she needs to see a doctor."*

"Anders is a doctor."

"Anders is not going to lay a hand on her."

"You sound like you're starting to care about her. Are you starting to remember?"

"Is that why you kept her here? As a ploy to make me remember something? Harm? Harm, answer me."

"Make sure she's okay."

"Now you sound like you're starting to care about her."

"Make sure she's okay, and I'll make you a deal."

A deal? Don't, she wanted to say, but her voice came out twisted and tongue-tied when she tried to talk. *Don't make a deal with him. You don't know what I just saw.*

She thought she heard other things, too. Her mother talking to someone else. She kept saying a name that wasn't Lona's, but when Lona would open her fever-heavy eyes, she didn't see anybody else there.

Sometimes, in the middle of her delirium, she felt things she was sure were real: the scratch of a cool wash cloth wiping the backs of her knees where sweat had pooled. Or lullabies. She could swear that the lullabies were real. There was an Irish one, with a high note at the end, and the voice that sang it cracked when it tried to hit it. *Was Zinedine singing to her?*

She didn't know how much time had passed. A lot, it felt like. She could sense the room getting darker and then light again; she could hear the door open and close. A tray of food was brought in; she could smell warm bread and potatoes – but later someone returned – *"You haven't touched a thing"* – and the smell disappeared.

Gradually, things slid back in focus. Objects stopped floating in front of her; the headache that had built itself up behind her eyes from the strain of trying to distinguish between reality and fiction began to subside, cell by cell.

The first clear thing she saw was a glass of apple juice, looming large in front of her lips. A hand under her neck lifted her enough to take a drink. Once she realized it tasted normal – none of the sourness of the soda – she gulped it down, managing to sit up and grasp the glass with both hands.

"There you go." Zinedine let go of the glass, but kept her hands cupped a few inches underneath Lona's chin, ready to catch the container if Lona dropped it. When she finished, Zinedine used a cloth to catch a dribble of juice that had run down the side of her mouth. It was an intimate gesture, especially coming from a woman who didn't remember her.

"You had a bad reaction to what he put in your soda," Zinedine explained. "It was supposed to help you sleep for a few hours, not put you out for almost a day. Plus, you probably didn't have enough food in your system. Listen to me – I sound like my mother. She always blamed any illness – cold, flu, sprained ankles – on young girls not getting enough food."

Lona coughed; she'd gulped down the last dregs of the juice too fast. "I know she did. She still does. I met her."

Was it her imagination, or did Zinedine recoil, just the slightest bit at the idea of Lona spending time with Maggie?

"How long have I been out of it? How much time has passed?"

"About fifteen hours."

Her heart leapt and then sank. Fifteen hours would have been more than enough time for someone to contact the police – if anyone even realized she was missing. Ilyf and Gamb would have left for New York and Fenn – she brushed the idea out of her mind. Fenn wouldn't be trying to contact her. Julian would eventually realize something had happened to her, but even when he did, what good would it do? She'd left no evidence behind for where to go looking.

"Thank you for taking care of me." She allowed enough gratitude in her voice to be polite, but no more.

"You were sick," Zinedine said simply, and she hesitated, just a stutterstep, before asking her next question. "What did he show you downstairs? When you went down with him, what did Harm show you?"

She didn't want to think about the girl with the braid. Instead of answering, she held the glass toward Zinedine for another refill, drinking slowly to buy some time.

"Was it part of the Julian Compact?" Zinedine pressed on. "Please, it's important. I've been waiting to ask you for hours."

The juice suddenly felt slimy in her throat. That's why Zinedine had been such a dutiful nursemaid – not because she was worried about Lona. Because she was worried about the information Lona had.

"I apologize that my long sleep inconvenienced you," Lona said stiffly. "That must have been difficult for you to have to wait until I regained consciousness."

Zinedine looked at the floor. "I'm sorry. I'm not very good at this yet."

At mothering? At talking to other humans? Lona didn't care what Zinedine was or was not good at. She was thinking about Katie again. She was thinking about how the last time she'd ended up in a Path-related lab, she'd watched someone die. Katie reminded her of herself, six months ago, when she was someone else's plaything. She couldn't go through that again. She had to get out. The room had stopped swirling in front of her, but when she swung her legs over the side of the bed, the floor rocked.

"I don't think you should get up yet," Zinedine cautioned. Lona ignored her, holding the nightstand for balance. "What are you doing, Lona? If you want something I can bring it to you. You don't need to get up. At least keep your eyes on something that's not moving – it will help with the dizziness."

She didn't want to admit Zinedine was right, but the

headspinning did subside when she fixed her eyes on the soccer ball in the poster across the room. She removed her weight from the nightstand one ounce at a time, until she was sure she could support herself standing. Then she tried to envision the room as if it weren't composed of furniture, but of tools. There were the right tools in here to help her escape. She just needed to think.

The sheets? The sheets. She could strip the sheets from the bed, and she could knot them together like in old prison movies and she could – but as soon as she looked at the window, she knew she couldn't. The bars on the window were far too narrow for anyone to fit through. *The chair?* Could she swing the chair at something? At the door, or at whomever came through the door next? But when she tried to lift the chair, she saw it was bolted to the floor. Of course it was. *The spoon on the tray left over from Zinedine's last meal. She could use the spoon to loosen the bolts, and then she could* –

She took the spoon from the desk and, ignoring Zinedine's raised eyebrows, kneeled on the ground. The chair was affixed with a bolt on each leg; she could barely wedge the spoon under one. It dug into her palm, bending uselessly into an L-shape. What she needed was a wrench, to loosen the bolts, or the claw end of a hammer. But as long as she was wishing for something it might as well be a key. She took mental inventory of the items still in her possession. Her coat was gone, left in the apartment downstairs, which meant her phone was gone too. She was still wearing Fenn's shirt, which meant she still had a birthday candle. She could sing her way out. She could light it and wish her way out.

Maybe the bowl end of the spoon would be stronger than the handle. Or maybe if she threw her weight against the chair, she could loosen it from its bolts.

"Stop," Zinedine said quietly. Lona felt pressure on her wrist – Zinedine, kneeling beside her, her chapped hand clasped over Lona's. "It won't work. I tried that. I tried all of that when I first got here."

Lona shook her off and braced her shoulder harder. Throwing the chair at the door would be stupid – she saw that now. But maybe, if she could fit a leg of it between the window pane and the bars, if she could use it like a crow bar to pry the bars off. The building was old. The bars looked rusty. It might work.

"Whatever you're thinking, it won't work," Zinedine said again. "Even if you could get the chair off the ground. It wasn't bolted when I got here. They bolted it after I tried to throw it at a guard. I've tried everything. I used to get forks, too. I don't get those anymore."

Zinedine's tone was reasonable, but it only made Lona angry. Zinedine had tried everything to get out of this room, she said. *Why hadn't she tried everything to find Lona?*

No forks. No weapons. No hope. She thought of Warren, in his soft room with his soft clothes. She looked down at Zinedine's feet. Tennis shoes with laces. So they hadn't removed that way out for Zinedine. Did they not think she would try it? Or did they simply not care?

"Lona?"

Lona ignored her, all of her muscles straining against the chair. *Did it move? Did she just feel it give, the slightest bit?*

"*Lona.*" This time, Zinedine tried touching her shoulder, and

Lona wrenched her body away so quickly that she nearly fell over, and Zinedine's hand was left suspended in the air. "Lona, I have to tell you something. About Harm."

"I know. He's sick. I knew him before."

"Not that." She shook her head. "He made me promise. He said if I could mimic my research on the Julian Compact – if I could help them figure out what they're doing wrong – then he would let us go. Both of us."

A deal. That was the deal he'd made. Aspirin and freedom for evil work.

"You can't." For a minute she forgot that she was angry at Zinedine. "Zinedine, you can't – you don't know what they're using it for. It's horrible. It's—"

"I know," Zinedine said. "I know it is. I don't have any other options. I have to try, if I can. The memories of my research are dim, but if I dedicate all of my energy to remembering—"

"Why don't you remember *me*?"

Zinedine stared at her. The words had erupted before she could think about them. She didn't even try to keep the bitterness out of her voice. "Whatever tests they did on you, or however long you've been here, or whatever else – I'm your *daughter*. How can you not remember *me*?"

Zinedine swallowed. "It's not that simple, Lona."

"It seems pretty simple for most mothers." Anger built in her blood, and she welcomed it. Anger was better than what she felt running below the surface, like water below a thin pane of ice. Feeling angry was better than feeling abandoned. She had run all over the state, all to find a person she didn't even have proof existed. She had put Fenn in harm's way, and then she

273

had lost him in the name of this quest. She had followed the breadcrumbs like a good little Gretel. And her mother didn't even remember laying them out.

Zinedine backed away, sitting down on the single bed. Since Lona didn't know what else to do, she sat on the chair, the one that was still bolted to the floor, the immovable force that would keep her in this room.

"How did you find me?" Zinedine asked. "I didn't ask you that before."

"I had your memories," Lona responded dully. "I saw you in your lab, the night that I was born. I saw you stab a syringe into your stomach, and I saw them put you in an ambulance to take you to the hospital. You used my birthday as a password. That's how I found you."

"In my lab?" Zinedine repeated. "You dreamed of my lab?"

"Mostly. Your lab and then this apartment building. That's how I found you."

"What did you see, when you dreamed of this building? This room?"

"No." Lona was irritated by the quizzing, by the fact that Zinedine still seemed more interested in her research than in Lona. "Not the apartment itself. The courtyard. You were playing soccer with your dad, and there was a big dog. A German Shepherd."

"Daisy," Zinedine whispered.

"Yes. Your dad was mad because she was in the way."

"I don't think you're looking at this the right way," Zinedine said. She was beginning to smile. Why was she beginning to smile?

274

"The *right way?*"

"No. You're focusing on the wrong things."

"You're telling *me* I'm focusing on the wrong things?" Now she really needed to get out of this room. Not even to escape from Harm. Just to escape from Zinedine.

"I think the important thing is that I remembered I would forget you."

The statement was ludicrous. "You remembered you would forget me. I don't know what that even means."

"It means I must have known my memories would be erased. So I gave you a way to find me. I gave you a way to find me that was time-released for seventeen years, so that by the time you left the Julian Path at eighteen, you would have been dreaming of me for a year. I must have wanted you to have enough memories that you could identify who I was and come find me."

"Congratulations to me. I did find you. And you didn't remember me."

"Lona, you can't blame me. My memory is like a piece of paper that someone punched a bunch of holes through and then lit on fire. It's not my fault that I don't remember everything. I remember *pieces*. I'm remembering more every hour that you're here. I'm remembering everything that I can."

Lona snorted. Zinedine was acting like she'd done a selfless, thoughtful thing by giving Lona her memories. She hadn't considered that it could be dangerous for Lona. She hadn't thought about how Lona would feel, haunted by the past of someone she'd never met and couldn't find. The act was selfishness disguised as selflessness. "*Pieces*. Which pieces do you remember?"

Zinedine ignored Lona's sarcasm. "I remember my work. Parts of it. I remember developing the Julian Path. I remember the fights we had. About dumb things. Things that seemed so important, like whether Julian should be seen cursing in the Path. I thought he should – that removing the curse words from the Path used up money and technology we could have better spent elsewhere. Warren said that the general public would find him more likable if he didn't."

"Warren?" Lona started at the sound of his name being spoken with affection. "Were you friends with him?"

Zinedine didn't answer, so Lona talked louder. "Warren said you broke the rules." That's what the hospital aide had written, in big, loopy print. *Ned Broke the Rules*. Warren's sad memory.

"I suppose I broke a lot of the rules." She gestured to the room that surrounded them as if to say *I wouldn't be in here if I hadn't broken the rules*. "Trying to steal research that belonged to the Path – broken rule, even if it was my work to begin with. Destroying the evidence of that research – broken rule. Broken rules everywhere.

"In Warren's mind, the biggest broken rule was probably the fact that I stopped believing. That would have been more than a broken rule to him. That would have been a betrayal."

"You stopped believing?" The phrasing irritated her. It sounded so reductive. Believing. That word was used with Santa Claus. With the Tooth Fairy. It was a fantasy word, but this wasn't a fantasy. "Believing in what? In the Path?" Zinedine nodded. "Why?"

"Because of you."

Zinedine said the words so simply. An honesty that reminded

Lona, in some intangible but real way, of the bare honesty with which Fenn spoke. "Because I wasn't supposed to get pregnant with you, and when I did, it wasn't supposed to change me. But it did. Because I couldn't imagine not having you. Because for all the ways I knew I would be a bad mother – that I was going to work too late and let you crawl around in an un-baby-proofed lab – I still wanted to be your mother. Once I believed that, I couldn't imagine taking away children from other people. Not the way we were going to. Not from the people who wanted to keep them."

"I thought you didn't remember me," Lona whispered. She was afraid to move. Zinedine was still, too.

"They let me touch you." Zinedine's voice was barely above a murmur.

"When?"

"Before they took you from me. They let me touch your hair. It was so soft. I forgot about that. Until you were sick today and I was doing it again. It was *so soft*."

Lona shook her head, blinking back the tears forming in her eyes. This was the tender memory she'd wanted from Zinedine. But to have it now, with everything that had happened in the past sixteen hours, was so complicated. She could see that Zinedine was hoping for something from her now. A hug? A smile? She couldn't make herself respond in that way yet, though. Not after their first meeting had been so strange. She needed to stay focused.

"Warren was mad because he thought you were going to recommend shutting down the Path," she said firmly, keeping herself from too much emotion. "The program you designed."

Zinedine opened and closed her mouth, swallowing whatever hurt she felt because of Lona's dismissal.

"He must have thought I betrayed him in so many ways," she said finally. "Abandoned all of my scientific principles."

"You sound like you're sorry. For what you did."

"In some ways. As strange as it sounds. We were a small team back then. And Warren – his son had just died. He was – I can't even describe it. He was an entity of pain. It just – it just sort of emanated off him. I know you can't possibly understand. Not after the things he ended up doing. But I loved him, and in the beginning, at least, I would have done anything for him."

Suddenly the words Zinedine was saying seemed to come out of her mouth in slow motion, landing heavily on Lona's ears. Her mother had loved Warren. Would have done anything for him. They were a small team. That's what Jeremy had said, too. That's why he'd always thought Lona's father was Zinedine's lab partner. Because Zinedine was always working. Except Zinedine hadn't mentioned Edward Lowell a single time.

"He was my father, wasn't he?"

Zinedine's face froze, a plaster mask. "What?" she asked, but Lona knew she'd understood every word.

"Warren. Is my father. He was married, but you had an affair."

Zinedine had begun shaking her head back and forth midway through Lona's last sentence, and she was still shaking it now. "No no no no no," she said.

"You can tell me," Lona said. "What does it matter – you don't have to protect him anymore. He's in a coma and he'll probably never wake up and realize that I'm his daughter."

"I'm sorry, Lona, I thought you knew already," Zinedine said.

"Warren isn't your father. Your father is Julian."

Lona tried to lean back in the chair, but the rungs didn't seem to be quite where they were supposed to be. Everything was off. Everything in the world had shifted just a few inches to the left.

"Julian," she said, and the name came out like it was a nonsense word. "Julian is my father. That was the real rule you broke, wasn't it?"

"The first rule of any scientist. Don't get emotionally involved with your experiments."

"Julian is my father?" The more times she said it, the more ridiculous it seemed.

"He didn't know," Zinedine said quickly. "He knew I was pregnant, obviously, but he couldn't know that it turned out to be you. He wanted to get married – it was a very Midwestern chivalrous idea of what should happen when a girl got pregnant – but I wasn't interested. I told him I would leave if that's what it took to make him not feel like he had to commit to something out of guilt. And that's what he thought had happened, I'm sure. I left, to protect him."

Zinedine was the person Julian referred to before he left at Christmas. That was his last relationship, almost twenty years ago. "But. . ." Her words came out sluggishly, as they waited for her brain to process the information. "Julian? You were in love with Julian?"

Zinedine lifted her palms into scales, trying to weigh the truth of the statement. "In love? Not in love, though I probably thought so at the time. But I was spending twelve hours a day with him, and he was the only person close to my age."

She must have seen Lona's dismayed expression, because she amended her explanation. "He was kind, and he was easygoing, and unlike my colleagues, he didn't take himself too seriously, which was refreshing. And he liked me, and it happened, and I didn't regret it for a second. But, Lona – we never would have gotten married – even if nothing had happened to me. It wouldn't have been a neat little fairy tale."

Of course it wouldn't have. Lona never got the neat little fairy tale. She only got the messy complexities.

Every day of her life, for sixteen years, was spent learning about her father. She knew his friends, and his school, and his teachers, because they were her friends, too. She remembered how he'd rearranged his room when he was nine, moving the bed to cover the crack where Nick had thrown a baseball. And the way, when his parents had discovered it, his dad laughed and showed him that the den sofa was covering up a rug stain from where a pen had exploded.

She knew everything about her father's life, because she had lived it.

"Are you okay?" Zinedine asked. She hadn't tried to touch Lona again, but she sounded worried.

"Did everyone know? All your coworkers?" How thorough had the betrayal been? When Warren had taken Lona away from her mother, did he know he was taking her away from her father, too? Warren and Julian were supposed to be friends. They were all supposed to be friends.

"I didn't tell anybody, but I feel like Warren suspected something. My parents knew I was seeing somebody, obviously, but they didn't know who. If they'd known what happened, they would have taken care of the baby." She corrected herself. "They would have taken care of you."

That's why the Architect had sent her to the Path center. All evidence of Zinedine's rule-breaking had to disappear. Putting Lona in the Julian Path was the only way to hide her. To replace her identity with a randomly issued set of letters. To ensure that nobody would find her because nobody would come looking. It was icy and calculating.

But it was also, perversely, kind. The Architect believed that the Path really did represent the perfect childhood experience. He'd placed Lona there, thinking that she would be cared for. He'd placed her there and she'd been with her father.

"Are you okay?" Zinedine asked again.

"I don't know."

"That makes sense. I don't know if I'm okay either." She smiled, nervously, and extended her hand toward Lona. She looked so hopeful. Lona reached out and took it, and Zinedine's eyes filled with tears.

"It was my hair?" Lona's own voice was shaking. "That's what helped you remember? It was really just touching my hair?"

Zinedine flushed red, looking embarrassed. "And one other thing, which sounds ridiculous, when I say it out loud. Superstitious and unbelievable."

"Doesn't all of this sound unbelievable?"

"I remembered saying a name. I had a visceral memory of saying a name. When I was touching your hair, I wanted to say it again."

"What was it?"

"The one I gave you. After my grandmother. Jane."

Jane. A four-letter response to Lona's deepest wishes. Her identity, given to her by the first person who ever touched her or loved her.

"Do you like it?"

Lona tried to speak, but couldn't for the lump in her throat. She nodded instead, leaning in closer to Zinedine, who wrapped her in her arms. She still smelled like verbena flowers, and the faint memory of home.

48

There was a strange rhythm to the next days. Zinedine spent them in a lab downstairs – it was a room that Lona hadn't seen, the one behind the white room where the experiment on the girl Katic had taken place. Buying their freedom, one molecule at a time. But it was hard for her – like dragging memories through mud, she said one evening when she returned, exhausted, at the end of a day of research. She might have been the one who designed the Julian Compact, but that was seventeen years and several lifetimes ago for her. She didn't remember doing it and she'd destroyed her own research notes. Now she was trying to replicate what she'd so carefully destroyed, for a cause she didn't believe in, for a daughter she'd just met.

"And it doesn't help that the only diluents I've been able to find that work with the active materials are dangerous, and flammable as hell," she'd complained last night. "Even if I can get volunteers to retain their injected memories, what's the point if, while you're preparing for the injection, the syringe bursts into flames?"

Was it strange for Lona to feel happy, during this time?

Not completely happy, of course. Still, during these short conversations with Zinedine, she couldn't help but marvel at the wonderful mundanity of being able to talk with her mother. About her work. About anything. About peanut butter and banana toast, which Lona loved and everyone else always thought was gross. Zinedine said it had been her favorite snack growing up.

But Lona's days were more nebulous than Zinedine's. She wasn't trying to design an injection, or minimize the fire risks of a liquid. Her only use was collateral use, a catalyst to Zinedine's productivity. She spent time reading, and pacing from one end of the apartment to the other. And most of all – though she was angry with him, though she didn't trust him, though she was afraid of him – she spent time with Harm.

He'd opened up the whole apartment for Lona and Zinedine, not just the bedroom Zinedine had been sleeping in. Now Lona had a living room, and a kitchen with chipped countertops, and a guard posted outside. Harm would come to visit and stay for hours, sometimes leaving when Zinedine came back upstairs at the end of the day, sometimes staying for a twisted tableau of family dinners.

The first time, he'd knocked on the door and handed her a bouquet of flowers. Carnations, red, something that you would buy in a hospital with a get-well-soon teddy bear.

"Did your etiquette book say flowers were a nice way to apologize for something?" Lona had asked. "Did it bother to mention that not imprisoning someone was also good etiquette?"

"I'm trying, Lona," he said.

"You're always trying," she spat back, but she let him in

anyway, because it seemed better to have him here, in the apartment, than it did to have him alone doing things she couldn't see.

He wanted to impress her. It was the strangest thing, but she could tell, from the way he made a show of telling her things he'd read, or the way he liked to talk about how he was in charge of the work on the Compact. He brought her things, too. Not just flowers, but music or movies or, like today, a board game, one where the object was to travel around the board collecting various colored cards, all the while trying to send your opponent back to the beginning.

"Gray card." She held her hand out. "I landed on 'Color of your choice'."

He searched the stack for a slate-colored square. "You're going to win this round."

"It's mostly luck. Your turn now."

He rolled the dice for longer than he needed to. "Zinedine calls you Jane sometimes." The dice clattered on the board; one rolled onto the floor and Lona picked it up.

She tried to keep her voice even. "I guess she does."

"Why?"

Because that's my real name. Jane. She had whispered it to herself, practiced saying it as if it were an introduction. *Hello, it's nice to meet you. My name is Jane.* "Because it's what she would have called me. If she'd kept me. If I hadn't been in the Julian Path."

"I know." He landed on a square that required him to go back three spaces, but gave him an extra turn. "But it's not your name *now*."

She wasn't sure how to answer. Harm could still be unpredictable and she didn't feel like arguing about something he couldn't possibly understand. "Is it raining outside? It sounds like water on the windows."

"You didn't answer my question."

She picked up the dice to hand them to Harm. "I'm changing the subject. There was probably something about that in your conversation book. How to gracefully change the subject when someone brings up something you don't want to talk about. Your turn."

"You don't belong with Fenn."

She froze, with the cool white cubes in her palm. "What did you say?"

"You said it was my turn. I was trying to change the subject."

"I meant it was your turn in the game."

"You and Fenn don't belong together. I could tell that when we were at Julian's house." His glacier eyes were staring at her steadily.

"How would you know that?" Harm didn't know her – he'd spent a few weeks with her six months ago. She'd tried so hard not to mention Fenn here, not to give Harm any reason to know where she was weak.

"I know that because you're here. And Fenn isn't. Fenn is too afraid. He's boring."

Lona stared down at the board, as if she were trying to plot her next move. Really, she was trying to take in what Harm had said. *Fenn is too afraid*. It was almost what she'd told him when they broke up – that he wanted normalcy too much. But Harm's interpretation was a perversion. She'd never thought of Fenn as afraid. He was brave in a different way – braver than her, even, for the way he was vulnerable, for the way his emotions were kept at the surface. And not boring. Simple isn't boring. Making a book of childhood photographs wasn't boring. Knowing when the night air tasted like peppermint and when it tasted like cloves wasn't boring.

For the first time since she'd become Harm's hostage, she allowed herself to think about Fenn, and when she thought about him, she missed him, and when she missed him, the feeling cut through to her tendons, to the bone. She should have listened to him that New Year's Eve on the porch, when he tried to tell her they were just having a fight, one that might look better in the morning. She should have listened to Gamb when he told her she was daring Fenn to leave. She should have given him the patience that he'd given her, instead of acting like the only way to pursue her mission was full speed.

"That made you upset, didn't it?" Harm had cocked his head to the side, a curious puppy. She didn't have the energy to explain human emotions to him, to watch him collect her feelings like specimens in a glass display box.

"No," she lied. "But this game is too easy, and it's late. Can we go check on Zinedine?"

Katie was in the chair when they got downstairs, after working their way through the maze-like basement. Her head drooped forward, her eyes were closed, the bangs of her hair were drenched with sweat. A wave of nausea rolled through Lona's belly. She and Harm had arrived just in time to watch the last thing she wanted to see: another trial.

But no, now Katie's eyes were opening and Zinedine was kneeling next to her, talking softly, taking notes. The trial must have just ended. Zinedine handed Katie a glass of juice, patting her arm and then leading her over to a cot in the corner of the room. The lab had grown more cluttered the more time Zinedine had spent working in it. Over to the side, lined along the wall, were bins and containers of whatever materials she was working with – jars of a clear, kerosene-smelling liquid that must be the flammable diluent Zinedine talked about.

When it appeared that Katie was sleeping, Zinedine looked up and saw Lona. Her face broke out into a tired smile. "Jane! Am I late? I don't even know what time it is." She had bags under her eyes, which were run through with red.

"It's after eleven. I asked if we could come down and check on you."

Zinedine put her arm around Lona, a distracted half-embrace, and somehow the casualness of the gesture was more intimate than if it had been intentional. "Thank you. I don't know how I'm still standing."

"How did today go?" Harm interjected.

Zinedine's smile faltered a little as she turned to Harm. "Fine. Good, even. She remembered a crumbling wall and someone screaming."

Someone screaming. Lona didn't know what her mother was putting into Katie's head – she'd never watched the Paths herself. The descriptions sounded like things you work to forget, not to remember.

"Did she remember who was screaming? What about the alley?"

"No, but it's progress."

"How much of the wall did she remember? Did she know where she was? I need to know exactly what I can tell my contacts about how the experiment is going."

"She's doing the best she can, Harm." Zinedine gave Lona's arms a final squeeze and began pulling on a set of gloves she'd removed when talking to Katie, ready to head back into the lab. "So am I."

49

~~Dear Fenn,~~
~~Dear Fenn, I just wanted~~.

Lona set down her pen in frustration. Zinedine was allowed pens again. It was decided that her risk had been greatly reduced with Lona's arrival and the deal that had been struck. The pen didn't make Lona a better writer, though. It didn't make it easier for her to express herself. Fenn wouldn't have had that problem. Fenn would have been able to write down exactly how he felt.

She took the birthday candle out of her pocket where she always kept it – a totem, a wish, a piece of luck – and rolled it between her fingers. The memory of frosting always made her fingers shiny with grease. This time, as the wax passed over her skin, part of it seemed to unroll into a thin strip, over her hand. She was dissolving the memento.

No. No! The thought made her panic – the last tangible connection she had with Fenn until she got out. If she got out. She tried desperately to clump the wax together again, but it wasn't working.

And wait – when she looked closer, she saw that it wasn't

a strip of wax at all, but a strip of paper, thin and soft and almost the same shade of green as the candle, which is why she hadn't noticed it before. It was sopped through with oil, nearly iridescent, but she recognized the paper as a scrap of the wrapping from her birthday present. There were gray marks on it, evenly spaced. Writing. Fenn's. Without allowing herself to hope for what it might be, she held the paper up to the lightbulb of the lamp next to the coffee table. A list, written so small she had to squint.

Lona's birthday. Tasted like:
Sugar
Warmth
Desire
Peace
Home
(Cake)

As gently as she could, she traced the words. He must have written it before he came out and found her on the porch, and they decided the night tasted like cloves. Or maybe after she had already gone to bed. She replayed the evening hungrily, trying to recapture moments she hadn't realized were important at the time. Reading Fenn's birthday list felt like reading a message in a bottle, something that had been written a long time ago and traveled miles to get to her.

Was there something else at the bottom? She held the paper closer to the light, and leaned in so close she could smell the memory of the buttercream. It looked like there were more words, below "cake". Just a few of them, but they were in Fenn's handwriting and figuring out what they said seemed like the most important thing in the world.

Suddenly she was smelling something besides buttercream. Something charred and blackened, and her fingers were getting hot – and she looked down and Fenn's list was disintegrating. She'd rested it on the open bulb, and now the paper was dissolving in her fingers, disappearing before her eyes. Lona frantically pulled it away and blew on it – but nothing she did helped. Before her eyes Fenn's words vanished.

"What are you doing?"

She hadn't heard him come in. Usually Harm knocked first – an elaborate ruse of politeness, making it seem like she could choose to let him in. Now he was standing just a few feet away.

"Nothing." She tried to keep the tremor out of her voice, looking down to where the tips of her fingers were black and charred.

"You're not doing nothing. You're doing something, at least."

"I was writing a letter." She looked back to the paper still lying on the table, where she'd never managed to complete more than a sentence. "What do you want?"

"Was the letter to Fenn?"

Why did he always ask her about Fenn? To hurt her? Did he bring it up specifically because he knew it was an open wound and he wanted to watch her writhe under the salt? "What did you bring today? A game? Cards?"

He didn't answer. "Harm? What did you want to do today?"

"Where do you think you'll go?" he asked. "When you and Zinedine leave, where do you think you'll go?"

Like so many things he said or did, the question seemed a non-sequitur. He shifted his weight from one foot to the other; the motion made Lona uneasy and she finally figured out why: it was because Harm himself looked uneasy. He usually looked like fluid motion, but now he just looked nervous.

"Back home, I guess," she said.

"With Fenn and Gamb and Ilyf?"

"With Gamb and Ilyf at least," she corrected him cautiously. "Or maybe Zinedine will get an apartment." Lona was still seventeen. Was Zinedine her guardian now? Would they tour a college campus, or have mother–daughter shopping trips? She couldn't picture Zinedine at a mall.

"Where do you think I'll go, when you leave?"

What was he getting at? "I don't know, Harm. I guess you can go wherever you want. You will have fulfilled your mission, right? They'll probably give you a medal."

He made a small sound. It sounded like a laugh but there wasn't any mirth in it.

"Do you think I could go with you?"

She started to laugh, until she saw he was serious. "Do you *want* to go with us?"

"What if I want to go with *you*?" His glacier blue eyes were staring at her, melting. Time stuttered as Lona figured out how to respond. "What if I don't have anywhere else to go? Please?"

The "please" left her speechless, off balance. Before, when she first met Harm again and he poured her ice water in his little apartment downstairs, she thought his voice sounded brittle. Maybe brittle was the wrong word. Brittle things, when you broke them, shattered into nothing. But this, behind his words – if you broke what Harm was saying, it would shatter into sadness.

"Lona. Before, when you asked what I meant?"

"What you meant when?" she asked carefully.

"When I said that it was easy to tell you were in love with Fenn."

She swallowed. "When you said I didn't realize I was in love with him," she supplied. "When I asked whether you wondered what it was like to love someone and not know it."

"Yes. That."

"I remember."

He took a step closer. The coffee table was between them, but he was skirting it, moving haltingly around the side. "I always admired you." His face seemed to be tinted just slightly red, as if he were blushing. But Harm wouldn't blush. He might surprise her in a thousand ways. But Harm wouldn't blush. Would he?

"You admired me?"

"You were . . . whole. You weren't broken. It always seemed so easy for you, to find your own path." She wasn't imagining it. There was the most delicate pink tinge spreading up from Harm's shirt collar, flushing his cheeks.

"None of you were broken," she told him, but the words sounded hollow even to her. Of course they were broken. She'd said the same thing a hundred times herself. The Strays were all broken, and none of them were more broken than Harm.

"I don't know if I can love anybody, Lona. I don't know if love is . . . in my skill set. But I figured that if I'd ever been in love – even if I didn't know how to identify it, and even if it was only my limited version of it – I thought it would have been with you. That's why I wanted you to come here. I wanted to see you again. And I wanted you to see me, how much better I'm doing. How hard I'm trying."

She shrank back involuntarily, stumbling against the sofa. Harm in love with her. Harm the sociopath. She still thought of him as the boy who had used his teeth to rip his way to freedom and send himself into an institution. *And to save me*.

"You're joking, right?" She wanted this to be a joke, a prank, a mindgame. She wanted to be able to forget he'd ever said this, and that she'd ever seen his eyes melt into a pool of sadness. "You're practicing your conversational skills."

He arranged his lovely features into a smile. "Joking. Of course I'm joking." But then he looked away from her and brushed his palm in front of his eye.

Was he – she could barely believe it, but it was true. Harm was crying. Standing in the living room he had lured her to as a prisoner, Harm had silent tears streaking down his cheeks, rivulets of water down cold marble. When he realized she was staring at him, he covered his eyes with one hand, and that made him look like a child.

She couldn't stand to see it, this naked emotion, this flayed vulnerability. She took a hesitant step toward him and then another, and then, because she didn't know what else to do, she reached to his hand. He flinched when her fingers brushed against his wrist, as if she'd struck him with a hot iron. *The touching*, she reminded herself. Pathers were raised without touch. They feared it, and no one likely feared it more than Harm. The first time Fenn stroked her hand, she felt exquisite tremors for days. Harm never had that. Harm had probably never been touched at all.

She reached out again, this time even more slowly. With just her index finger, she slowly traced a path down the tendons connecting his wrist to his knuckle, on the hand still covering his eyes. "It's okay, Harm." She never knew why people did these things, said things were okay when they weren't, but she found herself doing it now, lying to soothe. "It's okay."

Harm dropped his hand, and his eyes were bloodshot. The blotchiness should have marred his face, but instead it made him look human. Lona remembered hearing a story once about the old master painters – how they would deliberately paint a flaw into each of their works, to prove that they knew they were unworthy, that they had no aspirations to be God. The flaws were what made the paintings beautiful. Harm's tears were his flaw.

"I'm really messed up, aren't I?" His shoulders were jerking up and down.

"I guess we all are. All of us who were in that program." She moved her hand to his again, and this time he didn't pull away. This time he watched her cover the back of his hand with her palm, sucking in sharp mouthfuls of air, his shoulders heaving.

"None of you are messed up like me," he said through choked sobs. The brittleness had completely shattered; there was only sadness now.

"You don't have to be," she whispered. "You could come with us. You could come with us right now – we don't have to wait for Zinedine to finish her work."

"I can't."

"You can! Harm, it wouldn't be hard for you to come up with a story. You could say you needed to take us somewhere to trigger Zinedine's memories. Or that she needed supplies. Or that – Harm, you could think of a million excuses, and then we could just *drive away*."

"Do you think I could? Do you think I could start over?" He sounded small and pitiful, the shards left over after a stone had cracked.

Suddenly Harm's face was centimeters away. He smelled like soap and something soft. Baby powder. More innocent than she ever would have imagined. Waves of pity ran through her body. Pity, revulsion, fear and sadness. *He deserved to have one experience that was about the softness of the human experience, not the harshness*, she thought as she felt his face come closer. *He deserves something that feels like the opposite of pain.* And then his lips were on hers.

The door flew open. Lona instinctively jumped away from Harm, but there was no need – Zinedine didn't seem to notice what she had interrupted. Her cheeks were pink and her eyes had a wild, off-kilter look to them, and she was out of breath.

"Zinedine?" Lona moved toward her in case something was wrong. "I thought you said you were going to work through the night. What are you doing back so—"

"I did it," she interrupted. "I did it all. Today Katie remembered everything."

50

"I was in a room. It was in a basement, I think, or at least in the interior of a building, because it had no windows."

Katie paused to drink from the water Zinedine handed her. Her voice was raspy, it sounded like she'd been awake for days. Again, her shirt was soaking with sweat, and her hand trembled. "There were sixteen other people in the room, and we were debating how to proceed with a mission. Everyone was military or suits – everyone was a man, except me."

"You weren't a man?" Harm asked.

"I was wearing a skirt and high heels."

"It was a scene from Secretary of State Ursula Vaughn's time in office," Zinedine interjected. "Katie even remembered the brooch she was holding that night."

"Did you see this?" Harm turned to Anders, who was standing behind Zinedine. "Is it true?"

Anders cleared his throat. "We can confirm the brooch memory. I found a picture of that night from an angle that had never been published – it's in her hands, under the table."

"It was a good luck charm. I knew it had belonged to my mother," Katie said. "I don't know how I knew that but I knew."

Harm and Anders's eyes locked from across the room. Finally, almost imperceptibly, Anders nodded his head. It was a benediction. A release. Harm had succeeded. Harm would get his medal after all.

Then Anders laughed, a full baritone chuckle. Lona had never seen him laugh; it was strange to see him happy. He clamped a hand on Zinedine's shoulder, shaking her back and forth in a vigorous congratulation.

Under the vise of his hand, Zinedine looked frailer than Lona had seen her look all week. At first she thought Zinedine was just exhausted, ready to collapse from lack of sleep. But then she saw the expression on Zinedine's face. It was uneasy – a grimace of resignation more than a look of triumph. She looked at Lona and shook her head sadly.

This wasn't a win. Not like Harm and Anders would think it was. Zinedine had managed to do what they asked, but what if what they asked was wrong? She'd given them what they wanted, but at what cost?

At the cost of our freedom, Lona mentally answered, and she tried to convey that to Zinedine, too, by reassuringly nodding her own head up and down.

The morality was in a gray area, but then, wasn't life in a gray area too? Isn't that part of what she'd been thinking about, with Fenn? That neither one of them had been completely right or completely wrong? *Hadn't she just let Harm kiss her out of pity?*

"You saved us, Zinedine," she said pointedly. "Thank you for doing what you had to do."

To Lona's left, Harm spoke for the first time since Anders had nodded at him. "I need to go call them." He looked weakened, too, but in a different way from Zinedine. He looked like a marionette whose strings have finally been cut, who now must learn to walk on its own, with unsupported joints. "I need to go tell them it's over."

It's over. Lona wanted to repeat the mantra after every thought. Zinedine did what they asked and it's over. *She would go home and it's over. She would get to see Fenn and it's over.*

"Are you okay?" she asked Zinedine, when Harm had left the room to make his call and when Anders was using his own phone to call a taxi for Katie. The rest of the basement was silent. Lona didn't know what time it was, but she knew it was late. Katie had been the only volunteer in the building.

"I'm tired, Lona." Zinedine rubbed her face with her hands. "I'm just so tired."

"Do you want to lie down for a minute?"

"No. God no. Let's go. Let's go right now." She wrapped an arm around Lona, leaning on her for support. "Anywhere you want to."

Lona put her arm around Zinedine's waist. They had the same stance, she noticed. They both turned their right feet out, just a little, cocking their left hips. She tilted her head down to her mother's shoulder.

Harm reentered the room a few minutes later, but instead of stopping to talk to Lona or Zinedine, he started directly for Anders.

"Harm, wait." He turned to her but didn't seem to want to make eye contact. Was he embarrassed, about before? There'd been no time to say anything to him since the kiss in the apartment – everything had happened fast. Maybe he assumed their conversation was void now – that she'd only invited him to leave with her because she was trying to escape. "Harm."

"I need to talk to Anders," he said.

"Wait." She grabbed his sleeve, and lowered her voice to a whisper. "Harm. Upstairs—"

He shook her off. "I need to talk to Anders," he said again.

She watched as he bowed his red curls in close to Anders, and the doctor nodded solemnly – once, twice, four times. It was probably just official business, bureaucracy, nothing to worry about. But she couldn't help notice that Anders's eyes kept sneaking over to Zinedine.

"Zinedine," Anders called loudly. "Would you come with me for a second?" Zinedine raised her eyebrows and looked uncertainly to Lona. "It's nothing," Anders assured her. "We just want to make sure we understand all of your methods, before you leave. It won't take long. And, of course, we'll figure out how to keep in touch, for follow-up questions later."

Zinedine squeezed her hand reassuringly before following Anders to the back room. This was normal, of course. Harm had said they could leave right away, but Katie had only woken up thirty minutes ago. Of course there would be things to go over. If Lona craned her neck, she could see her mother and the doctor talking. Her mother was pointing at something; Anders was nodding, there wasn't any reason to be suspicious.

"Lona?" Harm was standing beside her, closer than she'd realized.

"Congratulations, Harm."

"Thank you." Was that a smile or a wince?

"Upstairs—" she started again.

"We don't need to talk about it. You said I could leave with you so I would help you escape. But now Zinedine has solved the problem."

"You could still leave with us, Harm. As soon as Zinedine is finished, we could all—"

"We don't need to talk about it," he said again. He looked as tired as Zinedine. More, even. "Let's just sit down. Can we? And talk for a minute about normal things."

"Sure." She didn't know what else to say. Had Harm's feelings really changed so much in half an hour? Why was he behaving so differently from how he had in the apartment?

He led her back into the break room, sitting down across from her at one of the shellacked tables. The last time they'd sat here, he'd put something in her apple-flavored soda. Today he didn't offer her anything to drink, folding his hands on top of the fake wood. Normal things. He'd said he wanted to talk about normal things.

"Are you and Anders going to go out and celebra—" she started to ask. He raised one hand and shook his head. No. That wasn't the kind of thing he wanted to talk about.

"What do you want to be when you grow up, Lona?"

"You mean after college?" She adjusted her brain for this radical topic shift. "I don't know. I hadn't really thought about it. I like math. What about you?"

He shook his head again; he didn't want to talk about himself. "Do you think you'll study math in college? And have tests, or work on projects?"

"I guess so." He seemed to be looking over her shoulder, at

302

something behind her. She suddenly realized that she'd chosen the wrong seat. From where Harm was sitting, he had a direct line of vision to Anders and Zinedine. From where she was sitting, she could only see Harm. "What are they talking about back there? Are they almost done?"

"Do you think you'll make a lot of new friends there?" he asked. "Do you, Lona? And maybe you'll all go to each other's houses over breaks?"

"Harm, just come with us and pick your own college. Study whatever you want. I'm going to go check on Zinedine; I want to know if she needs anything."

"Don't."

She looked down and saw that he'd clamped his hand over hers, with more strength than she would have expected. "I wish I could go with you. It turns out they don't let you leave."

51

"Harm. Why hasn't Zinedine come out yet? What are they doing back there?" His fingers were too hot; her wrist was burning. "Let go of my hand."

His eyes flicked up, above her head. She wrenched her neck around. Zinedine, coming toward her, followed by Anders. Lona relaxed for a second until she saw Zinedine's face – tight and drawn, so pale she could see the blue vein along her temple. She started to stand up, but this time it was Zinedine who stopped her.

"It's okay," she said. "Don't follow me. He's just taking me upstairs to sign a few things. I'll be back soon. I love you. It's okay."

"No!"

"Don't," Zinedine said again. "Don't."

Anders led Zinedine out the door, into the bank of pods. Lona watched until she could no longer see them in the darkness, then she listened to their footsteps. They stopped early, before they would have reached the stairwell. Anders wasn't bringing Zinedine upstairs to sign some papers, and he definitely wasn't bringing her back down. They weren't about to go home. There weren't fairy tale endings. The compact was broken.

Harm wouldn't look at her. Harm was still silently sitting, looking down at the table. *Help us!* she wanted to scream at him. Last time he had helped her, with his clawing and his teeth and his uncoiled rage, but now he was just sitting there. Civilized.

"What's it going to be?" she asked him. "Erasing another part of her brain again? Destroying her memories? Are there other programs she started to build that you need help with too? Anders is putting her into a pod right now, isn't he – or getting a remmersing prod."

"We'll still let you go, Lona," he said. "That's what Anders told her. That you would still be allowed to leave, if she came along quietly."

"She did what you asked her to, Harm. She fixed the Compact. She made it work like you wanted it to."

"We feel that she's still necessary," he said. She could tell he was quoting something – someone. These weren't Harm's words. "They want her to continue developing and testing new Paths. They don't believe her use has run out."

"She did everything you wanted – you have to let her go." It wasn't fair. She'd had her mother for only days. She reached again for Harm's hand, but he pulled it away.

"It's what she agreed to, Lona. It's the contract she signed up for."

"When? When did she sign up for that? After you modified her memory to forget about me? After she thought she didn't have any reason not to sign her life away for your stupid Path?"

"I have to, Lona." His voice was flat, expressionless, but there

305

were tears pouring down his face in rivers, a granite statue in the rain. "I have to. It's what they want, and I have to do it for them. I can't go back to where they would send me."

"Then don't go back!" From the room with the pods, she thought she could hear the clicking sounds that would have come from a pod being adjusted. "Help me escape – we'll all leave together."

"I can't. I don't know how to. I thought I could but I don't know how to be that kind of happy. I don't have a choice about following these orders."

He could learn what it meant to be that kind of happy – she was sure of it. She just needed a little more time, to show him how. But there wasn't any more time. Once Anders had placed a remmersing prod to the base of Zinedine's skull, there was nothing more Lona could do.

"It's inevitable," Harm said through his thick veil of tears. "I can't let you help her, and I can't stop it. Unless there's an act of God, unless this building burns down, right now, nothing can change what's going to happen to Zinedine."

It was just like last time, again. Just like six months ago when she was trapped in the room with the Architect, except that no one was going to save her or Zinedine. She'd barely met her mother, and now she was going to lose her again.

"Help!" she screamed, even though she knew no one could hear her. "Help me!"

She wrenched her arm away from Harm, and something clanked into her abdomen. Something hard and metallic. The lighter. The heavy weight of Fenn's birthday lighter, tucked in the zippered pocket of his flannel shirt. And the candle next to it, half-burned and worry-worn from all the times Lona had stroked it.

Unless this building burns down. That's what Harm had said. Was the phrasing a coincidence, or did he know about the lighter? If he saw her light it, would he try to take it from her, or watch it burn? Was he trying to save her?

She couldn't waste the seconds to figure it out. The lighter was smooth and cold and heavy in her palm. She flipped the top open and thought of Fenn, singing Happy Birthday, of the taste of frosting rolling around on her tongue.

She lit the candle – the nubby green lump of half-melted wax – and tossed it into the air, through the door behind Harm, where Zinedine had conducted experiments on Katie. It arced, end over end, until it landed on one of the drums full of diluent, the flammable building blocks of the Julian Compact. For a second it was just a small flame, a flame to make a wish on, as it ate its way through the red plastic. "Get down!" she yelled. And then the room exploded.

52

She couldn't see anything – the air was black and orange, so thick she wanted to peel it away; she clawed in front of her face only for her fists to close around vapors. She moved her hands across the floor and they came up bloodied – the explosion had knocked out a window and the floor was covered in shards of glass. Something was in the middle of the room that didn't belong there – a long wooden object. It was the support beam that used to be on the ceiling. One end of it had been knocked down, slicing the room in half at a forty-five degree angle, engulfed in flames. She was on the right side of it, though. She was on the side with the door – she could escape.

Shouts poured out of the pod room, Anders's voice and Zinedine's. Lona heard her mother screaming her name. "I'm fine," she tried to yell back, but smoke caught in her lungs and she erupted in coughs. "I'm fine."

But where was Harm? She'd thrown the candle past him, she'd told him to get down, and now she couldn't see him. Had he been knocked out by the blast? *Had he been* – no, she wouldn't allow herself to complete that thought. She hadn't killed Harm. Not today.

"Harm?" she coughed again, and pulled the hem of her shirt up to her nose, trying to breathe through the fabric. "Harm?"

Something moved, on the other side of the fallen support beam. Harm was still alive, crouched to the floor like Lona. When he heard her call his name, he moved toward the fiery barricade, but it slipped before he could reach it, sliding down another foot along the wall.

"Crawl under it," she croaked to Harm. There was enough room to do that now, but there wouldn't be if the beam fell much further – not with the flames licking off it the way they were. "Harm, you have to come with me now." The smoke filled her lungs, curling around her tonsils, coating her throat, ravaging her vocal cords.

A popping sound came from overhead. The fire was eating away at whatever held the beam in place – any minute it would crash to the ground. A shower of sparks flew off a live wire swinging from the ceiling. Why wasn't he moving? The only way out was past the beam, and Harm wasn't trying to get around it. He was backing away from it; he was standing up, into the space where the smoke was even thicker.

"Lona?" Zinedine's voice again, closer, choking.

"I'm coming," Lona called over her shoulder. She hoped Zinedine heard her; her voice seemed swallowed in the deafening roar of the flames. It was hot, so hot – now when she touched the ground it felt like putting her hand on a simmering pot. "Get out now – I'll be behind you."

She turned back to Harm. "You have to come now," she begged him. "Before it's too late!"

The room had completely filled with smoke; her eyes were

weeping tears. She desperately sucked filtered air through her shirt. There was no point – every breath she drew was poisoned. She could barely make out Harm's outline, still standing on the other side of the barrier. Except for his hair. His beautiful red hair stood out through the thick gray of the smoke – but it wouldn't for long. The fire was closing in on him, the flames that were exactly the color of Harm's hair. If they got any closer, she wouldn't be able to see him at all. The fire would completely swallow him. He tilted his head up and raised his palms toward the sky.

"It's too late," he said. He wasn't yelling, but she could hear him somehow, even over the scream of the fire.

"It's not too late! Just crawl under, Harm!" Her chest ached, from soot and heat. She wasn't going to be able to talk much longer. She looked behind herself for the door and couldn't see it. She was going to have to crawl out by feel. "It's not too late!"

"It's too late for me," he said, and then he was engulfed in flames.

53

Sirens were getting closer; she could hear them winding through neighborhoods as she stumbled into the grassy courtyard. Empty. She'd thought there might be a crowd, gathered to watch the building burn, but in a night sky bathed orange with fire, she saw only the still swingset and the empty parking lot. And then Zinedine, running toward her, streaked with ash. "Jane!" she screamed. "Jane!"

"Mom." The word came out like a croak, but it did come out, as Zinedine folded Lona in close, stroking her hair with calloused hands.

"Shhhhh," she whispered. "Shh shh shhhhh." That was the comfort sound that Touchers had made when Lona was on the Julian Path, and for the first time, Lona saw where it had come from – how the hushing murmur from the right person sounded like warm wind and security. "What happened?" she asked. "I couldn't get to you. Anders ran off and I couldn't find you."

The noise of the sirens became deafening before Lona could answer – two red fire engines pulled into the parking lot, and a team of shouting men in reflector yellow poured out of them.

"Is anyone else inside?" one of them called. "How many people are left in the building?"

"One—" Zinedine started to respond, but Lona shook her head.

"Nobody. There's nobody left inside."

A brief flash of pain traveled across Zinedine's face and she closed her eyes.

"Do you know how it started?" he asked. "Do you know what the source is?" Lona shook her head back and forth; the words wouldn't come out of her scorched throat.

After the fireman ran on, Zinedine didn't ask any more questions. Instead she draped something warm over Lona's shoulders and they stood silently, side by side, watching the fire fighters swarm the building, call out orders, try to contain what was already ruined.

She was exhausted, a dish towel wrung out, a bowl that had been scraped clean. Harm's face, disappearing into the flames, and the look of serenity he'd been wearing.

Dully, she realized that the warm thing Zinedine had draped over her shoulders was her own coat – the blue wool one she'd worn when she first arrived at the apartment however many days ago, and which Harm had taken from her before she got sick.

"I grabbed it earlier," Zinedine explained. "It was hanging on a hook; I took it to keep from breathing smoke. Is it yours?" Lona nodded, pulling the material closer around her chest, smelling the chemical scent of the white foam that the fire fighters were spraying around the building. It must have acted as a suppressant; wherever it touched flames, it expanded, turning them into pillows of fluff.

"This was in the pocket," Zinedine continued. Lona turned to look at what she was holding – a small black rectangle. Her phone. "I turned it on to call the fire department – it had been off." She held it out and Lona took it from her, the buoyant colors on the screen making her head ache like too-sweet candy.

"We should also call—" Zinedine struggled to complete that sentence. "We should call someone. For Harm."

Lona didn't know who to call either. There was no one, really. There were government agents who would come and pick up his body, or what remained of it – the charred skeleton the firemen would eventually uncover. And there were people who would know how to codify his death, who would know which standard-issue gravestone in which public cemetery he would be issued. There was no one to call to mourn him, though. "Jane?" Zinedine asked. "Do you know who we should call?"

"Please don't call me Jane." Zinedine pressed her lips together as Lona tried to explain why the name she'd been so happy to have now felt wrong. "It's – it's a good name. And I'm glad it was your grandmother's. And sometime I want you to tell me all about her. It's a really good name. It's just not mine. Not my real one."

Zinedine nodded slowly. "I guess we can't go back."

"We can go forward."

"We can go forward. Lona."

Ironic. Wishing to know her name is what started this, one month ago. But suddenly, after everything that had happened, it seemed – not unimportant, but not a part of her, either. Not something that would define her. The only connection she felt

313

with it, besides the fact that it had come from her mother, was the name's third letter, the "N". "Jane" could have been a Path name, after all. The Pather would have been born in October, on the first day of the month, instead of on December 15. But the Pather would have lived in Sector 14, just like Lona had. And Fenn, too.

What did that mean, symbolically, she wondered. What would a numerologist say about the coincidence? Did it mean Lona would have been the same person, no matter where she'd grown up and what experiences she'd had? Would she still have fallen in love with Fenn?

"Lona!"

She looked up, confused. It was his voice. His voice, ragged and ripped in parts, coming from behind the fire trucks in the parking lot. She must have conjured it, she thought, invented the sound out of thin air. But she hadn't – it was him, looking thin and sick, bags under his eyelids. When he saw her, he let out a guttural cry, and he didn't stop running until he'd crashed into her and his arms were so tight around her she almost couldn't breathe.

"How are you *here*?" she asked. "Fenn, what are you – how did you *find* me?"

"Your phone. They traced the last time you used it, before it was turned off. They traced it to the closest tower, but it was miles away. And then there was nothing, not until ten minutes ago. The police said someone used it ten minutes ago. What happened? What is this place?"

"You've just been driving around looking for me? You've been . . . circling the radius of the tower looking for my car?

How far did you drive?"

"I've driven a thousand miles in circles," he said. "Eleven hundred, the odometer said, and I don't know how far Gamb and Ilyf and Julian have driven – we were all looking separately. I would have driven a thousand more. I didn't know what else to do."

"What if I wasn't close by anymore? I could have been halfway across the country."

"Then I would have driven three thousand miles to cross the country," he said, as if the answer was obvious.

Several feet away, Zinedine looked like she was trying not to listen. She should introduce them, even as strange as these circumstances were – but she couldn't, not without knowing what he was to her.

"I thought you weren't looking for me." She wanted to avoid his green eyes, so she could get the words out, but she forced herself to look up into them. "I thought you'd given up."

His eyebrows were pushed together. "What are you talking about?"

"That night." She forced herself to continue on. "The night before I disappeared. You told Ilyf not to worry about me. And when I called you, you were, um, out with Jessa."

His face softened and he gently reached up to run his thumb along her chin. "I was driving around in Jessa's *car*," he explained, "because Jessa was the only one who drove to the restaurant that night. The rest of us had walked, but Jessa had her car, and Jessa was nice enough to volunteer to drive me ninety miles home."

"You drove to the *house*?"

"The second I hung up the phone with Ilyf, I told Jessa that I needed her to drive me home so that I could stand outside of the door until you got back. And I told Ilyf not to worry because I wanted one of us to have a clear head in case something had happened to you. It wasn't going to be me because I was completely out of my mind for the entire drive. When we got there, your car was already in the driveway. So I left. So you wouldn't think I was bothering you. Jessa dropped me off at my dorm."

"Oh." Oh. She leaned her head against his chest and inhaled. Her nostrils were too scorched, she realized. She couldn't smell the grass of his skin, not through the ash and chemicals.

"Lona, I've been terrified every minute of every day," he said. "Can you tell me what happened?"

"I will. Eventually." He nodded. "First, I want you to meet my mother."

54

Spring came late this year, but by the middle of April the brown landscape had finally given way to green. There were buds on the trees down by the creek, which is where Lona stood with Fenn. And with Gamb and Ilyf, Talia and Gabriel, Zinedine. And Julian.

Her family, all of them, both biological and collected. Later, she was going to have dinner at Maggie and Jeremy's house. Her grandparents – grandparents; she was still getting used to these words – would have come this afternoon if she'd invited them, but it seemed like the memorial should be for people who were tangled more deeply in the Julian Path.

It had taken several weeks for Harm's remains to be sorted and sent to her. Whatever they'd managed to find arrived in an opaque plastic box, which she'd never opened, which now lay below the ground next to the flat, mossy rock. Fenn hadn't understood why she would want him on the property at all, so near them. It wasn't that she wanted him nearby. She just wanted to bury him by the water, where it was fresh and clean and always beginning again.

"Did you want to say something?" Fenn squeezed her hand.

"No." She should have brought something to read. They had Bible verses for funerals, or poems. She probably could have found an appropriate one in the Walt Whitman anthology Dean Greene had sent her last week when she'd contacted him about summer enrollment. But eulogies were supposed to explain who the dead were, and so Lona felt like anything she might have said or read would have been dishonest. She didn't know who Harm was, not really. She doubted he'd even fully understood himself. She hoped he'd found some peace.

"I would like to thank him," Zinedine said. "For bringing me back my daughter. Whether he meant to or not. And I'd like to say goodbye."

It was the second goodbye, of sorts, for the day. That morning Lona had gone to the hospital with Zinedine and Julian to visit Warren. He'd never woken up. He wasn't going to. He was going to lie in a hospital bed in his baby blue tracksuit, a perpetual clean slate for the rest of his life. Lona didn't think she'd need to see him again – it was too hard to think about which Warren was beneath the closed eyelids: the one who asked for stories, or the one who had set off every event in her life. She was ready to stop worrying about the sins of the past.

Julian was having a harder time with that concept. His hair had grown whiter in the past four months. When she'd told him that Harm was dead, he had cradled his head in his hands and sobbed. And when she'd told him that she was his daughter, the tears had continued to flow but they had been happy. "My life of supposed perfection," he had said, "and you are the only perfect thing to come out of it." Now he stood on her other side, holding a sealed envelope to lay at Harm's gravesite. Lona took his other hand in hers, and he managed a watery smile.

"Does anyone else want to say anything?" Lona asked. Ilyf and Talia had each lain flowers; Lona sensed that Julian wanted his last correspondence with Harm to be private. "All right. Then I guess—" She wasn't sure how to finish the sentence, and she could feel her eyes start to fill with tears. "I guess—"

"Cupcakes," Gamb supplied. "You guess cupcakes."

Cupcakes. That's right. Tomorrow was Gabriel's birthday, so Talia had brought them. Because life was unbearably strange and sad, but lucky people still had birthdays, and sometimes there was nothing to do but eat cupcakes.

"Gabe, your dinosaur chariot?" Gamb squatted low enough for Gabriel to clamber on to his back. "RAAWRRR!" he growled, charging up the hill while Gabriel held on to his neck and laughed. "RAAAWRRR!"

"No, that's fine, Gamb," Ilyf sighed, beginning to pick up the shovel and blankets they'd brought down with them. "The rest of us wanted to carry everything else on our own."

Lona let the others go ahead of her, pausing to rearrange the flowers and tuck Julian's letter in a crevice below the rock where it would be protected from rain. Then, as slivers of sun began to peek through the trees, she followed the sounds of their laughter up the path home.

Monica Hesse

Monica Hesse grew up in the cornfield American town of Normal, Illinois, spending most of her childhood pretending to be Laura Ingalls Wilder or Anne Frank. She is a feature writer for *The Washington Post*, where she has covered everything from political campaigns and the Oscars to the cultural meaning of Doritos. She lives in Washington, DC with her husband and a big black dog named Sheba.

Follow Monica on Twitter: @MonicaHesse